Niko

Dimitri Nasrallah

ESPLANADE
Books

THE FICTION SERIES AT VÉHICULE PRESS

The author wishes to thank the Canada Council for the Arts and the
Conseil des arts et des lettres du Québec for their support.

Published with the generous assistance of The Canada Council for
the Arts, the Canada Book Fund of the Department of Canadian
Heritage and the Société de développement des entreprises culturelles
du Québec (SODEC).

Esplanade Books editor: Andrew Steinmetz
Cover design: David Drummond
Set in Adobe Minion by Simon Garamond
Printed by Marquis Book Printing Inc.

LIBRARY AND ARCHIVES CANADA CATALOGUING IN PUBLICATION

Nasrallah, Dimitri, 1978-
Niko / Dimitri Nasrallah.

ISBN 978-1-55065-311-3

1. Title.

PS8627.A78N55 2011   C813'.6   C2011-901216-2

Published by Véhicule Press, Montréal, Québec, Canada
www.vehiculepress.com

Distribution in Canada by LitDistCo
orders@litdistco.ca

Printed in Canada on FSC certified paper.

Praise for *Niko*

"Nasrallah possesses superb powers of description. With a few deft strokes, he delivers a character's essence and motivations. His idiosyncratically scarred landscapes shimmer in exotic hues. . . . [His] startling achievement is to cause us to perceive the group differently, to remind us that every crowd of refugees consists of scores of people like Niko and Antoine."
–Donna Bailey Nurse, THE GLOBE AND MAIL

"By alternating the focus from one character's inner life to another's, Nasrallah creates a series of cliffhangers which propel the story forward. But the pleasure of reading *Niko* comes from more than just its fast pace. In this novel, Nasrallah has created complete worlds that you carry around in your head after you put the book down, worlds to which you want to return."
–Eric Boodman, MONTREAL REVIEW OF BOOKS

"*Niko* is relevant and engrossing reading – it's a particularly alluring read. Nasrallah gives us the space to contemplate his characters, who are refugees and immigrants who struggle towards uncertain futures, uncertain even in the relatively safe haven of Quebec society."
–HOUR MAGAZINE

"I was taken aback by Nasrallah's ability to infuse every scene, act and thought with emotion. By the time I reached the novel's dramatic finish, I'd shed more than a few tears."
–Olga Kidisevic, BROKEN PENCIL

"*Niko* is tragic, spirited, resilient and very affecting. Economic with words and avoiding much embellished language, the novel's arc is finely crafted and gallops along."
–Martyn Bryant, ROVER ARTS

"Written in swift, clear prose, this book clips along nicely, covering vast personal, political and geographic territory. It is also a tremendously tender book. Love pulses from cover to cover."
–Michael Bryson, UNDERGROUND BOOK CLUB BLOG

BY THE AUTHOR OF

Blackbodying (a novel)

for Kika and for Luca

If you are united to God, it is by grace, not by nature.
If you are humbled, it is by penitence, not by nature.
Thus, this double capacity.

–Blaise Pascal

Niko's Origins

PRESSING AN EAR to his mama's belly, the little boy listens again, hunting for signs of a beginning.

Mama kisses the top of his head and warns him that enough is enough. She has tried to keep typing with his head under her elbows, to no avail, and so she is left with little choice but to brush him away. Though she would much rather proffer her affections unconditionally, between the growing baby in her belly and working from home all day, the insistence of the little boy often leaves her feeling strained. "Go play in the other room," she instructs him. She must finish before the courier arrives to collect her work. "Go see Baba."

Doing as he's told, the little boy runs into the next room, if only to please his mama, who recently informed him, during a mild outburst he's since taken to heart and she's since regretted, that her delivery of his new friend depends entirely on how he behaves. Fearing he'll lose the friend he so desperately wants, the little boy has gone out of his way to be good.

He runs into the next room and pounces upon his baba like the cunning tiger he imagines himself to be, and roars proudly into his father's neck. His baba, who up until then was lost to a hypnotic plume of black smoke outside the window, bridles and guffaws under the sudden weight of the little boy, who has gotten heavier and rounder, a bit like his mother, in the months since the schools closed.

Baba, who lies on the sofa most days now, takes him by the armpits and raises him over his head.

"And what's your name?" Baba chides him, as part of a routine of questions that the boy has grown to expect, even anticipate.

"Niko!" the little boy shouts his name. His name is not really Niko, but Nakhle Karam, the same name that his father Antoine was given at birth, and the same name as his grandfather and great-grandfather were given before him. It's a name that's been handed down to every first son in his family, all the way back to the first Nakhle, who worked in Adam's fields. Or so Baba tells him when he tells stories. But it's a name none of them has ever worn.

"And how old are you, Niko?"

The little boy shouts, "Six!"

"And what would you rather be doing right now?"

"Going to school!" But none of them can spend much time outside. The little boy is trapped inside this apartment most days. It's December, and he's been waiting to attend his first class of the school year for more than three months. Soon, his parents fear that the year may be cancelled again.

From the kitchen Mama protests that she has a deadline to meet, and that if her husband and son can't keep quiet for the next hour, then one of them will have to drive to the television studio in person to drop off her work. And the other, she adds skeptically, after some thought, may not get a new friend after all.

The little boy covers his mouth with his hands. Not only does he want his new friend, but he also does not know how to drive. His baba brings him down to rest on his chest.

"And will you be a good student?" Baba whispers.

He promises he will. Together, Baba and the little boy lie on the sofa and watch the black plume of smoke trail off in the blue sky. The boy gazes wonderingly at the horizon. Then Baba burps. Baba has the worst breath of any man he's ever met. Baba looks sad lying on the sofa. He used to run a camera equipment shop at the base of their building, but a few weeks ago the storefront was bombed out. So the little boy snuggles under his father's arm and feels conflicted, because he does not like to know that Baba is still sad about his store, especially when he enjoys how Baba now spends his days in the apartment with him, four stories up, watching cartoons. And so the little boy changes the subject to a recurring conversation they've been having behind his mother's back recently.

"Boy or girl?" The boy knows there is no answer yet, but he likes to ask anyhow to hear the stories Baba will make up.

"Ah, yes, the question of your new friend," Baba says. "Well, you know, it's funny you should ask. Yesterday, I was driving to Jounieh, you know, for a job, and who stops me at the checkpoint but God himself."

"Stopping cars?" The little boy looks stunned.

"Yes, God himself waves at me from the checkpoint to stop my car, and so I stop, and he asks me to roll down the window, and so I roll it down, and then of course he asks for my papers, and once he sees that I am one of his, only then does he smile at me and puts his rifle on his shoulder and we begin to chat."

"What does he say?"

"You know, things you expect God to say. This war is taking too long. My condolences for your shop, Antoine. It's a nice day to drive to Jounieh. Things like that. Then he says, well, what can I do for you, my friend? So I tell him, I want to know: will I have a son or a daughter? So he laughs, he says to me, you know, no one in Beirut has any patience left, and it's true, so we laugh together, and then God says, you will have your answer soon enough."

"Then what?" the little boy asks excitedly.

"Then nothing," Baba says. "He slaps the hood of the car twice, bam bam, and I drive away."

"What did he look like?"

"Oh, you know, nothing special." Baba considers a worthy description to fit an already tall story. "He has the beard and the eyes, you know they feel like sunlight when he looks at you, like his eyes have been watching you all your life."

Mama holds her belly and shouts. "Stop telling him stories. He believes every word you feed him." Then she's back to clacking away at the typewriter again.

13

Baba sets the boy down on the carpet. The little boy crawls across the room and grapples with the large knobs of the television, to see if any channels have come through the perpetual snow. He's in luck. Quickly, he finds a madcap episode of Tom and Jerry and immediately delivers all of his attention to the cartoon. Soon his father, with nothing else to do, is watching the show as well.

During the last three months of sitting in the apartment, the little boy's friendship with this cartoon cat and mouse has deepened; he finds Tom and Jerry to be dependable animals, defiant and full of life every weekday afternoon, provided the channel comes through. He prefers Jerry to Tom. When neither is around, he has told Baba that Popeye amuses him as well, though he still does not like spinach. Also, though the little boy would rather reserve his final judgment for several more episodes, he doesn't mind laughing with the Pink Panther, whose sole occupation, it seems, is to paint a world of blue back into pink.

As he follows the cat-and-mouse adventures he forgets the world outside, with its black plumes of smoke and intermittent gunfire. Then there is a knock at the door, and Baba gets up and peers through the peephole.

"It's only the courier," Baba says, sliding the bolts from their locks. "Elise," he calls into the kitchen. "For you."

Even though it's only the courier who has come to collect his mama's pages for the day, the little boy abandons his cartoons and rushes to the bedroom, where he shuts the door behind him and he lies on his bed, which is right next to his parents' bed. He is intensely shy around adults. His head propped against the wall, he opens a tattered copy of *Le chat dans le chapeau* and studies the pictures he already knows so well. He also owns a hand-me-down copy of *Green Eggs and Ham*, and though it's in English he still enjoys the illustrations, which he often compares, with great care, to their counterparts in the French Dr. Seuss. Would he eat green eggs or green ham? Never.

Later in the afternoon, when he opens the bedroom door again and finds his mama and baba have fallen asleep together on the sofa, he quietly mounts the fire-red Miele canister vacuum in the hall and, activating its wheels, he turns the appliance into a fire engine. He is small enough to straddle its hood, and normally he can replicate a revving engine simply by turning it on. This he does not do then, with his parents sleeping peacefully. He knows that they do not sleep well in the cellar at night. So, as quietly as possible, he pushes the vacuum cleaner throughout the apartment with his feet, now an ambulance, now a police car, now an army jeep, pretending to suck up soldier figurines with the hose attach-ment, as if they are the dead below.

Riding the vacuum cleaner, he wonders what else he can do to pass the rest of the afternoon. The possibilities are limited: he is the proud owner of a fly swatter. When his parents nap, he often spends time hunting flies around the apartment. Usually, the flies buzz away before he can manage an ambush, and he's forced to plot his trap all over again, in another corner of the apartment. But once or twice he has succeeded, and so he keeps trying. Later in the afternoon, the eternal afternoon, he will ask Baba if he can ride the old tricycle back and forth across the balcony, even though his knees now scrape the handlebars. He would be happy to just stand out there and fire caps at birds through the lattice of chicken wire that obscures the balcony from end to end.

His parents still sleep, and there are no flies in the apartment. Tired of pushing the vacuum cleaner, the little boy lies down on his bed once more and thinks that, if all else fails, he can always go back to watching Mama's stomach grow, and again he hopes, with all the sincerity of a prayer, that he has behaved well enough for his mother to give him a new friend. If she's making him a new friend, through a mystery he cannot even begin to decipher, he knows only that he won't be so alone anymore. He falls asleep this way, waiting patiently just as God told his baba, imagining new friends climbing out from his mama's belly.

Later, Baba rocks him gently awake and places the still sleepy boy upon his shoulders. As he yawns, they duck through the doorway, and in the kitchen he sees that his mother has cleared her papers from the table, to a pile atop the fridge, so that she can prepare supper.

"Come," Baba says, "let's go downstairs and have a cigarette."

Baba bends down like a camel to set the little boy back on the floor. Niko scrambles from his father's shoulders and bounds across the hall to fetch his plastic ball.

"Don't stay too long," Mama calls, because soon supper will be on the table.

The little boy runs down the stairs ahead of Baba, eager to venture out into the parking lot behind their building. Once, the back door of his father's shop opened directly onto the courtyard, and the little boy used to play down there every day. Now the little boy only gets outside every few days, and he kicks a plastic ball against the wall as Baba has a cigarette in the blackened doorway of his old life. Then Baba ventures deeper inside and looks around, remembering what the shop looked like with counters and displays. The storefront is boarded over. From the street, no one can tell a store ever existed here.

At the sound of the ball bouncing off the wall, more children run down to join in. They too have been standing on the balcony, staring out through chicken wire. Four buildings line the courtyard, each at least six stories high. Baba says that, if not for the gaping hole of bright blue sky above, the parking lot would be almost as safe as the cellar.

Within minutes, there are four boys taking turns kicking that plastic ball against the wall. Four years old or fifteen, age doesn't matter as they play rounds of soccer or hide-and-seek between parked cars, until they are beckoned back indoors, sometimes by their parents for supper, or sometimes by the caustic drill of a machine gun's stutter, the shrill whistle of a shoulder-mounted missile, the throaty guffaw of mortar blasting through the side of a building. Today's game ends when the little boy's errant kick drives the ball into the side of a neighbor's Audi, leaving a dent in the door. All the other children scramble away, and as his baba rushes out from his old store, Niko knows that, no matter what happens now, his mama will be angry with him, and his chances at new friendship diminish before his eyes.

One day in January the schools in their neighbourhood of Hamra reopen. That morning, Baba takes the little boy out on the balcony and has him pose for several pictures, because the first day of school, he says, is an important day in a student's life. The little boy hasn't seen his father this proud of him in many weeks, and he decides that Baba is happiest when he has an excuse to use the camera.

"Perhaps this will be the most important day you have lived so far," Baba muses. "You never can tell." He tilts the camera and asks for a big smile.

The little boy smiles, and Baba clicks away. They set the camera on a tripod and pose for a family portrait: Baba, Mama, belly, and the little boy together. One, two, three, four. Then he kisses his mama and her belly good-bye and follows Baba down to the parking lot, bounding down the stairs two, three steps at a time. In the parking lot, other boys and girls appear dressed in their finest clothes, pressed shirts, shined shoes, combed hair, new notebooks, ready to attend classes.

They drive through checkpoints, to the front gates of the school. Even though the little boy has been here before, he cowers shyly behind Baba's legs as they enter the building. It has been a long time since he has seen so many people in one building. His Baba leads him down a long hall to a door covered with colorful drawings, where Niko meets his teacher, Madame Murr, a young woman with thick eyebrows and a bored smile. She asks him to sit cross-legged in a circle of fifteen other children, all as excited and nervous and frightened and eager as he is.

The school day is only four hours long, yet they still manage to do a lot, and after his initial reluctance to be left alone subsides and his father has slipped away from the bench outside the classroom door, the little boy is pleased to be in a room with so many other children his age.

Their first school day begins with a game that involves whistling, which only two students can do well. The little boy, though he tries, is not one of them. One girl asks how pushing air through pursed lips produces sound. The teacher has no answer for that. "It's one of the magical qualities that fills our otherwise normal lives," she says. The girl decides right then and there that she wants to be a magician when she grows up.

The teacher says, "The best way to start a life in magic is to learn how to whistle."

Together, they all push air through their teeth.

Once they've tired of whistling, they learn the words to the national anthem that no one sings anymore. After a round of practice, Madame Murr brings out a record player from the cabinet, and the class listens to the official version. The second time through, they all sing along.

Then it's time to have a snack and play outside. The school has its own courtyard, where giant willow trees grow. Niko joins others who jostle in line to swing from vine to vine. The courtyard also has two large sandboxes, a slide, monkey bars, a swing set, and a merry-go-round. Over the course of the half-hour break, he plays on all of them, laughing and shouting and jumping. If only every day could bring such pleasures.

After the break, he and the rest of his class (for they are now, after the recess, an unbreakable bond in everything they do) take assigned seats around two large tables for an Arabic lesson. On the board, the teacher writes a letter from the alphabet: *aleph*. The little boy copies it onto draft paper. One long line.

The Arabic lesson ends, and Madame Murr draws the class's attention to the wooden shelf at the back of the classroom, where fifteen yellow flowerpots, filled with soil, wait to be seeded. One by one, each student walks over and chooses a pot. The teacher passes around a bag of seeds. With his thumb, the little boy pushes the seed down into the soil.

A bell rings and the little boy's first day of school comes to an end. He is finally in school, though it passes quickly, too quickly. By and by, mothers, fathers, and housekeepers pass through the room to pick up their children. Soon, he's the only one left. Niko sits outside the classroom, alone, studying the drawings pasted on the door by the previous year's students. Soon, he imagines, his work will be up there, too.

He walks through the corridors to the bench right in front of the school's main doors. He sits there instead. An hour passes, and the little boy's stomach rumbles with anxiety. It occurs to him, for the first time, that maybe his parents have forgotten him. Where could his Baba be? The little boy thinks of going back to the classroom to ask Madame Murr that very question, but here she is, walking down the hall.

"I've been looking for you," she says. "You should let me know whenever you decide to walk off. There's a war beyond the school walls, let's remember."

He nods, aware that she's aggravated with him. He apologizes; he can't bear to have an adult disappointed in him. She says nothing. He needs to go to the bathroom, but now he's afraid to ask. Madame Murr takes him by the hand to the superintendent's office. The superintendent sits him down.

"Listen," he says, "your father, he can't come. I will drive you to your grandfather's."

As they walk to the superintendent's car, the little boy apologizes yet again for not waiting in the right spot.

"Don't worry about that," the superintendent assures him.

As the car maneuvers through the streets, the superintendent and the little boy pass an apartment building where a gaping hole of twisted balcony railing gives way to the innards of what was once a family's living room. On the next balcony over, an elderly woman hangs laundry to dry. Some of the other buildings they pass are unscathed. Baba once told him this is because the landlords can afford to pay for security.

The superintendent drives by the Corniche for a few blocks, where the sea breeze coming off the bay would normally fill the air with the smell of salt. But nowadays people only drive here to throw out their garbage, and the harbour is now a landfill. Waves push plastic bags and swollen islands of toilet paper against the rocks, like tangles of seaweed. With his hands pressed against the window, the little boy squints to see if he can recognize the logos on the bags. What store have they come from, he wants to know, and has he been there with Mama. Food is expensive, she often complains. The little boy doesn't like powdered milk. He gags every time he hears his Mama boiling water, portioning the powder into the glass.

Soon they pass the little boy's church, its dome and big doors standing unharmed among the rubble. Should he tell the superintendent that they're passing through his neighborhood? The superintendent looks worried; his eyes are darting around every corner. He's driving cautiously. Even though it's bright out, the streets are empty.

If we're going to visit Jiddo, the little boy decides, then my parents must be there as well. He speculates that they've all planned a surprise party for his first day back at school. He hopes someone, maybe even his jiddo, has decided it's time to pay for lamb. He's had weeks of thin chickens. Now they're passing Mama's bank, and now they're in familiar territory: the cigarette store, the pharmacy, down the street the little boy spots the side of their building. Militiamen and Red Cross ambulances have blocked off the street. He wonders if a car has exploded on their street. As the superintendent pulls away, down another street, the little boy sits up on his knees and looks out the back window at the mess they're leaving behind.

Soon they arrive at his jiddo's apartment. Waiting in the doorway, Jiddo, his mama's baba, the oldest and wisest man the little boy knows, steps outside as soon as the Citroën pulls up to the curb. Somewhere not too far off, a machine gun sputters. After Niko gets out of the car, the superintendent speeds off without waving goodbye.

The little boy asks his jiddo if he can expect lamb for dinner, and Jiddo says dinner can wait. "We have somewhere to go."

"Where is Baba?"

"Waiting for us. Come, we must go, quick. They're all waiting."

In his jiddo's car, his thoughts racing with possibilities, the little boy can already smell a restaurant with lamb and a toilet, where he and his family can sit down and eat and laugh and celebrate his new skill, whistling, and the growth of plants. He expects that other students might be there as well, celebrating their first days of school with their own families.

They're driving fast again, now past a group of boys dodging into doorways, pistols in hand. Jiddo, whom the little boy loves for his long stories and his many vests and for the smell of his pipe, says almost nothing during the drive. Where are they going, the little boy wants to know. But Jiddo is reluctant to say anything at all.

Soon after they leave their neighborhood and arrive at a checkpoint. Jiddo shuffles through his fake IDs, while they wait in the line of cars.

Jiddo rolls down the window, holds his card out.

"Where are you going?" asks the guard.

"The hospital," says Jiddo.

The young man looks intently at Jiddo, then back at the ID card. He bangs the butt of his pistol twice on the hood of the car. "*Yallah*, get out."

Hesitant to leave the car, Jiddo instead tries to reason with the fiery young man by explaining how he must deliver this little boy to the hospital, to see his mother. He nods in his grandson's direction. The young man leans down and looks inside the car. The little boy holds so still the guard must feel that he is looking at a statue. In the end, Jiddo reaches for his wallet and produces several bills. The young man takes the money, counts it, and waves his pistol at his friend manning the barricade.

Now the little boy knows they're driving to the hospital to see his mama, and his mind is racing with speculations of brothers, or maybe even a sister, which wouldn't be so bad after all. They make a turn onto a road he recognizes from the visits his mama makes to the doctor, to check on the baby. The little boy shudders with excitement. Within the hour, he concludes, he'll finally meet his new brother or sister. He wants a little brother more than a little sister, but in the end he'll settle for either one. As the older brother, Niko plans to come home from school each day and share all he's learned. By the time his new friend has his or her school photo taken on the balcony, he'll know more than even his teacher. He imagines a boy and a girl, a brother and a sister, standing side by side on their balcony, with frozen smiles. He imagines an entire playground's worth of children, like the playground he witnessed earlier that day at the school, stepping out of his mama's belly and lining up to embrace him.

After they park the car, the little boy asks if he can pee against the hospital's wall, but his jiddo tells him, "No, there's no time."

Somewhere beyond the buildings, a thunderous roar blazes and the ground shakes. Jiddo picks up the boy and runs into the hospital. People everywhere scatter as a billow of smoke rises from the west. The little boy holds onto his jiddo's neck, wrapping his legs tightly around the old man's waist, more eager than ever to see his mama and his new brother or sister.

Once they pass through the hospital doors, Jiddo slows to a cumbersome jog, breathes deeply, coughs, and begins to explain to the little boy the situation at hand. "Inside," he warns, "you'll see things you may not understand, that I won't even understand. Nobody knows what the future holds. Our only choice in the matter is to live, to continue living, to find out how things are going to turn out. All we can do is hope."

As they pass briskly through the hospital corridors and up two flights of stairs, Jiddo gives Niko an urgent squeeze, as if to impress the sadness of their surroundings, and the little boy hugs him back, oblivious and joyful, eager to start this new episode in their lives. His jiddo, after all, is right. The little boy has no say in the matter: brother or sister, he will love them both equally. He already knows that hospitals are not only for new babies, but also for the sick and the elderly and those who stumble and split in the streets after explosions. And so he assures his jiddo not to worry by pressing his hot palms into the elderly man's neck. On previous visits to the hospital, his mama has instructed him to shut his eyes when passing a stranger who might rather not be seen.

Jiddo pats the side of Niko's head and says, "You have a good plan. Don't be afraid to close your eyes for a long time if that's what you want to do."

The little boy nods. "Tell me when to open them again."

Jiddo says the little boy will know on his own. If that's what his jiddo says, then Niko will know. Together they walk through a series of doors and curtains. Peeking through his fingers anyways, they pass a boy no older than the little boy, sitting in a chair with his eyes rolling back in his head. His face is almost blue. He must have missed the first day of school. If they were in a cartoon, the little boy imagines, he could paint the pink back into that boy, and he would beam to life all over again.

There's a man on a stretcher. He has no leg below the knee, just a pale bone snapped off. The woman holding his hand is covered in grey dust. The little boy closes his eyes and thinks instead of his yellow plant pot at school, its seed growing at that very moment. Will the soil bulge like Mama's stomach? Soon he will find out.

When Jiddo sets him down, he knows that it's officially time to open his eyes again. The little boy finds himself in a room with twelve beds. It is full of people who have big bandages. Many are sleeping. Baba is there, and so is the little boy's grandmother. He sees one of his cousins, covering his face. No one says a word.

In the bed lies Mama breathing coarsely. Her entire head, apart from the right side of the face, is covered in gauze. It takes the boy some time to come to terms with the fact that his mama is so broken. Suddenly he feels confused. He wants to scramble away, under the bed, out the door, anywhere. If he runs fast enough, maybe he can run back to this morning. But his baba and Jiddo catch him before he can escape. Baba tells the little boy that he has to say goodbye to his mama soon.

"But where's she going?" The little boy begins to weep. All of his muscles pull and he feels that if he cries any harder, he will implode, and so he chokes his tears to a whimper. He can't hide and this is no time to run away. If indeed this person is his mama, then he'd rather not cry in front of her. He turns toward his jiddo's thigh and bawls into the leg of his grandfather's pants. Jiddo strokes his hair. He buries his face in the leg of Jiddo's pants for what feels like a long time. Then Baba scoops the little boy up in his arms and whispers gently that Mama has something she wants to tell him.

He sets the little boy down on the bed beside her. How ghastly and pale and frightened she looks, like a ghost waiting to be set free.

"*Ya habibi*," she whispers. "My sweetheart."

She tries to move her arm from under the blanket, but fails. Jiddo helps her untangle the arm wrapped in white gauze from the sheet. Once free, her stained fingers touch the little boy's chin. She brushes the matted hair from his hot forehead.

"Be a good boy for your father," she whispers. "Grow up and be a good man."

On her left side, he now realizes she has no arm. Where did her arm go? He can feel her, ever so gently, pulling him closer, maybe to shield him from all that's happening, maybe to start all over again, some other time. Her warm breath on his cheek is a comfort. He crawls into the bed beside her and curls up under her arm. This is how he usually falls asleep when she reads to him at bedtime. He kisses her. He kisses her again and again. He wants her to know that he loves her deeply, without compromise. He holds her tightly. And then, exhausted, he falls asleep. They both fall asleep.

The little boy dreams he's swimming through the garbage bags in the harbour. When he wakes up again, Baba is holding him by the armpits. His pants feel damp. Below, the sheets are wet. Jiddo uses them to cover Mama's brown eyes.

Though the typewriter still sits at the end of the kitchen table, the stack of corrected scripts atop the fridge disappears. And, the little boy's school closes its doors again.

He remembers what God told his father one day at the checkpoint, that no one in Beirut has any patience left, and concludes that his impatience for simple friendship, coupled with his behaviour, which, to Niko's mind was good enough, but by God's standards must have fallen short of expectations, must have deemed him undeserving of new friends and having a mama.

To pass the time, for there is simply too much time everywhere he turns, Niko spends mornings following his baba through math exercises. They work together in the living room, where square patches of light filter through windows webbed with duct tape, to keep them from shattering all over again. "Languages," Baba tells him, "you can learn any day. But if you don't learn math when you're young, you'll never understand it." So they study simple addition and subtraction. When the gunfire in the street grows too loud for math lessons, Baba suggests they listen to some music instead. In the living room, Baba and the little boy lie on the sofa for hours, listening to the small stack of records Baba has saved from before his marriage. When one record finishes, Baba gets up to remove the needle and he says, "You know, Niko, these were my childhood." Then he sets the needle down on another album. "Now, they're yours. Under the circumstances, it's only fair that you have my childhood to share."

He sits back down on the sofa and, taking the little boy into his arms, begins to tell him a story about when he and Mama were young. When the shelling dies down, Baba checks the freezer. They should go out shopping, right away, before the fighting begins again.

Together, Baba and the little boy walk the two blocks to Abou Khoury's grocery store, waving white handkerchiefs to let the local snipers know not to fire. At Abou Khoury's, they wait in line to purchase eggplants and olive oil and chickpeas and yoghurt and large tins of ghastly powdered milk. Rarely, a bag of cashews or some colorful bubblegum, which at Abou Khoury's shop sells for the price of a birthday cake. As Baba haggles down the price of a bag of okras and Abou Khoury argues that a canister of propane is worth more than an evening with a prostitute, the little boy fondles a chocolate bar. Then he sets it back on the shelf. He knows that Baba will not buy him chocolate, nor can he ask.

By the time they return to the apartment, the electricity is out again. As the sun sets over the harbour, Baba and the little boy share a small meal, cooked by propane and eaten by candlelight.

After dinner, a woman from the second floor who has made a habit lately of visiting in the evenings, comes up to cut Baba's and the little boy's hair. The little boy sits on a stool in front of the bathroom mirror and watches her clip away. Hair falls into the sink.

As he lies on a cold mattress in the cellar of the apartment building with twenty of their neighbours, the little boy tries to will his mama back, to no avail. It's getting worse, all of it: Mama, school, the bombings. Sadness. He is eight years old and already bereft of the adequate magic to will what he wants into existence. He fears that she might never return, that there is nothing he can do to redeem himself. All he can do is follow his mama's advice; he lies in bed at night and imagines what it would take for him to be a good man, but apart from resurrecting Mama, little else comes to mind. Beside him, he overhears Baba talking with the woman from the second floor. They talk about Mama and about leaving the country.

When the bombs finally stop falling, they all go back upstairs, and Baba and the little boy discover a gaping hole in the wall of the bedroom, not too large but enough to hear the sounds from the street below. The room is covered in white dust. They go downstairs, and Baba and the woman from the second floor make telephone calls, because the lines are working for a change. Later on in the night, the little boy hides in his bed. He does not want his baba to leave the country. He does not want to stay here alone.

The next day is Sunday. They drive to the church, where Baba talks with the woman from the second floor again, who says she has news about leaving the country. The little boy wanders off, lights a candle for Mama. Once more, he asks for forgiveness. Little flames flicker in silence. On the drive back, Baba announces to the little boy that he may have arranged them passage to Cyprus on a ferry. The traffic moves slowly, and then stops altogether. Teenage checkpoint guards have taken the identity cards of four men and arrested them. Four men kneel off to the side of the road in a straight line. A guard fires into the air, pulls one captive to his knees. A different guard pulls a plastic supermarket bag over the captive's head, ties it tightly around the neck so that it inflates and deflates with every breath, like a giant heart. The checkpoint guards laugh and laugh and laugh as the man tries to breathe. Then they wrap a belt of dynamite around his neck. Baba and the little boy and everyone else caught in the traffic line listen to the fuse burn. The fuse is long and winding, like the war itself. Baba cups his hand over the little boy's eyes. There is little he can do to block the sound of the man's head exploding. Satisfied, the guards take down the checkpoint and light cigarettes as they wave the cars through.

His hand covering Niko's face, Baba drives over what remains of the body, thump thump, like a speed bump. Then they are speeding back to their apartment. In the bright afternoon, the wipers swing blood back and forth on the glass. A finger is caught in the wiper. Baba stops the car on the side of the road, picks it off, and drives away.

"Where is Cyprus?" the little boy asks that evening, as they take the steps downstairs, to the cellar for the night.

"Away from here," his baba says.

"Will we take our TV?"

"We won't take anything we can't carry."

That night as they cower in the cellar, Baba, the little boy, and the woman from the second floor hear not bombs falling, but a gunfight in their building as men from militias chase each other up and down the staircases for hours. They hear loud thuds, like shelves falling. Unable to sleep, the little boy listens to the footsteps for signals of an imminent ending. When dawn arrives, the footsteps stop. Baba and the little boy, huddled in the cellar with a dozen neighbors, begin the trip up the stairs to see what remains.

They find the door to their apartment has been kicked in. The dresser toppled over the sofa. Glass shards in the carpet. Hard circles of maroon punctuate the walls. Lamps are keeled over. Records broken across the sofa. Mama's typewriter in pieces on the kitchen floor. Even the sheets have been stripped from the little boy's bed, leaving only a bare mattress on the floor.

So, they sleep in the living room of the woman on the second floor, whose name, the boy learns, is Nabila. Ten days pass. One night, after a long telephone conversation, Baba says he has found "a way, but quickly." The next morning, they drive to the port of Jounieh, north of Beirut, where they stand at the loading docks under the blazing spring sun, waiting with several dozen other people for a ferry that is supposed to come take them away. Nabila comes too, and bids them farewell. Baba gives her the keys to his car and kisses her on both cheeks.

"Come with us," Baba says, holding her.

"My life is here." She kisses the little boy's forehead and leaves.

Baba has two large leather suitcases, and the little boy carries the knapsack he once took to school. Baba says that in the next country the little boy will go to school, whenever he likes. The little boy has brought his new pencils and notebook, so that he may be prepared.

By the time the ferry arrives the crowd has swelled to more than the boat can accommodate for the overnight voyage. Militia guards try to shape the crowd into something resembling a line. Baba and the little boy wait and wait and wait, documents in hand.

The line moves slowly. As evening arrives, Baba buys a sandwich for the little boy from a vendor who makes his living coming down to these docks and selling sandwiches to people waiting to leave their country.

When their turn arrives, a soldier tells Baba that there is no room to sleep any more passengers on this ship.

"But we don't want to sleep," Baba says. "We want to leave." He offers the soldier money, and then a gold chain. The soldier tells them they can sleep on deck chairs if they want. Baba readily agrees. Holding hands, Baba and the little boy board the boat.

As dusk falls, the ferry quietly pushes away from the shore. Niko looks at the city he has never once left and sees it as he has never seen it before. From the tranquil waters of the harbour, amidst the stench of bloated garbage, the bright flashes of gunfire and the fiery orange balls of smoke look like a bad dream. In deeper waters, Baba manages to secure them a deck chair. Under the stars, with the brittle snaps and punches of the city now fading, and the sea breeze now grown colder, the little boy realizes that for the first time in a long time he is spending the night outside. How expansive the sky looks from the sea. How tiny Jounieh's lights look from the water. By morning, at this rate, the city will no longer be there.

Baba pulls a wool blanket over their legs. He breathes a sigh of relief or regret – the little boy can't be sure. So the little boy closes his eyes and thinks of their nights in the cellar. If he shuts his eyes tightly enough, the little boy can move back in time. He plays in the courtyard, as Baba stands smoking in the doorway of his shop. Look at the gaping hole of blue sky above, how it glows against the concrete. Now he stands on the balcony, posing for a school photo with his baba, his mama, and her womb of possibilities. Now the little boy squeezes harder; and a little brother stands to one side. Mama puts away her typewriter and begins to prepare supper.

The city is gone, and in its place is a blaze of horizon. The ferry rolls up then down then up again upon the open waters of the

Mediterranean. All the other travelers on the deck are like them, whispering obsessively about possibilities for the future, if futures are possible at all. The little boy discovers the sea makes him nauseous. After an evening of lightheadedness on the ferry's slippery deck, he succumbs to a fitful sleep of exhaustion and dreams. Looking over the ship's railing, he dreams that among the waves he can see his pregnant mama sitting alone in a rowboat, holding her belly in her hands like a large vase. All around her flow shapeless waves, twisting and turning, building and receding. The ferry pulls away. When his mama is little more than the size of a coin, she tips sideways out of the rowboat. She flaps her arms like wings and bursts out of the sea like a seagull. She flies away.

The next morning he holds onto his baba's leg and looks over the railing. Out there, he watches an endless enormity of waves much bigger than anything he has ever seen at the port or at a beach. The air is stiff, cold, and full of salt. A ship's hand walks among the crowd, tells them they are passing through a storm, assures them this is normal. Until then, the little boy has never considered his preference for land, but as he struggles for adequate footing on the deck of this boat, embracing his baba's leg each time the white foam of a wave strikes the bow, he decides that he likes land better.

The wind sharpens. Rain lashes them. Together they huddle on their beach chair, a suitcase on one side for privacy, under a thin blanket they've been given to keep warm. The waves are simply everywhere, there and continuous. Niko fears this voyage away from home will be much the same: always there, always continuous.

The little boy's teeth chatter. He presses his face into Baba's chest for warmth, but finds only dampness. "Where will we live on Cyprus?" he asks his baba. The thin blanket snaps in the wind.

"Somewhere warm," Baba says. A thick wave crashes against the side of the ferry, sprays them both. Then he adds, "But let's see first if Cyprus will let us stay."

By afternoon the clouds have drifted off, and the sun dries the deck. The Cypriot shore appears as a thin brown line on the horizon.

An hour later, the ferry pulls into a port. At the dock, young men in uniforms greet the passengers.

"Visas!" they call out. "Have your visas ready!"

His baba grimaces. Hand in hand, Baba and the little boy stand on the ship's deck through the afternoon, waiting to make their case as the sun burns their necks. The guards take their time strip-searching every bag and every man. Few passengers possess the visas in question. As Baba and the little boy near their turn in line, they discover that the cost of a temporary visitor's permit, the only form of permission they will be given without a visa, is prohibitively expensive.

"Your papers," the guard says.

Baba hands the bored young man his passport.

"And what is your final destination?"

"We don't know."

"Today, nobody knows anything," says the guard. "One long line of idiots." He rifles through the passport. "Stand over there and get undressed."

Baba unbuttons his shirt. Soon he is naked. Exposed, he waits under the hot Cypriot sun with other naked men before an audience of hundreds. Eventually another guard arrives and asks the little boy to move from his father's side. He prods Baba with a nightstick, as if to see if he can tap something loose. A second guard tosses through the clothes and papers in their two suitcases, which lie open beside them.

"Okay, get dressed," says the guard. Quickly then, he frisks the little boy, who stands still and dares nothing. "Collect your things and wait over there."

He points to a hangar at the end of the dock. Soon, they begin crossing the sun-baked tarmac. They pass an old woman, stopped to catch her breath. A man holds her by the arm. They arrive to a crowd of dozens who have been directed to the hangar like them. Between the asphalt, the metal roof and the afternoon sun, the hangar feels like an oven, and the many smells of the long journey waft through the humidity. Rumours circulate that some are being told to board another ferry and go back. The hangar is for families only. Another rumour asserts that men or women without children have been asked to wait by a second ferry. Baba and the little boy sit on their suitcases and wait for what will come next, visitation permits or deportation.

Finally a jeep drives up, and an official in a grey suit steps down and welcomes the boat's passengers to Cyprus. "We sincerely hope you will enjoy your stay with us." Their stays cannot last more than thirty days. In that time, they must check in with the police once every seven days and they may not marry or work or purchase land. Any crime or suspicion of crime, and any failure to check in with police once every week, will result in immediate deportation. "But please enjoy your stay," the official insists, "and consider yourselves our guests."

At dusk, three trucks arrive. After paying the fee for a temporary visitation card, the travelers are herded onto the truck beds. They are escorted to the port gates, where lines of taxis manned by drivers who greet them in hollers of cobbled Arabic they have picked up since the beginning of the Lebanese civil war turned the Limassol port into a thriving industry. Foreigners, too afraid to question the fare, pay guest rates.

By the time they are outside the port perimeter, the sun has set. Only a bright orange stripe lines the horizon. A man who sits next to Baba says that he doesn't want to be at the port when night comes, especially with suitcases. He has heard stories that this is where travellers get robbed, just outside the port after dark.

"Where do people go from here?" Baba asks.

The man says he doesn't know. "One here, another there. Greece, Egypt, Tunisia, France, wherever the boats stop and there is work."

The little boy who felt so sick the night before and only slept fitfully is having trouble staying awake. When will they return to their apartment, he wants to know. But Baba has no adequate reply.

He carries the little boy and the luggage off the truck. With the help of an insistent taxi driver, Baba shuffles the boy and their bags into a Nissan. The driver asks if they want to go to a hotel. He claims to know one that takes in Arabs.

"No, that's okay," says Baba.

He produces a piece of paper from his pocket and reads the driver an address of a man who once employed him. As the car drives along the seafront highway leading into the city of Limassol, the little boy falls asleep to the passing yellow streetlights.

When the little boy wakes up again, Baba is undressing him in a bathroom he doesn't recognize. He yawns. The mirror in this bathroom has a long and winding crack running through it, he notices, a detail that would make him uncomfortable if he had more energy. But he is too exhausted to respond with any enthusiasm. Baba lifts him into the tub and scrubs him clean. His skin tingles in the warm water.

"Where are we?" the little boy asks.

"We are with friends tonight."

"Is this where we'll live?" The little boy looks around, at the shampoo bottle with foreign letters, at the parched sea-sponge.

"This is where we'll live tonight. Tomorrow, we'll see about the rest."

Baba towels him off. He carries the little boy to a strange living room and sets him on a loveseat that has been made into a bed. A man with a grizzled beard brings a bowl of cereal that Niko laps hungrily, for once food touches his lips he realizes that he hasn't eaten all day.

A cool draft flows in through an open window. Crickets chirp. Off in the corner of the room, he notices an upright vacuum stoically awaiting its next assignment, and this machine reminds him of the red Miele tucked away in his own apartment's bedroom closet. With a touch of sadness, he imagines riding that fiery engine across his living room carpet. Then he falls asleep.

*

Where will they go next? This is the question Baba wants to answer, as soon as possible. Every day Baba wakes up early and shares a morning coffee and cigarette with their host, whose name is Raymond. At a table behind the house, the two men sit in the morning sun while Raymond helps Baba navigate the city with a map drawn on the back of a cigarette pack. The little boy knows that Baba is worried about money. Every night, Baba counts his money in their room. Every morning, he asks Raymond if he knows of any quick jobs that won't attract the scrutiny of police. Then Baba walks the forty-five minutes to the office building downtown, where he waits in line at the long-distance calling centre. And so the little boy stays behind most days, passing the hours among the grass and trees of Raymond's property.

Raymond owns a small farm on the outskirts of Limassol. He has a face like Yasser Arafat that the little boy recalls pasted all over Beirut telephone poles. But Raymond is nowhere as intimidating. Raymond has lived in Cyprus since before the war. He fixes cars for a living.

Every morning after Baba goes walking into the city to make phone calls, Raymond takes the little boy into the garage at the back of his house to show him how cars work.

"Here is the engine and here is the exhaust," he explains. "The life of a car starts here and ends there. The beginning is a spark and the end is smoke." Otherwise, Raymond passes the time in the garage telling the little boy stories of when his baba was not yet married.

In the evenings Baba returns, and they drink little cups of coffee and smoke cigarettes. Raymond suggests the names of people that Baba can try calling, people at embassies and people who've passed through his home. Leaning forward as if he's about to share a secret, Raymond says, "You are safer sleeping on the streets of any country in the world than you are trying to build your future in Lebanon. No one here will block the road or shoot at me from a building."

Raymond has many people from Lebanon stay at his house. Apart from fixing cars, he makes money by giving the recently exiled a place to stay after they leave Lebanon. Why is he so fortunate while so many others live in despair, he asks, only to answer his own question. Because he had the foresight to leave before everything went down the toilet. He had the luxury to go to the embassy and apply for a proper visa, and so he is one of the few Arabs on the island of Cyprus who owns a farm. He laughs at his great wisdom. Now he profits from the mistakes of those who were too attached to their homes.

Baba slumps in his chair, depressed. "To work you need a visa. To get a visa you need to work." He is caught in the middle.

"Listen, my friend," Raymond says, "it's difficult to move to another country without walking through a wall of politics. But the difficulty is worth it. You go to the bottom, and you learn to be humble again, and you do it so that maybe you can one day live for yourself again. At least in the rest of the world, you can build a future for him."

And so the next day Baba walks down the hill to make more phone calls. He calls the names given to him by Raymond, relatives of relatives, friends of past associates, anyone whose number he can find among those who have already left Beirut. When he returns in the afternoon, Baba tells the little boy stories of phone calls to Greece, Italy, France, Spain, even England, where a second cousin, or an entrepreneur whose parents come from his father's village, or Mama's old classmate, or whomever he happens to connect with that day, ponders the possible opportunities that could befit a man with little education and questionable papers, who has spent his life running a camera shop.

"Why not go to Kuwait or the Gulf?" they sometimes suggest. They ask him to call back in a few days, so that they can ask around to see who's feeling charitable.

Then Baba walks his pride back to Raymond's house, where he recounts adventure stories to the little boy, partly to forget about the day and partly to allay the little boy's many questions about the cities he's called from his little booth at the telephone centre that day. After learning about car parts in the morning, the little boy spends his afternoons climbing the trees on Raymond's property and waiting for his baba to come back up the hill with new stories of what seems to the boy like a huge and magical world, and then he lies in the long grass as the afternoon wanes and imagines faraway places like Greece, where according to his baba the pigeons fly upside down; Italy, where the sun never sets; France, where the lions are friendly and often become lifelong companions to little boys; Spain, where trees grow taller than buildings; even England, where the schools teach students how to travel into space.

After fifteen days of making phone calls and fabricating stories, of tired legs and sunburned shoulders from walking up and down the hills, Baba and the little boy visit the Limassol police station for a second time. They wait in a long line of worrisome faces that the little boy vaguely recognizes from the ferry. It seems to him that any time they must wait in lines, they are also asked to explain themselves. He listens closely as a man ahead of them describes a city called Dubrovnik in a place called Yugoslavia, where the sea overflows with fish. He imagines walking on fish flapping beneath his feet, then picking one up in his hand and flying away.

Once their turn at the counter arrives, an unsmiling woman asks Baba his name: Karam, Antoine. She runs down a list of questions regarding his activities in Cyprus, where he can be reached should the police want to find him, the nature of his future plans.

Baba has many aspirations. "I would like to find work," he tells her. "And I want to put the boy in school."

The woman reminds Baba and the little boy that they cannot, under any circumstances, stay in Cyprus for more than thirty days.

Baba and the little boy leave the police station and step back into the blazing afternoon sun, for now they are deep into August, the most oppressive summer month. They walk along the cobblestone streets of two-story townhouses and past the occasional private garden, to a plaza that hosts only pigeons and cats at that time of day. The shops are closed and most working people slumber through an afternoon siesta or skim through worry beads or watch foreign football matches on little televisions.

They pass a school playground. Then they walk down a slope that leads to an olive grove.

"Will I go to school next year?" Niko asks. The boy, who is not as little as he used to be, has not attended a full year of school for two years.

"We must get you into school," Baba confirms. Above all, he fears his son has already slipped too far to catch up with other children his age. He does not want the boy's life to turn into one long quest for survival. As they walk along the dirt road that cuts through the olive grove, a small truck approaches and offers them a ride to the end of the valley, not far from where Raymond lives.

That evening, as the sun dips closer to the horizon and the temperature cools, Baba finds the little boy in the back garden of Raymond's house, throwing rocks at sparrows with the kind of incumbent hostility he recognizes as the first sign of a tragic awareness. Reality is often little more than a negation of dreams.

"Come, leave the birds alone," he cautions. "Let's go for a walk."

They walk toward the sunset. The dirt path that cuts through the grass comes to an end at a cliff's edge. Cast in long shadows, Baba helps the little boy scramble down large sun-bleached rocks to the pebble shores of an isolated beach below. Only small waves ripple in from the Egyptian coast. Baba removes his shirt and runs toward the sea in nothing other than shorts and tennis shoes, splashing and laughing and jumping. He dives in headfirst and seconds later resurfaces with a rusted Pepsi can in his hand, which he throws back to the shore.

"Come!" he beckons to the boy, pushing back hair from his eyes. "It's not too cold."

The little boy pulls off his T-shirt and then tries to find a path into the water that doesn't taunt or disarm him, even though he already knows from past experience that there is no cure for the sea's coolness.

"Don't wait for the sea to invite you," his Baba calls. "Run in with your eyes closed. Think about something else. The rest will take care of itself."

The little boy heeds his baba's advice, because if Baba says so then it must be true. He shuts his eyes tightly, thinks of Mama sitting at her typewriter in the kitchen, his ear pressed against her belly. He imagines that from the inside of that belly his little brother does the same thing, that they are connected at that moment by their curiosity for one another. And then he feels the pebbles beneath his shoes give way to splashes, and before he knows it he has run into the sea waist-deep. He lunges ahead and saltwater rushes up his nostrils and he coughs and mucus runs down his chin. It has been years, many years, since he has ventured into the sea. The last time he was four or five, a lifetime away, when he and Baba and Mama used to go the private beach club and he would wear waterwings and wrap his arms around Baba's neck. Now he is much too old for that.

"Come," says Baba, "I will teach you to swim." He takes the boy by the arms. "The first thing you must do to swim is relax. Don't fight. Come here." Baba puts one hand under the little boy's shoulders and another hand under the little boy's thighs. He raises him to the surface. "Now, imagine you are like the shore, a natural friend to the sea. Just relax." The sea licks the little boy's arms and spills in and out of his ears. Somewhere behind him a boat rocks, as the day's last fishermen cast a net into a phantasm of white light. "Close your eyes," says Baba, "and breathe in. Hold it."

The little boy closes his eyes and breathes in and forgets all about the precarious dilemma of floating a body heavier than water. Baba continues to soothe him with calm words. Eyes closed, Niko visualizes his father's words. He breathes. He follows the lights that appear beneath his eyelids. Green, orange, blue. How much time has passed before he realizes that Baba's hands no longer prop him up? The magician has moved back to admire his handiwork; all this time the little boy has floated of his own accord. Once he knows this, the spell vanishes and he sinks. Baba steps in and helps him find his feet.

"We'll try again tomorrow."

The next evening, when Baba returns from his downtown phone calls, they walk back down to the beach and try all over again. And so it goes the following evening, and the following, until the little boy has mastered the motion of no longer relying on his father's hand.

From Limassol they travel by ferry to the Turkish port of Antalya, where a waterfall flows directly into the sea. It is the height of tourist season and a summer heatwave blankets the city. They are tired from the voyage, the drawn-out voyage. They smell. The boat trip from Cyprus was crowded. As they walk through the seafront streets in search of a hotel, shopkeepers eye them suspiciously and handle them with condescension whenever they ask for help.

In the city's backstreets they find a hotel. Baba helps the little boy undress and shower. As Baba scrubs the little boy's hair, he recounts the only story he knows of Antalya, the tale of the great King Attalos the Second.

According to legend, Baba tells him, King Attalos challenged his men to sail the seven seas and return with news of a heaven on earth. When they ran aground in a land of cliffs and waterfalls and green trees and meadows, they said to themselves, this must be the oasis their king envisioned. And that was how Antalya became known as the place where the heavens meet earth. But he doesn't tell the little boy that there is no such thing as a heaven on earth anymore, at least not for them.

Soon after the little boy falls asleep. Baba sits in a chair by his bed and watches him. He considers again the King Attalos story he just told the boy and decides that the world is closed to them, that he's running out of money and ideas, and that the war they escaped might as well be tattooed on his face, because he is a man and he is Arab and he is moving into a part of the world that is suspicious of Arab men, a world that has little sympathy for grown-up men who have been touched by trouble, and now, even though leaving the war is the only thing he wants, he cannot escape its influence no matter where he goes. This leaves him in a somber mood. He goes out to the balcony and listens to the joyous tones of tourism, and yet feels that there is nothing for him and his son in those streets below. Maybe here he'll find some work at the back of a restaurant, but nothing for the boy and no chance of a future, only surviving.

The next morning, to ward off thoughts of impending failure, Baba ruffles the little boy's hair and buys him a döner sandwich and a Coca-Cola. Together they sit on the edge of the sidewalk and eat breakfast, as German and British tourists embarking on days of shopping and sun tanning step around them to admire new sunglasses and bathing suits and the cheap busts of gods that front all the shops.

The next night in Antalya, radio and television relay the news that a truck bomb in Beirut has killed over 200 American soldiers. The hotel manager asks them to leave.

"Is our money no good?" Baba raises his voice.

The manager threatens to call the police. "You make the other guests uncomfortable," he hisses. "Please, leave and don't make any trouble for us."

With nowhere to stay among the tourists, they get back on the first boat to accept them and travel to the furthest outreaches of the Greek islands, Rhodos. On the open sea, the little boy asks for another döner sandwich, and Baba begins to resent that the boy is always hungry, always waiting for his next meal. Meanwhile he himself hasn't eaten more than one meal a day since leaving Cyprus. Baba can no longer afford to be the person he'd like to be, not with this mask of the perpetual victim sewn fast to his face. He must accept his predicament and give up the luxury of pride, think like the scavenging man he has become. He has made errors in judgment. Traveling has proven more expensive than he anticipated.

He has traveled into a fog. His steps have become clumsy with desperation.

On the ferry, he overhears a Turkish fisherman who speaks some Arabic, and eager to speak his own language to another adult, he engages this reluctant man and soon finds himself asking insistent questions about the region, somewhere he might be able to find work for a week or two. The fisherman tells him of a nearby island called Karpathos where the locals often take seasonal help at that time of year to deal with the tourists. Because the island is small and so remote, the authorities there don't ask too many questions.

"You go there," the fisherman says, backing away. "Your troubles will disappear, I am sure." And then he leaves for another part of the boat.

In Rhodos, looking to save on ferry tickets, he offers to pay a local boat-owner to take them to Karpathos. But the Greek is hesitant to deal with this Arab who broaches him with frantic sign language, and so Antoine offers him a little more. Through a wave of the hand they strike a deal. The Greek throws their suitcases into his dinghy, and then pushes the boat from the shore.

The sea is choppy. The fishing vessel lunges violently through the waves. Once they are out on the water, the little boy turns olive-green and begins to complain that he does not feel well. The Greek is foul-tempered. He does not have patience for children and complains that the boy's crying is irritating. Spray from the sea soaks them. Without a cloud in sight, the sun and saltwater makes them wet and thirsty all at once.

If only he had saved the boy enough water, Antoine laments. He would sooner nourish the boy than educate him.

The Greek yells something, but his words get lost in the wind. When they strike the butt end of another wave, the little boy yelps. In all the commotion, he has bitten down on his lip. He screams, bleeds freely from the mouth. The Greek lurches back and threatens to slap the child if he doesn't shut up. Antoine smothers the boy in his salty sleeve to appease the Greek. Something must happen soon, he searches his mind frantically as he presses the sleeve into the little boy's gash, perhaps one of those unlikely pirouettes of fate that aggrandize the stories of old men and bloat them into legend.

By the time the boat pulls into the turquoise waters of the Karpathos shoreline, the boy's lip has bled dry. The sun, at its peak, has thrown flame after flame at them, without abating, as if they are cursed. Apart from the random squawks of seagulls, nobody can be seen anywhere on the shore. The townspeople have boarded up their shops for the afternoon and retreated to the white bungalows that skirt the hills rising out of the bay.

The festering Greek jumps out and pulls his dinghy ashore. Before Baba and the little boy have climbed out, he's yelling that he's had enough of them and that he can't believe how these Arabs have dirtied this little boat, his livelihood, with their filthy, devious blood. "My money," he shouts, slapping his palm.

Antoine has already paid the man, but he does not want an argument, for fear that he cannot win. The Greek can always go to the police. So Baba pulls the suitcases from the boat and pays the man more money. Not wanting to upset the Greek further, he attempts to ask for advice on where to go next, but by then the boat-owner has received his money and wants nothing to do with them. He traipses up the shore, crosses the road, and disappears into one of the narrow alleyways that punctuate the seafront taverns and shops.

The streets are empty. A Volkswagen speeds past, screeching as it turns the bend around the hill. And then all is quiet again. His son's chin and neck and hands are covered in blood. Antoine's shirt, too, is soaked in the boy's blood. Now the little boy complains that the sun is too hot, that he's feeling lightheaded. The boy, Antoine feels, is constantly complaining. He whimpers, asks irrationally for his mama, over and over again. Antoine looks around, sees little in the way of opportunity. What can I do now, he thinks. Feeling his face he realizes that he hasn't shaved in days, and that his cheeks bristle with the prematurely speckled beard that makes him look like an Arab derelict. The locals will mistake them for trouble. What can I do now, he worries.

Most pressingly, he decides, they need to find shade, drink water, and wash away the blood that stains them, and so he picks up the suitcases and calls for the little boy to follow him. They trample up the sandy shore and cross a slate-stone road that has long been bleached by the inescapable sun. How utterly hot he feels after the journey. Even the sea breeze can't sate the heat that has embedded itself under his skin. In the distance, he can hear the cyclical whine of the old windmills that skirt the hills. It has been days since he has eaten a proper meal, and he wonders now if the boat trip hasn't left him a bit delirious, because his thoughts appear to have filtered down to one thought that keeps returning to him involuntarily and with disturbing regularity: to wash away the blood, wash away the blood, wash away the blood that stains them. But first he must find shade. He looks back for the boy and sees that Niko has not kept pace with him, that he himself must be walking with the diligence of a man obsessed, and so he runs ahead and sets the suitcases down under an olive tree, and then runs back across the dusty street and picks up the boy. They arrive under the patchy shade of the tree. To his dismay, the boy looks as if he's been beaten and starved. His lips have cracked and his eyes are hazy. He kisses the boy, perhaps too fiercely, beckons him to stay alert.

"Let's go wash away this blood," he says to the boy. The boy nods.

Antoine rubs the boy's head. "And what's your name?"

The boy's eyes roll back into their lids, as if simple thinking will push him into exhaustion. "Niko," he says. "Niko Karam," he repeats. "Nine years old," he continues, anticipating the next question.

"Good boy. Now let's go."

Even though the stores are closed for the afternoon, Antoine knows from his time in Cyprus and Turkey that some of the owners simply lock up for several hours and sit by the quiet whir of a fan to read a newspaper or magazine. Hand in hand, they leave their suitcases and step back into the sunlight to walk the thirty paces to the bleached red walls and chipped columns that were once built to emulate the temples of Knossos. Antoine knocks on the first door, a little shop for ice cream and newspapers and cigarettes, and soon catches the attention of a man in an undershirt, who approaches the door with suspicion and begins to question Antoine in Greek. Unlike the Cypriots or the Turks, the Greeks here do not know a word of Arabic. Antoine holds up his hands and makes a scrubbing motion, but the man in the undershirt is warded off by the Arab stranger, and so he draws the shutters and returns to the back of his store. When at the next door Antoine picks up the bloodied boy so that he can demonstrate the distress of their situation, they are refused again. Door to door they go, searching for sympathy, or at least begrudging access to a bathroom. A kitchen sink will do just as well. He will settle for a garden hose.

At long last, a young woman is overwhelmed enough by the sight of Antoine and the little boy to help. She steps outside and motions for them to follow her. Antoine runs back to collect the suitcases, which have attracted the attention of a stray dog, and then they follow her through a narrow alleyway to the back gate of her café, where there is a small garden, a terrace of four tables and a shed. She unlocks the shed and offers them the washbasin. She explains something in Greek that they cannot understand, turns the taps on and off, and shows them some rags they can use to dry off. Then she leaves them. Soon Baba and the boy can overhear her in the café, arguing with an older man, perhaps a father or an uncle.

How much time they have here, Antoine does not know, and so he begins the laborious task of scrubbing the boy clean with only thin shafts of sunlight piercing through the ramshackle ceiling to guide him. That the water is yellow and tastes faintly of copper and salt does not deter him. After a while it is cool, and that is all that matters. After Baba has scrubbed the boy clean and washed his hair under the tap, he rubs his own skin clean and washes the sweat from his brow. The clothes they wear are ruined, and so they open the suitcases and change and, not knowing where to go next or how long they have in the shed, they take a moment to sit on a bench next to a pile of tires. Though it is only the middle of the afternoon, the day has felt like an eternity. In the dark of the shed the boy falls asleep, his head in his father's lap, and to pass the time until they are asked to leave again, Antoine contemplates whom to phone once they've found a place to rest their heads.

The problem, as Antoine sees it, cannot be solved in its current form. He cannot leave the boy alone for entire days, which is what the fishermen of Karpathos ask of him, if he is to fish with them. And though he has had the minor good fortune of locating a farmhouse and a family to take them in, he forever feels the situation is fleeting and that this host family's goodwill is bound to cloud inevitably, sometime, like any clear sky. Still, for now they have a small guesthouse and simple meals, and the little boy can spend his days playing with the children. But their new world, although momentarily tranquil, does not offer an antidote to their many problems. The fishing itself pays little, and the fishermen skim a little more off his pay at the end of each day. Add to this, Antoine is forever preoccupied with the matter of the boy's schooling. The boy cannot afford to miss another year of school, nor does he know the language used in schools in this part of the world. There are international schools in the region that will teach the boy in French or English, but those are expensive. Antoine cannot cover any of it without well-paying and stable work, let alone the spectre of no work at all. Furthermore, if the boy is to have a secure future, he must continue his studies in French or English, and he must go west. The Arab universities will not prepare him for the world at large. And yet, they would need to find their way to France, at the very least, to find such opportunities, if such opportunities exist beyond the ports and the customs. He cannot bring himself to return to the Middle East. He no longer believes in the future of the Arab world. Arab life – Arab animosity and Arab vengeance – has taken his livelihood, his wife, his apartment, most of his personal belongings, and the stamina of his will.

To add to his complications, there is the matter of their passports, which expire in three weeks. After that, there is only land, but no grasp of its rewards. So, despite the fish and friendship of this island, they must travel to the mainland, find an embassy.

And then there is the question of his savings. During his visits to the exchange bureau in Limassol and Antalya, he has noticed a disturbing trend in his bank account, an amalgam of Lebanese liras that plunges in value every time news of another horrific attack finds its ways from the streets of Beirut to the circuitry of international televisions and radios. What was initially intended to soften the transition of the first year abroad has quickly dwindled not through their spending, for they have been nothing if not frugal, but through the machinations of international currency fluxes. His life's savings have been slashed in half in a matter of weeks, as the war has attacked his bank account.

Antoine surmises that they have not escaped the war after all, that perhaps they may never outrun it. The problem of his country, this ever-complicated struggle to stay together in the face of adversity, has leached onto their skin and traveled with them. They cannot rid themselves of it. It stains them. So once Antoine Karam has left the offices of the island's only currency exchange, a room of decrepit furnishings with a whirring ceiling fan and a hairy, vile-looking man with an acid tongue who negotiates exchange rates like he's selling diamonds at a souk, he walks back down the winding streets, passing elders who drink wine on the stoop and boys who pull mules loaded with baskets of vegetables, and he thinks that all he has left are his phone calls. He must reach out, once again, and ask for the charity of others. It has become his curse in life, to request of people the one thing he disdains most: the helping hand that will leave him in their debt.

He trudges through the streets of Pigadia, Karpathos' main town, smelling like fish and defeat, knowing where he must go but not looking forward to getting there. Everywhere around him the street lamps flicker on, turning the island into a constellation of stars, a minor universe in the middle of the sea. Had he arrived here without his problems, Antoine would have very much enjoyed the slow pace of this hideaway. Maybe in another time, he and his wife and the boy could have vacationed here. More and more, he finds that the weeks of deliberation that have marked his time on this island have made him, above all, mournful. In the turmoil of trying to get from one life to the next, he has pushed his wife's memory into the corner of his mind. But on this island, his mind is like a whirling dervish that has tired; its spinning has slowed down and the illusion of ornamental symmetry has given way to the more chaotic form of flailing arms and garments. Without Elise, he finds the world to be one interminable difficulty, a struggle that a person of a certain age will consider insurmountable without a companion at his side. Above all, he misses companionship, the ability to deflect his quandaries to Elise, the gumption to take her worries and cure them.

Turning the corner at a bicycle rental shop, where a young Italian couple tests the seats of a two-person bicycle, he walks up the cement steps of the sidewalk to the phone centre he knows all too well, with its walls of phone booths. He slips into a stall and looks at that unassuming silver-plated rotary once again. Where will it lead him today?

How carefree the rest of the world appears, how unburdened. What fingers must have touched these very numbers in times of spiritual fog like his. Antoine dials his oldest friend, to whom he has been directing anyone who offers to call him back, but all he receives when dialing Beirut is a busy signal, the telltale tones of a country gone mad. The lines are down yet again. From the outside, his home city has become unreachable. Planes will not land there. Most of the time, the phones don't work. No point in writing letters;

who's to get them to their destination? Once you leave, Lebanon may as well be on another planet.

He pulls out his wallet and withdraws the piece of paper upon which he has written every single number he's dialed in the past months: his extended cousins, his aunts, his uncles, his nieces, his nephews, many of whom moved in the first years of the war and resettled in places like Marseilles or Dubai or Michigan, which he has heard is somewhere in the United States. Few of his relatives have anything to offer beyond sympathy and condolences. Some have moved from Beirut with their companies. They are allowed to work in their new countries, but once their jobs disappear, they too must leave. As temporary guests, they have no right to sponsor Antoine and his son. Others are like him, still traveling.

Once he has run through the list of numbers he associates with his side of the family, he goes outside, on the steps of the telephone centre to smoke a cigarette and watch the sun slip under the horizon. After the cigarette, he prepares himself for the more onerous chore of calling Elise's side of the family, whom he already knows from past calls will have less sympathy in store for him. To them, he has become an outsider, one of the circumstances leading to Elise's death. They took his ambition to leave Beirut as an insult, and those conclusions, he has learned since, have trickled into the lives of family members abroad. Still, Antoine has no choice but to ask for help. So he goes back into his booth and gets it over with.

Customarily, the first call he makes to the Badr side goes to Elise's cousin Youssef, in Jeddah, for it is through Youssef that he met Elise in the first place. To his surprise, Youssef claims he has been awaiting Antoine's call for days. "We may have an answer to your problems," he says. "Do you know Elise's sister Yvonne?"

Antoine remembers her only vaguely, as the one who rarely talks to the family.

"Yes, that's her," Youssef confirms. "Someone passed along the news of you and Niko. She phoned me to say that she and her husband want to help you."

"Where does she live now?"

Canada, Youssef tells him. "Do you know her husband? Her husband's name is Sami Malek."

Antoine knows of the Malek family. The Maleks once owned a big construction company in Lebanon.

Youssef Badr passes along the Malek telephone number. Hurriedly, Antoine takes it over to the operator's booth to gather the proper dialing codes.

"What time is it there?" Antoine asks, cobbling together the only Greek he has learned to articulate with the help of hand gestures.

The operator scans his map of the world. "Early still. Late morning."

What help could they be prepared to offer, he wonders, what chance or charity has landed at my feet. Antoine rushes back to the phone booth and dials the number he's scribbled on his palm. The line rings two times, then three. On the other end, a hand finally fumbles with the receiver, and a man's voice grumbles through.

"Sami Malck!" Antoine cries, surprised he would be that relieved to hear the voice of a complete stranger, a man whose family he'd only read about in the newspapers of Beirut. Nevertheless the voice on the other end still counts as family, his brother-in-law. They are connected by the pair of sisters they love, and at the sound of this man's voice, he suddenly feels as if the ghost of his wife has graced this call. No matter that this man's wife, from what he recalls, had distanced herself from the family ever since she was old enough to think independently. They are out in the world now, beyond petty histories. Custom precludes that they have an obligation to each other. And so Antoine introduces himself. "How are you, my brother?"

"I am alive," Sami says. "What more can I ask for?" They experience a pause, a natural delay in the line. "They tell me you lost your shop."

"My friend, I've lost everything."

It is then that Sami offers his condolences for Elise. "By the time news comes to us here, it's already months old. I heard that you left. Tell me, where are you now?"

"We've been traveling for nearly two months. We have been to Cyprus, to Turkey. Now we are on one of the Greek islands. Do you know Karpathos?"

Sami says yes, he knows of Karpathos. "They tell us you need help. Do you need money?"

Antoine hunts for a hint of condescension in Sami's voice. At the question of money from this man's mouth, he feels the hairs stand up on the back of his neck. His pride stretches and roars up like a lion awakening.

"No, no," he hears himself say. "Money can be found under rocks here." He laughs nervously, regrets that he has a nose that will not tolerate the stench of charity. Wanting to deflect the attention away from his situation, he begins talking instead about the boy.

"I am very worried for Niko," he confesses. "He has not been in school for two years. Soon, I'm afraid all hope of an education will be lost for him. For me, it doesn't matter. I look at my life compared to his and I can say I have lived, I had the possibility to grow up. But for him, I fear those opportunities may not come."

"Can you not immigrate?"

"Immigration takes time, it takes money. To be honest, Sami, when it comes to this journey, I have regrets. Perhaps I should have made more plans for what would happen. Still, you know, I am happy we are alive. I don't mind working for my money. I can build myself again. It will take maybe longer than I first thought, but it is possible. In the meantime, it is the boy's future that concerns me."

As he says this, Antoine hears a clamour on the other end, and for a moment he fears the connection will die in all the commotion, or that his story will go unheard. Then he hears a woman's voice shout into the phone.

"Antoine, are you there? This is Yvonne."

Straightaway he is taken by how similar Yvonne's voice sounds to her sister's. At those first calls of his name, he feels as if this phone connects not across the oceans but to another reality in which Elise still lives and his problems have more to do with ambition than survival.

In a tempered Arabic, Yvonne recounts the story of how she heard of Elise's passing, how she mourned and mourned and mourned, not only Elise but the whole of her family, whom she only spoke to sporadically, if that. "Here you have the opportunity to work and work, but there is no sense of family and, without family, no sense of purpose. Of course, I understand, we are here alone. This is to start a new life."

Their lives in Canada are safe but unfulfilling, and underlying the pragmatism in Yvonne's voice, Antoine can hear faint wisps of the sadness he once recognized in his wife's more downcast episodes. Leaning against the wall of the phone booth, he picks up the thrust of her message.

Presently she states her case. "Antoine, send Niko. Think about it. We will pay his ticket and we will put him in school, and in the meantime we will help you apply for immigration or give you the time to settle yourself wherever you want to live. You find the life you want, and in the meanwhile, let the boy have an education, warm food, and a stable home."

Antoine doesn't know how to respond to what is either charity or logic, he cannot decide. "Yvonne, I have to tell you," he says, "your voice reminds me so much of your sister's. This is a very generous offer."

"Think about it, Antoine. This is all I ask. Anytime you want, we are ready. We will buy the ticket the next day."

Antoine assures the woman half a world away that he won't say no just yet. They hang up. Their conversation has taken longer than he expected, and the fee quoted to him by the operator proves brutally expensive.

Outside, his pockets that much emptier, he sees that all remnants of the day have disappeared – the traffic, the sidewalk conversations – leaving in their place packs of dogs in search of scraps. Hurrying up the hill to the farmhouse, Antoine cannot dislodge that woman's voice from his thoughts. He cannot claim to know her, but he senses innately that Yvonne's striking similarity to his Elise, her frankness, is in itself something of a sign. After all, he cannot keep the boy locked away in his room for much longer.

Antoine returns to the guesthouse, finds the boy asleep on the floor, a cushion tucked under his head. The television glares with manic colors. He turns down the volume, then removes the shoes from the boy's feet. The boy insists always on wearing shoes. Perhaps an aftereffect of running to the bomb shelter in the middle of the night. Is it wrong of him to want to keep his son at his side, he wonders, as he picks the boy up off the floor. A boy belongs with his father, this everyone knows, but a boy also needs a family, friends, and the experience of an ordinary existence. Still, as he puts the boy to bed, he can't bear to conceive of a future for himself without Niko in the wings. Without his son, where will Antoine find the will to build a new home for them?

Propped up on the bed beside Niko, he smokes a cigarette to the light of the evening news on muted television. Pictures of his home flash past, a speeding Mercedes, a crowd warily circling the aftermath of an explosion. Here the scaffolding of an apartment building that once had walls, there a press conference featuring Amine Gemayel, apparently the new president since his brother was assassinated. Pictures, flashing pictures, the place he once knew carries on in pictures. None of it resembles home.

As they stand on the dock and look back to the hills of Karpathos, Antoine Karam announces that Niko is no longer such a little boy. He pats him on the head. The time has come to grow up.

Once again they've packed their two suitcases with the clothes and aspirations and doubts they've already carried this far, to board a ferry that will take them to mainland Greece. Unlike the day they arrived here, the sea is calm. If Niko leans over the pier and looks down, he can see his reflection in the sea, looking back up at him with curiosity. Does he feel older? He can't tell. In any case, he's been assured that he has no say in the matter. According to Baba, growing up is a test for each little boy and Niko's turn has arrived. He must be ready, and he must not fail. How this little island looks so much less daunting than when they arrived. There is the beach where they first landed, and there is the tree under which they first set their bags. Maybe if he looks closely, he'll be able to spot his own blood on the cement. But what will they find in Athens, Niko wonders. The world, he's quickly learning, offers so many different places to live. It's as if they've been trying out each one for comfort, for durability, like new pairs of shoes. But the summer has been long, carrying on as if it will never end. If only Mama could see what a good boy he's been since she's been gone. If only she could come back for a visit, an afternoon. A cold tea, maybe one meal. He understands that where she's gone offers no way back, but to him it seems unreasonable. The barrier between where he stands and where she rests is too rigid if it can't bend to missing someone. Even in Cyprus, he remembers, they were allowed to visit for thirty days. In Athens, Baba has told him, they can stay but not for long. They board a ferry. A deckhand loosens the hawser and soon they float away. He feels Baba's hand on his back, steadying him, guiding him. Baba, he thinks, his best friend. He turns around to kiss Baba's palm. The hand is no longer there.

The ferry backs out of the bay, pulling a trail of white foam across a gently rolling sea. Antoine looks down at the boy and remembers a time when he was Niko's age. His country was at war with itself then too — a different war, a much shorter war — but in many respects much the same war. For some reason — it could be the era or simple nostalgia — he remembers the civil war of his own childhood being, well, more civil, a power-struggle that seemed somehow easier for his family to avoid. Ah the fifties, he thinks back, now that was the time for a war as good as the Lebanese would ever muster, a war that could thrive alongside peace and prosperity. If only his son could have known him as a boy, if only he could have known the possibilities of a childhood only intermittently interrupted by war. Back then, the militias would respectfully take a break for supper, come down from your rooftop, sit at your table and charm your mother with compliments for her cooking. He remembers his own father, in his own shop, scooping olives by the handful for customers who would pay him in bushels of beets or live chickens or livers or whatever they had: money didn't matter back then. He remembers spending entire days at the sea skipping stones: time didn't matter back then. He remembers how, one day, his uncle led a herd of gazelles through the streets of his village, gazelles that had arrived by boat from the Dead Sea. He remembers riding his bicycle to the Dog River and back. He and his brother would travel even further, toward the hills, peddling fast, careening to the outskirts of their village. How many relatives they would pass along the way. It was impossible to venture out onto the streets and not pass a member of your family. Their village was full of aunts and uncles, so many he had: families were big back then, families had meaning and weight. Where were they now? Up the escarpment Antoine and his brother would ride, barreling into the valley, through a canopy of hanging branches that delivered them to the gate of the last house before the village frayed into arid wilderness. They kept cool under the swaying branches of willow trees. Antoine would show off his biceps to his little brother. He'd smear grease onto his brother's cheek. His little brother died of pneumonia.

The bittersweet moments of his youth come back to him as he stands at the ship's rail, looks out at the endless sea. What will his son remember of this time, and how will he judge the choices his father made? Niko may look back on a childhood adventure story, or he may look back and see evidence of a tragedy.

*

Aboard the ferry, after a self-service cafeteria supper of French fries, they walk the length of the boat and Baba tells the boy stories of Zeus, the king of the gods, who was saved from his father's mouth and raised by a goat. Baba knows a lot about the gods; to Niko he may as well be one, for without Baba he is lost in the world. Baba says that when he was just "this much" – the gap between his thumb and his forefinger – he read a book in school about the gods and their temples.

"Soon you'll go to school and see such books yourself," Baba tells the boy, gleaming.

But Niko wonders why a father would want to eat his own son, and the very thought makes him sad. Despite Baba's assurances, he can't shake the feeling that some horrible fate awaits them in Athens. He has overheard his father's most recent phone conversations. Baba doesn't have much money, and he talks with great persistence to the boy about school, even though Niko doesn't care much anymore if he goes to school or not. He was beginning to like Karpathos and its stray dogs and cats, the quiet beaches and the two television channels. And then there is this urgent matter of Baba needing to visit an embassy, a building on the mainland, as Niko understands it, where people go visit their countries. What kind of Lebanon fits into a building, he wonders. If they're already on a boat, he can't fathom why they wouldn't return to the real Lebanon, the one with their apartment building.

Then there's the curious matter of the two suitcases. Before leaving Karpathos, he noted with some suspicion that Baba had, for the first time, packed their clothes and papers separately. Niko's went in the brown leather one and Baba's in the black plastic one. As to what else they're planning to do in Athens, Niko has no idea. All Baba will tell him about this new place is that it houses many gods.

"But I want to stay with you," he blurts out, much to his father's surprise.

"You'll always be with me," Baba says. "With family, you're always united."

Then they descend into the hull, into their cabin and onto their bunk beds, and Baba assails him with stories of Poseidon, and soon Niko's lids grow heavy, as it has been a long day of waiting and waiting, with stories of this great man who haunts the waters around Greece.

The next morning, he spends the last hours of the journey looking over the railing, hoping to spy the god of the sea looking back at him from beneath the surface.

In the backseat of a taxi, Antoine wonders what kind of family Yvonne would provide for the boy. The taxi speeds through the hazy streets of Athens toward the Lebanese embassy. The driver curses out his window at another taxi and momentarily interrupts his considerations, then the driver claps his hands as if to say, "Finish!" And then they're careening through Messogion's midday traffic once again and Antoine is able to return to his thought.

Does Yvonne know about children, or is she nurturing a fantasy of motherhood? By his calculations she's still young; she can't be older than twenty-four. He knows, from her cousin, that she still takes classes at university. Would she grow bored with the child once the novelty of his presence began to interfere with a student's busy schedule? Antoine is hesitant to deliver the boy to a home of abject tolerance. He doesn't want to turn his son into an obligation.

In any case, in the back of this taxi that swerves around buses, he's only playing out the possibilities of a worst-case scenario. At the embassy, their passports will be speedily renewed and their fates, god willing, will change. But beyond that . . . The situation in Lebanon, from the outside, looks unfathomably dark. A massacre at one of the Palestinian camps has spiraled the entire region into a hellish pit of fear, and so the phone lines into the country have been disconnected for the past week. Furthermore, no ferries are scheduled into Beirut, from Athens or anywhere else. At the port he'd confirmed this with a ticket agent. As they drive to the Lebanese Embassy, Antoine Karam feels like the storm cloud of misfortune that has loomed over their heads ever since they left Beirut is about to rain down on them. They cannot return and, if their embassy fails them, they cannot move forward.

What about Sami Malek? Will he treat the boy decently? From what he has heard of Sami Malek, the man is much older, already in his forties. What does he know about caring for children? Antoine has the Maleks' promises, and beyond that he can only hope that they have the boy's best intentions in mind. With family, one sometimes has little choice but to make a leap of faith.

If the worst case is indeed upon them, then as soon as Antoine sorts through the complexities of finding a new country, he will either send for the boy or come join him. The Maleks have offered to pay for Niko's flight, but Antoine can't accept any such charity. His proud temperament stands in the way. When Sami Malek offered to pay for the ticket, he gave no firm reply, but the gesture has since left him feeling downtrodden. Antoine is steadfast; he can solve his own problems. It's the life of his son he doesn't want damaged. His own is not as important.

The boy who hasn't said a word since the beginning of the car ride now nestles under Antoine's armpit. Niko wraps his small hands around his father's waist. Antoine senses the boy's struggle to smother despair. He can feel his son's hot face pressing into the side of his shirt.

"Don't send me away," Niko pleads.

"Let's see what happens first."

At times like this Antoine does not know what can be expected of him, other than to be firm. He supposes he had to share the larger plan with his son at some point, and the back of this taxi was his next to last chance. And he has emphasized that this business of separation is merely a possibility that Niko should anticipate. Only if something goes wrong at the embassy, then and only then will the boy need to board a plane on his own. There is no other way. Without passports, without a country, he fears the authorities might take Niko away from him. This way, Antoine explains, he can be assured that Niko is in the relatively safe hands of his brother-in-law's family, who can provide him with an education, or at least a chance at a viable future.

"Don't send me away," Niko pleads again. In a panic, he apologizes profusely for having killed his mama.

"Shush," Antoine says. He assures the boy there was nothing he could have done one way or the other for Mama or anyone else.

"Then don't leave me alone," Niko insists, crying into his father's shirt.

After the taxi pulls up the tree-lined street of the Kifisia suburb and into the driveway of a two-story stucco building, Niko and Antoine climb out of the car and find the Lebanese Embassy's doors chained, the offices closed pending further notice. Not knowing what else to do, Antoine says they should wait there. He pays the taxi driver a price that once again seems too high, and the man removes their suitcases from the trunk and then drives off. Soon a security guard, who spies them through the many video cameras surrounding the door, walks up the drive and asks them, in Arabic, what they want.

"Passport renewal," says Antoine.

"Not anymore," says the security guard.

"When, then?"

The security guard removes a form letter from a folder and hands it to Antoine. He claims that the embassy officials would like every Lebanese citizen who visits this building to have this information. Having performed his duty, he leaves. Antoine reads the contents, as Niko tugs on his arm and asks what it says.

"It says that as long as there is no government at home, there is no embassy here." He crumples the letter and lets it fall to the ground.

They sit on the embassy's steps, and as Antoine looks at his hands for a long while, Niko spots a black cat in the bushes, its eyes trained on their every move. But he is in no mood to play with cats. He picks up the crumpled letter and throws it at the cat. It runs away. All around them a late-summer day has settled in and he sees some of the neighbourhood children riding past on their bicycles, laughing and shouting with glee in their own language about subjects he's not meant to understand, and at that moment he feels only contempt, a sharp pang of anger at what strikes him suddenly as a grave injustice. That one boy should be blessed with a bicycle and a family and friends and a warm supper, while another, namely him, should be cursed with a flight to the other side of the world, where he is expected to abandon everything he's learned for a life of isolation with a fake mama and a fake baba, is a travesty. He does not want to ride on a plane. He has never ridden on a plane before, and he does not consider this a suitable occasion to start. Who decides that one boy can have a home while another can't? He can't understand what he's done to deserve a lesser fate. If he could bottle this potent and yet frightening anger that burns inside of him, then he would throw it overboard the next ferry. But he can't, and so instead he bawls, because he is afraid of planes and afraid of losing his baba.

As he bawls a shocking and unholy sound shoots up from his stomach and releases a desperation Niko has never sensed before. Still it comes, and all the while Antoine sits beside him, silently staring at his hands and letting the cigarette between his fingers burn away. Passersby – a woman, perhaps a maid, pulling a grocery cart; two young men with books, perhaps university students, engaged in an animated debate – afford them curious glances. The sun beats down brightly come the middle of the day, and the old pine trees blaze lush and green in the arid heat. He wants to run across the driveway and climb the tallest tree, use its many branches to climb high above this unknown city where he can find an abandoned bird's nest in the boughs, and curl up in the shape of an egg. He would fall asleep there, wake up in another time and start over. He cherishes living, this much he knows for sure, but does he cherish the endless trials that have become his life? No, he does not want to ride on a plane. He refuses. He would sooner be shot in the face than leave his baba. He witnessed something similar once in a Beirut market, before his mama could shield his eyes. So immediate the after-effects of a shooting, so logical.

It is past noon now, and they haven't yet eaten. Niko feels bloated by hunger. Some twenty minutes have passed, and Antoine still sits on the curb beside him, oblivious to the passing cars and pedestrians, to the fact that many neighbourhood workers have come out of their offices for lunch, and many of the little restaurants across the street have set out their sidewalk tables with menus. But Antoine still holds between his fingers the burnt-out cigarette, now nothing more than a brown nub. His hand trembles in the light breeze.

"Baba, I'm hungry," Niko confesses.

Antoine puts his arm around Niko, pats his shoulder.

"Come. Let's go eat," he says in what sounds to Niko as the voice of defeat. They stand up and collect their suitcases, stable companions on this journey, and after waiting for the traffic to pass, jog to the far sidewalk, where they find a shaded table under a beach umbrella advertising Fanta.

"What should I eat?" Niko asks.

Antoine says, "Eat whatever you want."

"Any price?" Baba has worried over money in the past months and Niko does not want to give his father the impression that he is too young to help in such matters.

"Any price," Antoine confirms. "Money doesn't matter anymore."

When the waitress arrives, Niko hesitantly orders a cheeseburger and fries, and a Coca-Cola, anticipating his father's disapproval as soon as the words have left his mouth. But Antoine doesn't disapprove at all. He tells the waitress he'll have the same thing. And suddenly their situation feels a little less dire, as if by ordering the same cheeseburger and the same French fries and Coca-Cola, Baba confirms for Niko a bond that he has always wanted to extend beyond father and son, into just plain friendship. Maybe if he was older or Baba was younger, they would be nothing more and nothing less than best friends. Over the months, he has come to realize that it is this business of needing care that has made him a burden, and this sense of grave responsibility, once his trump card, that has led to his baba shipping him off. He looks at his baba bringing the burger to his mouth; he can't take his eyes off him. This is what pets do: stare at their owners. He can't help but feel like a domesticated animal, unable to fend for himself. If he was more Baba's equal, then they could travel the world together, indefinitely. They could build a house together, just cut down some trees and dig up the rocks and build a house deep in the forest, where no one would ever find them. No one would ever come round in search of passports or citizenship cards.

After their meal, Baba pays the waitress and hails another taxi. "The time has come to go to the airport," he says, inspecting Niko's eyes for a reaction. They drive and drive and drive, through the streets and plazas of Athens, which carry no meaning for them, only a hodgepodge of distraction between seaport and airport. Now their taxi speeds along a highway, and now the mirage of apartments and statues falls away, replaced by fields of wilting weeds and oil refineries. Off on the horizon, he begins to see the planes shooting off into the sky and fading away. Still others appear from nowhere and descend. Based on this evidence, he draws the conclusion that riding a plane is a matter of leaving the ground and waiting to disappear, a benign gesture, a totality, the fullest signature of complacency and defeat he can imagine. And for Niko this confirms once again that, unlike his Baba, he does not want to give up. He does not care about school or wealth or stability or all the other dreams his baba often tells him he is entitled to have. He does not understand how his father does not share his hope. In his opinion, all they need to do is hope more vigilantly in order to prevail. But for Baba, maybe the will is not there anymore. Maybe it's love that Baba doesn't share. Because up until Niko saw planes crisscrossing the sky, he earnestly believed that his father was undecided about the future, that in the worst case he was trying to scare him into behaving more like a man. He had taken this test; he thought he had passed. Evidently not.

At Baba's request, the taxi pulls up to the Departures terminal. The terminal is the biggest building Niko has ever seen.

They cross long stretches of linoleum with their suitcases in hand. Niko asks, "Where do the planes take off?" He's curious if they somehow land inside the building. Certainly there is enough room.

"Here, I'll show you." Baba leads him over to the windows at the back of the terminal, and points his finger at a jumbo jet slowly making its way toward the runway. The plane turns, waits for a few moments, and then fires its engines. It gathers speed, then momentum, and finally its front wheel leaves the ground, followed quickly by its back ones. Then it's off to who knows where.

At the sight of the plane disappearing, Niko looks at his shoes. Soon, it will be his turn.

"You'll be fine," Baba assures him, as if sensing his apprehension. "Trust me, you'll never know a bigger adventure."

"I don't want to go alone," Niko spurts out. "I want you to go too."

"Everything in its time, my son. You go first, and as soon as I find us a new home, I'll come for you. It won't be long. I promise."

Then Baba leaves to make the necessary arrangements, and Niko stays with the suitcases to watch the planes come and go. The airport is a busy place. All around him, women in blue uniforms and men with magazines push their luggage on large carts. Like clockwork, every seven minutes another plane lines up for the runway and flies off.

When Baba returns, he says, "Look, I can get you on a flight, but you'll have to leave soon."

"But where am I going?"

"The people who will meet you at the airport are family. Don't worry. You're in good hands. They're very excited to have you. The woman is your Tante Yvonne."

Niko doesn't know a Tante Yvonne.

"She's your mother's youngest sister. She moved to Canada with her husband when you were very young. Her husband is my brother-in-law. Sami Malek." Baba pulls out a sealed envelope from his blazer. "Here, give him this when you arrive." He slips the envelope into a little travel knapsack he has just bought for Niko. "For the plane. Look, here you have juice and a book to read, and here is a banana. This, here in the front, is your passport. Be very careful not to lose this. Do you understand?"

Niko nods. They walk through the terminal to the flight's gate.

"Don't look so sad. You'll be happy while you're there. It will be like a vacation."

They arrive at the gate where a demure female employee, who has pinned her hair back tightly and who speaks three languages, greets them by pointing out the nearby duty-free shop as the best place to spend the remaining forty-five minutes before the flight boards. Once she views Niko's ticket, she assures him that one of the stewardesses will accompany him from takeoff to landing.

After a quick browse through the duty-free, where Baba buys him a large Swiss chocolate bar for the flight, they sit along a row of plastic chairs and wait for the boarding chime to sound. "See," Baba says, "you won't be alone even for a minute. The nice lady will look after you on the plane, and she'll make sure you get safely delivered to Tante Yvonne."

Niko stares at his shoes. It's not the flight that troubles him, but its destination, a destination so far away from the only other person he knows.

"You'll see, it will be a great adventure," Baba says once more. "The biggest adventure of your life." He begins to tell Niko the story of the world's largest white bears, long considered the great fishermen of the North, bears who swim with spears and travel in large herds across the ice sheets of Canada. But whereas Niko once looked forward to his father's tales of far-off places, now he's not sure that he believes anything his father says. Soon the chime sounds for his flight. They approach the gate.

Baba bends down and says, "Okay, be a good boy. Remember, you're a guest in their house and in their country." He smothers Niko in a long embrace. Then he shows him his mother's wedding ring, a silver band. "Take this. Keep it with you always."

Antoine tucks the ring into his son's bag. Niko nods, finds he can't stop nodding.

"Listen, don't cry. You're a big boy now," his father reminds him. "You'll be fine. I'll see you soon."

Baba kisses him, a warm hairy press of the lips against his hot forehead. In turn, he kisses his father back. The stewardess has arrived. She stands at their side, waiting to take Niko by the hand. Leaving Baba behind, they walk down the corridor and board the plane, where the stewardess offers him the window seat. Outside is the tarmac, a bus with stairs driving past, some men sharing a cigarette break. He feels as though he'll never see any of this again. Once they take off, the plane will disappear. The engines rev. They're moving now. Now they're picking up speed. Now they're off the ground, and his eardrums bloat with pressure. Now he finds it difficult to swallow. And now they're gone.

Carrier Pigeons Always Fly Home

AUGUST DRAWS TO A CLOSE and September begins. Niko attends school for the first time in three years. His days quickly settle into a monotonous routine. He's expected to sit in a room and answer questions in a language he doesn't know, all the while being prodded along by teachers whose sole purpose is to keep him in step. There are so many strangers. They're everywhere. His Tante Yvonne looks alarmingly like his mother. Her husband says little, other than to deliver curt instructions. They have cleared out a corner of a room in their one-bedroom apartment, and there, under a window, using old sheets they have made him a small single bed.

Since Niko doesn't speak the language, he can talk to no one. His classroom is filled with students trapped in the same predicament. They come from parts of the world he never even knew existed. There is a girl from Mexico whose forehead is blotched with a large purple stain. There are two Africans, black as night, an older brother and a younger sister; he has a temper and she has trouble learning. There is the cavalry of Koreans and Chinese who all sit together in the back and want as little to do with the class as possible. There is a twelve-year-old girl from Spain who is almost two feet taller than everyone else and who has an abnormally long and slow-moving face. There is a seven-year-old boy from Pakistan who wears the same clothes every day. In Canada, there is no such thing as war, but in its place are innumerable rules. He must go to school every day, he must learn the language, he must listen to strangers.

"Repeat after me," Madame Robitaille commands in shrill French. "*Est-ce que je peux aller à la salle de bain?*"

"*Esse que peux aller la salle du bain?*" they all mangle in unison.

The French language: it has become the central obstacle in this new and unwanted life. There are laws governing language in this province, Madame Robitaille warns them every morning after the bell, just as there are laws governing crime. "Otherwise," she extols, conspiratorially, pacing at her desk with a long pointer in hand that makes her look like a prison guard, "we have no way of understanding each other." And so whenever their voices ramble off in foreign tongues, she snaps them to attention with a quick whack of her desk. Every morning, she writes at the top of the chalkboard, 'Without trying, you will never learn.'

The classroom is tiny, an afterthought of the building's construction packed with fifteen children ranging from six to thirteen. The air roils with the dust of foreigners in the mid-morning light. The only time they ever see any of the other children at the school is for lunch and recess, and it is then that they, with no grasp of the ways of local children, are most vulnerable. And so they often eat together, at a corner table in the cafeteria, feeding on smelly lunches that look vastly different from the sandwiches and juice boxes the local students bring. Pushed together by circumstance, they form an unwanted minority in the school. At their corner table, they develop a haphazard, bastardized pseudo-French scaffolded by crude drawings, hand gestures, and loud noises to talk to each other. Attempts at friendship seem only to open them up to the cruelty of the natives.

One day in late winter, as Niko's counting off for the Pakistani boy all the countries he's seen, an older Québécois boy with broad shoulders and an angry face picks up Niko's lunch, throws it on the floor, and steps on it. The entire cafeteria erupts in laughter.

"See!" the bully shouts to a friend, "I told you I'd do it." Then he walks away.

In heavy boots that are a bit too big for his feet, Niko returns to his special classroom hungry, having eaten only a few crackers from the lunch of a Latvian girl who felt sorry for him.

That afternoon, with his stomach churning, his broom-closet classroom turns into a caustic straightjacket of masculine and feminine words. Madame Robitaille snaps at him, "*Nicolas, où es-tu?* Pay attention!"

Until they learn this language and all its rules, Madame Robitaille tells them all again, they will not be able to learn anything else. A waft of urine circulates through the classroom, the wet fear of one of the younger children, who don't yet know how to remove snow pants on their own.

Seizing on the window of opportunity, in broken French Niko asks if he can go to the bathroom. "*Est-ce que je peux?*" He waits sullenly for the verdict.

Madame Robitaille frowns at him, maybe because he has hopelessly confused his expressions or because she spots he's either lying or the source of the acrid smell. "*Allez vite, Nicolas.*"

Niko leaves the classroom and traipses down the long hall, with its puddle-stained marble floors and rusting blue lockers, to the boys' washroom. He'll never be a Nicolas. His teacher can't make him French no matter how hard she tries. There, in the washroom, against the persistent background noise of a dribbling urinal, he looks into the mirror as if looking for an answer. To his dismay, the face staring back at him shows signs of a Nicolas breaking through. His cheeks are beginning to broaden and his lips are slowly filling in. He has become a bit taller even, a giraffe in the making, the first giraffe of his family. He is already eleven years old. If he's not careful, he'll no longer look like the boy his baba knows.

And yet, another part of him is in awe of the changes in his face. It's the school and the cold city beyond it that are affecting him in strange ways, turning him into Nicolas whether he likes it or not. When he lived in warmer climates, his body never needed more hair than it had. Now hair is beginning to grow on his arms and legs, everywhere, as if his body needs to warm itself.

'Would you eat green eggs and ham?' he asks his image in the mirror. Never. But maybe today he would make an exception after all, as he's starving. Food is more important than French, and it's the school's fault that he hasn't eaten. Where was the lunch monitor when that stupid boy was stomping on his sandwich?

He scuttles back to the classroom, where Madame Robitaille's voice dictates more rules of the French language, and there he quietly removes his coat from the hook outside the door, and then he turns the other way and runs as fast as he can to the double doors leading into the back field.

Outside, the morning snow has stopped coming down and in its place a glacial silence presides over an overcast day. Warm breath billows before his eyes. This is the brief period of being out of doors when the reality of coldness still hasn't settled into his skin, his favourite moments of being outside. But he knows that without his overlarge and stifling coat, the cold will get inside him very soon and he will feel deathly sick again and he does not want that, so he puts his coat on and fastens his scarf.

To his left, cars rush back and forth across the boulevard, splashing snowbanks with brown slush.

Digging his hands into his pockets, Niko walks around the building and then runs down the block to the bus shelter. There, he learns that the next bus won't pass for another eighteen minutes, which is too long to wait given that Madame Robitaille and the French police will soon be – if they aren't already – on his trail, and so he runs for another block, past the brown snow banks and parked cars and duplex homes with old brownstone bricks and leafless maples, and this is how he arrives at a busy street he's never seen before. Midday is in full swing here. Delivery trucks double-park in front of stores, and deliverymen in dirty white aprons carry crates of vegetables.

Out of the corner of his eye, Niko spots a deliveryman spitting out a cigarette before disappearing into the back of a truck. It's not too wet, so he scoops it up and runs further down the street. He likes smoking. Baba smokes and his uncle Sami smokes too, and every once in a while Niko will steal a cigarette from the ashtray atop the fridge.

Niko dips into an alleyway where a cat scrambles away in surprise. By a restaurant dumpster, he sucks on the wet cigarette and breathes it back to life. If only he could do this with everything. Sometimes he wonders if Baba is still alive, because he never calls. And then Niko coughs and wonders where to go next with his new-found freedom. A delicate snow descends from the grey clouds, to no one else's dismay but his. He must decide where and how to eat. Other than a bus pass and two pieces gum, his pockets are empty. He has no money.

Walking along the busy street, he finds a Provigo supermarket and decides he can do much worse than walk around the aisles of a supermarket and look at shiny packages. One of his very favourite aspects of Montreal so far has been the grocery stores overflowing with incarnations of foods stuffed with chocolate, marshmallows, Cheez Whiz, or whipped cream. He can spend an entire afternoon comparing chocolate bars and devising ways to save enough of his meagre weekly allowance to buy them.

Inside the store, he cuts past the fruit and vegetable stands to the aisle where a wall of breakfast cereals awaits his inspection. Immediately he looks for his favourites and notes the prices – a habit he's picked up in the months since he's begun accompanying his aunt Yvonne on her weekly shopping excursions. Count Chocula, Froot Loops, Cap'n Crunch.

In the next aisle he discovers a long line of chips. At this time of day, there are few people in the store and, with the aisle otherwise empty, he quickly removes a small bag of Ruffles from the shelf and stuffs it inside his coat. The next aisle is filled with soft drinks, and there he finds a can of Dr. Pepper that fits snugly in his pocket.

After walking through several more aisles to appear as inconspicuous as any shopper who intends, after all, to buy nothing, he pushes past the cash registers to his final exit. Then Niko is outside again, where the streets boom with cars and trucks jostling for free lanes. Locked away in the classroom, he misses so much of the day. And they're not learning anything that interests him anyway, only a language others have told him he must pick up if he is to stay here. And since there is no plan for him to stay here any longer than he has to, learning that language is a waste of his time.

A firm hand grabs his shoulder and turns him around, and when Niko looks up he sees a supermarket security guard.

"I saw you," the guard hisses. "Come on, where is it?" He shakes Niko's jacket, and out falls the bag of chips. Frisking him, the guard finds the can of pop as well.

"Now you're in trouble, you little shit," he smiles in a disturbingly self-satisfied way. "Let's go."

The guard drags Niko by his coat's collar back into the Provigo, and pulls him up a set of stairs to a mezzanine, where they enter a small white room filled with little television screens. He sits down, rewinds a tape, and plays it back for Niko. "I see everything from here. I'm the eyes and ears of this whole store, so you'll never ever get past me. You steal, you pay the price. You done a bad thing, boy, and this happens way too much here. What do you have to say for yourself?"

Paralyzed, Niko looks straight ahead at the little screens, watching shoppers go by.

"You poor, hungry?"

"Maybe."

"Yeah me too, shitstick," the guard replies, rolling his eyes. Then he sits down at his desk and begins to fill out a report. "Okay, Boss. You leave me no choice. I've got to call the cops. If it was just chips, then maybe we could talk. But a Dr. Pepper, too? You going to jail."

He gets on the phone to get an officer down to the Provigo for a petty theft.

"Are you pressing charges?" Niko overhears the operator say through the receiver.

"Well, we'll see what his parents have to say," the guard says. "Kids gotta learn it's a store and not a free-for-all."

Once again Canada has snared him. The security guard hangs

up the phone and swivels to face Niko. His nametag reads 'Walter'. "Well, Boss," Walter says, "looks like this little snack of yours is gonna cost you a field trip."

A squad car arrives ten minutes later and, from their perch in the mezzanine office, Niko watches the two officers walk casually down the meat aisle to the back of the store, as if they've done this hundreds of times before. He hasn't said more than a word since he left school. He doesn't have enough French to get along in this city. But more than that, he fears if he begins to speak that he'll buckle in fear, for this matter of skipping class has escalated beyond anything he could have envisioned. If he understands his situation correctly, he's about to go to jail. His aunt and uncle are going to come down hard on him, and his father, wherever he is, is sure to view this as a major disappointment.

Now he's beginning to feel a little ashamed for having shop-lifted in the first place. He doesn't know what drove him to do it, only that an urge to take back from the world a little something that has been taken from him overwhelms him from time to time. The police enter the small grey room without knocking.

"Allo, Walter," one of them says, shaking hands with the security guard. "This is your troublemaker?" All three stand hovering over him.

"Mmm-hmm," Walter says. "I think we should teach him a lesson."

"So this is trouble, my friend," the second one says. "Stand up. Put your hands behind your back."

Handcuffs latch around Niko's wrists, and the guard chuckles, and then they begin the walk back down the stairs and through the grocery store to the car. As they escort him through a gauntlet of staring mothers and awestruck children and shocked grand-mothers and snickering teenagers, all of whom have stopped their shopping to judge him, he tries unsuccessfully to bury his face in his jacket.

"Oh no," says one of the policemen, pulling back his head. "This is part of the fun. People must see you for what you've done."

Soon they're back on the wet sidewalk outside the store, and then Niko is having his head ducked into a police car, just like on TV. The backseat of the car is warm, and there is a cage separating him from the front seats. As one of the officers drives, the other gets on the radio with an operator. With the intercom in one hand, he turns back and begins asking Niko questions: his name, his age, his school, his phone number, where they might be able to reach his parents.

"Don't call them. Please."

The second officer turns to the first. "Ah, see, he *is* scared! Good. They're always scared of the parents." Then he turns back. "I either get the name from you or from the school." He checks his watch. "By the way, it's 2:30. School's not over yet. You've had a busy day. Tell me, are you a troublemaker?"

Niko shakes his head.

"Then what are you? Just trying it out for the day?"

"I guess so."

They arrive at the station and the police help him out of the car because it's difficult to maneuver with handcuffs on, and then they walk him up the steps and through the steel doors into the station, where they park him in a chair and go fill out a report with the secretary. When they come back, they look at each other and then at him and then the man says to the woman at the desk, "Shall we put him in a cell while he waits?"

"He probably has a history of running away," the woman says.

"Okay, kiddo," the man says tartly. "While you're in here, why not think about what you've done."

"I don't want to be here."

"No one ever wants to be here," the woman says. She looks at her watch. "Your parents should be here soon."

"Hopefully we won't have to see you in here again," the man says.

"Can we get you anything?" the woman says, her voice softening a little.

"Paper?"

"Sure thing, darling. If you want to draw, that's fine by us. Sure beats shoplifting and cutting school."

The officers disappear down the grey corridor. Soon the woman, perhaps feeling more charitable towards him than the others, comes back with a notepad and a short stub of a pencil.

"It's not crayons," she says, "but it's the best we've got."

Niko takes the notepad, and after the policewoman leaves he sets it on his knees and flips through the empty pages. What can he draw? Looking around the stark room, he sees a dreary downtown police station, with cops at their desks and sad-looking people waiting to go to jail. The walls are covered with graffiti. Near the ceiling of the far wall, there is a bright hole of fading daylight.

He gets up and begins to read the walls, for these are notes left behind by people like him. The police say that he has to wait for his parents to come, but they don't know that Sami and Yvonne aren't his parents. Niko sits down and spontaneously begins to do what prisoners before him have done on the walls. *Dear Baba*, he writes in a slanted and airy Arabic on the blank paper:

> I am in jail. It's your fault. I left the school and stole
> food from the supermarket. Do you remember what I
> said last time? I don't like it here. Well, it's still true. I'm
> still in the special language class, where the teacher
> doesn't like me and I don't like her or anyone else in
> there. I don't like Tante Yvonne or her husband Sami, and
> I don't like Montreal. They say I need a parent to leave
> this jail, and until one comes to get me I can't leave. So I
> am writing to say that you must come now, otherwise
> this is where I'll be forever. Anyways, I think soon it will
> be time to live together again. I don't need money or
> food or anything special, so you don't have to worry
> about me eating all your food like last time. I can
> do better. I'm bigger now, and I can work too. So we can
> both make money to buy a house where we can live

forever. So you don't have to worry about me, because I don't even cry anymore. That's how good and grown-up I am. I promise. But maybe you don't need me to have a job. I think you must have a good job at a camera store right now, and that you're building a house for us. One day when that house is ready you'll come get me, and then we'll go live in the new house. Until then, I'll be here in jail, waiting for you.

He signs the letter, *Love, the last Nakhle*, just so Baba sees that Niko remembers and can never forget where he came from, and then he tears the page out of the notepad and tucks the letter in his coat pocket. Lying down on the bench, Niko stares at the ceiling, since there's little else to do and because his anxiety over the last hour has made him really tired. How long has he been here? He looks at his watch. Fifty-three minutes. They feel like fifty-three days. His eyes hurt. He hasn't slept for fifty-three days.

Later, when the female officer returns to rattle the bars of his cage, he wakes up confused and realizes that the hole in the far wall has grown dark.

"Up and away, kid. You're free to go," she says. "Let's go."

In the open room filled with desks and busy police officers filing reports and processing prisoners, she delivers Niko to his aunt Yvonne, who greets him with a stern glare that screams, You're in so much trouble once we get out the door!

"Thank you," she says to the officer, "for making sure he doesn't get into any more trouble."

Then she lifts Niko out of his chair by the earlobe and leads him outside. She's a small woman, but she has a stronger grip on his earlobe than he'd imagined she could have. She pulls him toward the car, unlocks the passenger door, and shoves Niko inside. There's a vein in his aunt's forehead that throbs like a heartbeat whenever she gets angry, and just then it's beating feverishly.

"I thought you were hurt. What's gotten into your head? Do you know how hard it was to get you into that school? And now they're threatening to kick you out. If your father were here, he would beat the stupidity out of you."

"I'm sorry. I was hungry," Niko stammers. "No one likes me at that school. They threw my lunch on the floor and they all laughed at me."

His aunt sighs, because this is not how she'd imagined life with her nephew. They pull out of the parking lot and begin the drive home.

"Well, it's the only kind of school you can go to here. You just have to live with it."

Soon they pull into the dark parking garage under their building on a Montreal North street.

"Of course, you're going to have tell your uncle what you've been up to all day," Yvonne says, turning off the engine. "He doesn't know where we've been, or why there's no dinner waiting."

They take the elevator three floors up and walk the narrow hall of ragged carpet to their front door. The apartment has only three rooms: a living room, a bedroom, and a small kitchen. His aunt and uncle sleep on a pullout sofa in the living room, Niko has the bed in the corner of the bedroom, which doubles as his uncle's office during the day. When they walk in, his uncle Sami is sitting at the kitchen table in his undershirt, his belly hanging over his belt, eating a cucumber and watching television.

"Where have you been? You left no message, nothing. There's nothing to eat."

"Your nephew," Yvonne announces vindictively, "decided to try something different today."

"What did you do, Nakhle?" Sami leans forward, scrutinizing Niko.

Faced with the domineering gaze of his uncle, Niko can't find the words to say or justify what he did, and he knows that no explanation he gives will soften the blow of the trouble he's about to receive.

"I'll tell you what he did," Yvonne steps in. "This boy decided to leave the school to go steal food from a supermarket. Like a beggar! Do you know where I found him? In jail!"

"You were in where?" When Niko doesn't answer, his uncle slaps his cheek. "Answer me."

"In jail," Niko protests. "I don't like that school."

"For stealing food!" His uncle smacks him again, this time hard enough to bring tears to his eyes. "Now everyone at your school will think we're poor."

"We *are* poor," Niko cries. "You sleep on a couch. It's embarrassing."

"Do you know what you're doing to yourself, to us? You're not a citizen, we're not citizens. You go to jail, they don't even have to keep you in the country."

"I don't need to live here," Niko shouts back.

"Where will you go? Your father can't even find the time to call and say hello."

"I'll go back home!"

"Wake up. You can ruin our lives, too. They'll kick us all out without a second thought, if they want to. Do you know how hard it is to become a citizen? You're going to ruin everything we've worked for, and for what?"

"A bag of chips," his aunt says. "He'll ruin everything for a bag of chips."

Sami sits down on the sofa and pinches the bridge of his nose with his fingers. "They will have this file on you forever. When they turn you down for citizenship, when you apply for universities, every time you apply for a job."

"I wanna go home. You're not my parents. You can't tell me what to do."

His uncle says nothing to that. Then his aunt says, "Go to your room."

In the bedroom office, Niko closes the door and tumbles down onto his unmade bed. It's been a long day, too long, one of the longest since he arrived here. He can hear the muffled sounds of his aunt and uncle talking quietly on the other side of the wall; there is no such thing as a little privacy in this apartment, unless you are in the shower, and even then they ask him to keep the door unlocked, just in case anyone has to use the bathroom. As he turns over and gropes in the dark for his headphones, he can't help but think that maybe he was just a little wrong for doing what he did today. But he felt free for those twenty minutes between leaving school and entering the Provigo.

Headphones on, Niko presses play on the cassette deck and lies back to stare up at yet another ceiling, and he thinks that ceilings are everywhere in this new and inhospitable country. The thin pre-recorded sounds of Casey Kasem's weekly Top 40 show funnel into his ears. Since moving here, he's spent a lot of time fiddling with the radio, the only apparatus that no one else in the apartment ever bothers with, and so he likes to think of the little machine as the only thing he owns. On his tour of the airwaves, he's discovered a good many songs and personalities, but his favourite among them, by far, is Casey Kasem, because he hosts a countdown show that to Niko makes listening to music a mathematical competition fought over weeks and months. This is why he likes music, he would say if anyone bothered to ask him, because it can win or lose, climb up or slide down. Plus, Casey Kasem has a very friendly, almost fatherly voice. Casey Kasem doesn't sound like he would ever get mad or worry about something as petty and abstract as citizenship.

Niko doesn't really see why a person would need a piece of paper to prove that he belongs somewhere. His stomach rumbles; but he's too afraid to venture out into the kitchen now. Casey Kasem and last week's countdown keep him company. It's company he's grown to depend upon. Every week, at the end of his show, Niko awaits with baited breath Kasem's signature sign-off, which has grown into something of a secret pact between himself and the radio-show host. Every Sunday at around noon, after the Number One song has played and the show has come to an end, Casey Kasem says, "Until next week, it's your best friend Casey Kasem signing off." His best friend. It's true.

*

In the next room, Yvonne turns on the television so she can talk to her husband without being overheard. The voice of a late night news anchor fills the room with background chatter. Upcoming charity events, sports and weather.

"I'm worried about him," she whispers in the blue glow of the television light. After all this is over with she still has another hour or so of reading for her second-year psychology course. She will be ragged tomorrow for the exam after work, the day is ruined and it hasn't even started.

"He's beginning to get into this kind of trouble more now. Last month he took money from my purse."

"I'm worried too," Sami says, watching the news. "I'm worried for us. It's not a good situation. We have to get him back to his father as soon as possible. For his sake, and for ours."

"Has there been any news from Antoine?"

Sami shakes his head.

In the next room, they hear Niko's mattress begin to creak rhythmically. They move to the kitchen table.

"He's getting to that awkward age," Sami observes.

"Antoine has sent nothing?" The creaking is exasperating. She turns up the television to drown it out. "No number or address?"

"The last phone number we have is still not working. They say to stop calling, he's not coming back."

"Something's not right. Otherwise we'd hear from him. He used to call every week. Now, we've heard nothing for how long?"

"Since Christmas. Three months."

"Where could he be?"

"I suppose he could be anywhere. In the meantime, we have this problem here."

There is nothing Yvonne can say to explain away her nephew's behaviour, or his continued presence in their lives. Her husband quietly holds her responsible for the whole ordeal. They have been generous, more than generous, in opening their home to her nephew while Antoine finds his feet again. But instead of finding a place to settle down and start a new life, Yvonne now suspects that Antoine has disappeared for good.

"It's strange to think that we don't even know very much about him," Yvonne finally says. Her brother-in-law is a man she'd only ever met a handful of times. If pressed, she doesn't know if she'd be able to recognize him on the street. She lights a cigarette. "I hope he's alive."

"Inshallah," her husband says.

"I don't know what to do with Niko anymore," she admits. "I don't even think he likes us. He won't listen to us. His father won't talk to us. I don't know what's to be expected of us."

"I'll tell you one thing," Sami says. "He's going to destroy our chance at citizenship."

"He'll ruin his own life, never mind citizenship." She grimaces at her husband. "How come the police have to call me at work to come get him?"

"Well I'm sorry, but while you worry about him, I worry about us. Who has to work so we don't starve?"

"Don't exaggerate things. I work all day *and* I go to school in the evenings. It actually makes things worse for him and harder for me when you act like you won't have anything to do with him beyond providing food and shelter."

"You said it yourself. He needs his father. I'm trying to find his father before he goes and does something really bad."

"He needs a father. For now, any father. He won't listen to me. You need to be a man about it. It's been eight months he's been living in our house."

"You said," he scolds, his voice a manic whisper, "when you convinced me to bring him here, that you would take care of him. You wanted to help your family, so I say, go ahead and be a mother."

"It won't work if you behave like a hostile stranger. He needs discipline."

"I told you, I didn't want to be a father again."

"Then be a grandfather, an uncle. Be something more than what you are now."

"Let's leave it," Sami says.

But Yvonne won't let it go. "You certainly weren't much of a father to that boy of yours, so why bother now."

Sami puts his head down. "Let's not bring Ziad into this. That's none of your business."

"Of course, whatever you like. Apparently my only business is making you dinner and raising our nephew on my own because you want nothing to do with anyone but your own ambitions."

"What do you want me to do? I'm over fifty years old. I can't be his father. This was not part of our plan."

"It was your plan," she stammers, "not ours. I'm supposed to live with your plan."

"This is really beginning to affect our lives." He speaks to her now in the tone of her own father, with whom he used to work. "It's difficult enough getting a new start, but to do it with an anchor attached to your foot is practically impossible."

"His mother is dead, and his father is out there obviously having his own troubles. She was my sister, and he is your nephew."

"Go on, tell me. Tell me what you want."

"The boy needs borders, a man to stand up and tell him, 'no, don't do that,' 'yes, do that but better.'"

"I wake up every morning and it's a struggle just to survive to the end of the day. There are clients, contracts, blueprints, applications, judgments, fees, bills, taxes. When I was a boy, I watched my father work with his hands, and beside him worked his brother, and that was how I knew my uncle. They built things. I did the same work they did. There was no question that what belonged to them would one day become mine."

"Just show him the right path." Yvonne looks at the clock. "I still have to study."

In the next room, the creaking finally subsides.

In due course Sami and Yvonne get up from the table, and initiate the tired routine of cooperation they've cultivated since Niko came to live with them. Sami pulls the cushions off the sofa to pull out their mattress for the night, Yvonne collects Niko's winter clothes from the floor in the front hall, where he hastily shrugged them off before running to his room. Hanging up his coat, a piece of paper falls out of one of the pockets and lands at her feet.

She picks it up and returns with it to the kitchen table, curious to take a peek into the otherwise private life of the boy in the next room. In the light, she sits down and begins reading, struggling through the bad handwriting, misspellings, and worrisome Arabic grammar.

"Well," she says to Sami as he makes the bed, "you could do worse than sit down and teach him how to write properly."

"What is that?"

"A letter, I think. To his father."

"Oh, really? What does it say?"

Yvonne sighs and hands the crumpled piece of paper to her husband. As Sami looks over the letter, Yvonne pulls out her university books. She changes out of her clothes and into her night-gown, and climbs into bed with a textbook.

Sami puts the letter down. "Hopefully one day soon Antoine will call."

"We have a forwarding address. We could try writing again."

"With these shipping companies, you never know."

"We don't really have much of a choice."

He folds the note and puts it in his wallet, and then he begins to undress for bed. "Sometimes I don't know what's worse," he says to his wife, "life during wartime, or life afterwards."

Sami climbs into the sofa bed next to his wife, and tries to fall asleep as she studies to the low murmur of the TV. But he can't get comfortable, and after tossing and turning for a half-hour, he sits back up, dons his reading glasses, and begins writing his own letter to Antoine. The opening credits of the late-night movie flicker upon the screen. Yvonne licks the tip of her index finger, and then turns the page.

Darkly tanned, Antoine Karam overlooks another port of Algeria. The ship has arrived full circle to the city from which it departed last March. It is now July, and the white apartment buildings of Béjaïa rise up along the lips of the bay, interspersed with palm trees that dot the hills. Here, out in the royal blue waters of the harbour, they will anchor till nightfall. And then the work of unloading the cargo can begin, and then after that he will finally get paid.

By the time the ship docks at three in the morning and they set foot on land for the first time in ninety-seven days, a bright moon is gazing at their backs and seagulls caw in the distance, and there isn't a single coin left in any of their pockets. The men around him whisper giddily of whores and hashish. But the money earned has been too long coming and he has had to work for it much too hard, and so when Antoine looks to the hills of Béjaïa he thinks only of finding a room and, after a long shower, of a stable day's sleep. For the four months' work he is owed approximately 200,000 Algerian dinars, which by his calculations – an accumulation of hearsay from the other sailors on the ship – should secure him a small apartment for almost a year, in which time he should be able to find a proper job on land. He has been putting the details of his plan together every night of the last four months he's been out at sea. The authorities in Bejaia he's been told are easily bought. If you have money, then you can do anything you want. He might be able to find a foothold here, in this French outpost.

Briskly they unload the cargo that they first loaded six days ago in Dakar, a shipment of oil drums that they must lug to a line of flatbed eighteen-wheelers pulling up to the dock. The drums originate from all over Africa, even inland, bleeding out to the coasts, where ships like theirs dock at obscure ports and collect them from turbaned men atop Datsun pickup trucks, who often as not wield machine guns. Then they take the barrels north, and try to avoid pirates along the coasts of Mauritania and Morocco. In the dark cover of night with only a distant spotlight to guide them, the sailors work diligently toward dawn, when their work must be done and they must disappear. Once the last of the eighteen-wheelers had driven off, Antoine and the rest of the sailors line up in front of a small trailer office, where each man signs release forms and receives his pay. By the time his turn arrives to enter the trailer, the sun is peering up from the edge of the world and the morning's shift workers are milling outside the port gates. The door opens and a man who appears disappointed shuffles out like an unfed cat. Antoine is ushered inside.

"Sit," orders a grizzled Frenchman, hunched over mounds of files. Looming in the background is a brooding bull, a security guard.

Stubbing his cigarette into the ashtray, the Frenchman looks up at Antoine and says, "Name?"

Antoine gives his full name.

"Work number?"

He hands over his identification pay card, given to him by his captain for this very procedure just the day before. The Frenchman skims down a list of names.

"Ah, here you are. It says you have a letter waiting for you." He opens the left-hand drawer and, rifling through a thin collection of mail, removes a white envelope.

Antoine takes the envelope and pushes it into his dirty pocket.

"So you've been working on board the *Miranda* since March. According to our calculations, that means you are owed 181,000 dinars."

Antoine peers over the man's hand to see if he can catch the numbers on the paper. "It should be a bit more, no?"

"The port takes a tax on your work, and of course we take a fee for reserving your pay and collecting your mail."

As the Frenchman counts out eighteen 10,000-dinar bills from a thick wad, the brooding bull edges behind Antoine and rests a thick hand on his sore, overworked shoulder, as if warning a matador not to taunt him.

"Go on, take this money. Take this money, go have a nice meal, get drunk, find a whore, relax a little. It won't matter as much in a few days. There's always more work."

There isn't much he can do at times like these. Antoine sighs, stands up and leaves.

Outside the trailer the sun has started to rise over the horizon. After paying off the guards at the port gates, so they can overlook his long-expired passport, he begins the ten-minute walk across the sea wall to the city's empty beach. His legs feel queasy on land, especially after a night of no sleep. He stinks to the point that he would like nothing more than to escape his own presence. The fog of his exhaustion thickens in the bright morning sunshine. At the other end of the balustrade, Antoine reaches the stairwell that leads down to the sand, and there at the bottom he slumps against the sea wall, where there is still plenty of morning shade. Apart from a few dinghies belonging to fishermen heading out for the morning catch, this breadth of beach is his. He would like to sleep for a few hours here in the warm morning air, among the plastic bottles and lost shoes and burnt baskets that litter the shore cured with salt and filth, but not with all this money in his pockets. After all these months of hellish work, the thought of being robbed terrifies him. He's hungry, and in a little while he'll have to spend some of his money on food.

How in the world did I end up here? Antoine asks himself. He leans against the sea wall. It's as if without Niko his life has only gotten more difficult instead of easier. He has no compass. Nothing he does edges him forward. It's as though he's utterly powerless before the conventions of the world, continuously taking second place to the rubrics and restrictions of others. Devilish employers, petulant border guards, unsympathetic bank tellers, suspicious landlords, disappearing family, brutal police, blank-faced embassy functionaries, and, behind it all, a stream of violent news from his homeland, coupled with his own guilt. The world has made him small, a speck without any influence.

But maybe it's the exhaustion talking. Antoine takes off his shoes and airs out his feet. One of his small toes has been going green for some time, and the skin around the others has begun to flake away. He stands up and, not wanting to worsen the condition of his foot, hops across the sand and trash to the first waves. There, he sets his foot down in the saltwater and suffers the satisfying singe of disinfection. Then Antoine bends down and washes the oil stains from his hands as best he can.

As the morning sun fully emerges over the horizon and the city and hills are bathed in the first full light of the day, Antoine wades through the small waves and lets his foot burn underwater. Behind him he hears the call to morning prayers coming from the city's mosques, and then the city slowly jostling to life. The cold water, the warm sunlight, the breeze have all given him a second wind, and it is then that he recalls that he has yet to open the envelope in his pocket that cost him thousands of dinars in pay. He pulls out the envelope and looks for the sender. The letter is from Sami Malek. He knows that it cannot contain good news. It has been more than four months since he last spoke to the Maleks or Niko. Given how quickly the job had come to him, there was no way to tell them he wouldn't be in touch.

And now, after all his torturous endeavours he has little good news to report, only that he can't take Niko off their hands just yet. He knows that he has overplayed their sympathy, and now he can feel the frustrations of the letter reverberate through the unopened envelope. He walks back to dry sand, sits down against the wall, and tears it open.

Inside, he finds not one but two letters. The first is from Niko. He reads it carefully, and after having read it a second time to confirm all its grim detail, he moves on to Sami Malek's letter, ready for more bad news. *Antoine*, the letter begins, in words written by a firm and determined hand:

> We haven't heard from you in a very long time, and so
> I've had to resort to writing you this letter in the hopes
> that it will somehow find its way into your hands.
> First, let me just say that we hope you are safe and in
> good health. As you can imagine, there are times when

we are desperate and we fear the worst. We are particularly worried about the wellbeing of Niko, who does not understand – like we do – that the world can be a very complicated place.

To him, your absence is our fault.

You must want to know more about your son's life, even if it is not currently possible for you to speak to him.

He thinks he's here waiting for you. He believes in you and only you, and without you it's hard for him to believe in anything or anyone else.

We live here in a one-bedroom apartment. We cannot afford more right now because we work very hard and we're trying to save as much as possible for the future. It's not easy for us to have you disappear like this without any word.

What are we supposed to do with your son, and for how long? We are prepared to give him a house and education, but we need to know your plans.

Earlier today, Niko got into trouble with the police. He left school without permission and stole food from a supermarket, and he ended up arrested. Luckily, children here cannot stay in jail, but I tell you from my own experience, this is the time of his life where it can all begin to go wrong. If he stays on this path of petty crime and disrespect, there's no turning back.

Please, if you read this letter, call us or write us. Let us know that you exist and that you still care. Give your son faith, in himself, in you, and in your plans, and give some sign or signal of how to proceed.

Yours,
Sami Malek

After reading Sami Malek's letter, Antoine folds it in half, pushes it into his breast-pocket, and looks again at the crumpled one from his son and concedes that the life he's slipped into, which hasn't allowed him the opportunity for a telephone call in four months, is his own fault and no one else's. On the endless and turbulent seas, he has no sense of time, nor does he have any use for it. To keep track of the hours and days and weeks, as any of the other seafaring men will attest, is self-immolation. Still, he can't help but look down at the crumpled paper, his son's bad handwriting, the news that Niko has gotten himself into trouble, and think that it is he who pushed that boy into the jail cell.

Antoine walks up the stone steps of the sea wall to the streets of Béjaïa, where cars race past and, beyond that, the markets bustle with morning shoppers, covered wives swatting away flies as they search through barrels of dates and bins of sardines. Deeper in the morning souk, amidst shopkeepers negotiating energetically and the occasional three-legged cat brushing past, he finds a street vendor who sells him a lamb stew and couscous, which he takes into a nearby alley to eat bitterly in a quiet stairwell.

Someone else might say, you know, Antoine, you're a good man, you've given that boy an opportunity, and if he takes that opportunity and flounders in a jail instead, well, it's his own fault. But Antoine would have never let this happen if Niko was with him. He's already subjected Niko to far too many of his own troubles. His misfortunes are an infection. He has been reeling from regret to regret ever since he lost his camera shop.

They want him to call. They probably want to tell him that they can't take it any longer, and that he needs to solve his problems, which have unjustly become their problems. As Antoine desperately laps at his food, he tries to calculate how much such a call would cost him. More importantly, he has nothing good to say, no ambition to underscore and no grand plan to tell them, and so he cannot bring himself to say anything at all. It would be shameful.

Down the alleyway, Antoine hears footsteps; someone is coming. Soon he sees an old Muslim with a crooked back coming up the narrow path between apartment buildings. He pulls a mule, and they struggle against each other every step of the way. Nevertheless, they steadily crawl up the steps to Antoine.

As he passes, the Muslim meets the forlorn face of a tired and brooding Antoine and asks, "Why do you look so sad, my friend?"

Antoine can't muster the patience to name all of what overwhelms him. "Because I have nowhere to sleep. I need help. I have no home."

"Then it's my duty to offer you a home," the old Muslim sighs. He gestures with his hand. "Come, stay with me. It's not far. My wife will wash your clothes."

At the sight of the Muslim's hand pointing up the hill, he very nearly faints. That hand points to some magical trick: the first act of genuine, spontaneous kindness Antoine has witnessed in two years, falling at his feet out of nowhere.

"If you are too tired to walk, then climb on my mule," the old Muslim says.

And so Antoine rides on the mule as it trudges up the winding stairwell to the Muslim's house. By then he has slipped into the equivalent of a lucid dream, made more entrancing by the balancing act of riding a mule and keeping his eyes open but seeing nothing. His last words are, "I have money to pay you."

Then his eyes roll back in his head and Antoine slumps forward. The old Muslim pays him no attention, continuously coaxing the stubborn mule up the alleyway.

Antoine doesn't remember how he got into the attic room, who undressed him or who washed him, or how he got to wearing a clean nightgown. He wakes up in the dead of night, three or four in the morning, the hour when practically nobody is awake and the world is completely dark, and then, without getting up, he falls asleep again. The next time he wakes the room is stifling hot, his head hurts, and he can't piece together much, after unloading at the docks.

He's no longer wearing the pants that carry all his money. Erratically, he shoots up, and limps around the room. To his relief, he finds his clothes folded and pressed on a wooden chair, and the rolls of bills along with the crumpled white envelope all sit on a small table. He counts out the bills. All his money is there. Someone has also left behind a jug of water. Thirstily, he gulps half of it down.

Antoine sticks his head out the window to see where he is, and from up high he sees a courtyard and white walls and balconies baking in the high sun. Back inside, he discovers a small door no taller than his chest on the far wall. It lets onto a rooftop, where he finds a rickety table and chair that stand in the shade, and beyond that in the glaring sun, a pigeon coop the size of a large shed.

There is a knock at the door. An elderly woman shrouded in black cloth comes in, carrying a tray of cold broth, bread, and mint tea.

"I heard your footsteps through the floor." She sets the tray down. "Go on, eat."

He is made dizzy by the smell of food.

She walks to the far wall and opens the little door to let in some fresh air. Hesitantly, his fingers touch the bread. "Thank you," he begins to say.

The woman raises her hand and brushes away his gratitude. "It will come back to us, either in this life or the next."

After she leaves, Antoine decides to take the tray on the rooftop and eat with the pigeons. Food has never tasted so good, and he eats too quickly. He dozes for the rest of the day, only periodically getting up from the bed to drink some more water. It's been months since he's had any real privacy. Slowly, the evening drifts in, like the tides he knows so well from sea life, and the waning sunlight casts long flourishes of devilish shadow across the buildings. Then the serene sound of the mosques calling denizens to evening prayers resounds through the alleyways. A breeze floats in from the Mediterranean. Within a matter of minutes, the day's heat rises, leaving his room feeling cozy and even more private in the magic light of the early evening. He goes out onto the rooftop and finds the bright blue afternoon suffused with the beginnings of summer dusk. The rooftop gives way to other rooftops, and beyond that, the hills on one side and the sea to the other. Feathers scatter everywhere, and the pigeons appear excited by the onslaught of night. The birds brace themselves, chirruping away in their pen of chicken wire and old boards. Their sound soothes him. Perhaps in a place like this, he thinks, what is seemingly his first optimistic thought of the last few days, I can come up with a plan to turn things around.

The door creaks open behind him, and Antoine turns around to find the old Muslim standing there. In his hands he carries a bucket of seeds.

"I didn't want to bother you," he says in Berber's Arabic. "You looked at peace."

"It's very peaceful up here."

"It's the birds. They have a calming effect on the soul."

He tosses whole handfuls of seed into the cage. The pigeons flutter to and fro, pecking at every last seedling to hit the ground. His name is Mohammed Ahmed.

"You're not from here." Mohammed says. "I can see it in your face."

"I come from Lebanon."

"Ah, Lebanon. You're like them." He gestures at the cage of pigeons. "They come from Lebanon, too. They're traveling birds. They came here on their own, like you. The man who sent them said, 'they'll come, you'll see', but I didn't believe him. And then, three weeks later they were here, on my rooftop, and so I built them this home. They're carrier pigeons, sharper than the wind."

Antoine is impressed. "You send them out on their own, and they know how to find their way back here?"

"I'm free to write to whomever and wherever I want. People come to me from all around to send letters."

"How do they know where to go?"

"I hold them in my hands and whisper softly in their ears, and then they know."

Mohammed Ahmed finishes feeding the pigeons, and then he pulls out a pack of Marlboros and the two men have a smoke together as the day in the souks below draws to an end, with bargain hunters going home to be with their families and merchants closing up their stalls and sweeping their sidewalks. Soon the smell of cooked meat rises up through the alleyways.

They smoke cigarettes as the sun disappears, and Mohammed Ahmed tells Antoine about his son, who was recently killed in a factory accident. "He was about your age, and he used to stay in that room. I care for the pigeons now because he's gone." His wife, he confesses, is deeply saddened still by their lot in late life.

"My lot in life saddens me as well."

"I saw this in your face when I met you on the stairs. I thought, this man, I must help him."

"Don't you think that somewhere life must be easier than this?"

"Somewhere," Mohammed Ahmed grins, revealing the big gap in his mouth where his two front teeth should be. "Somewhere, but not here." He points to the sky with his cigarette. "Who knows? Maybe there."

They talk for a little while longer, and then he invites Antoine down to his kitchen for supper. His wife, whose name is Fatimah, is roasting a chicken that he slaughtered earlier in the day, and she would benefit from the distraction of a stranger.

They go downstairs, and Mohammed Ahmed reaches into the cabinet and pulls out a dusty bottle of arak, and they sit down at the table and he pours two drinks into decidedly large glasses, and he dons that toothless grin once again, leans across the table, and cautions Antoine to not tell the prophet what they're about to enjoy. Then they drink while Fatimah dices onions. After the first drink they have a second, and then Fatimah brings the chicken to the table and Abou Ahmed cuts into the darkly roasted bird and portions out a full breast to his guest.

After they finish the meal, they remain at the table, drinking and talking and smoking well into the night. Even Fatimah takes a glass. Eventually the sound of stragglers down in the streets gives way to crickets chirping from electrical wires, and drunkenly rising from the table with a slight stumble, Antoine bids his hosts good night.

"Is there anything more you need?" asks Mohammed Ahmed. "Please, don't be shy. What's ours is yours."

He can't think of anything, and so he simply shakes his head and begins to walk up the stairs, but then he turns back and catches his host leaving the kitchen and says, "Do you have paper?"

Mohammed Ahmed smiles, finds a notepad and a blue pen in the next room and brings them back. "Just don't send off all my pigeons at once."

Antoine stumbles upstairs, where in the dusty dark the air hangs heavier than it has all day because, to him, this is now a room with a more tragic past than the one he brought into it, and in his dizzyingly drunken way this makes him feel better, or at least simply not care as much right then, because at least the room knows bigger sorrows than his own. He sits down at the table where he imagines Mohammed's son must have sat many times, composing letters that he then tied on to the legs of pigeons. Montreal, he thinks. It might as well be on another planet.

He looks out at the view Abou Ahmed's son must have looked at, a series of windows, TV antennas, laundry, and he begins to write, his hand unsteady because it has been well over a year since he has written anything and his fingers are not used to the refined grasp of clean and disciplined penmanship. To begin, he writes not to anyone in particular, but simply to perform the act he once enjoyed as a young man, again, as exercise. What comes out is a litany of confessions; there's an overwhelming relief in setting his problems down to paper, as if they fall off his fingers and lock into the shapely, incongruous letters, burdening the blank page with their weight and leaving an impression clean through to the other side.

Then, just as quickly as he began writing freely, he stops, rips the page out, stuffs it in his pocket to work on later, and begins the more formal act of writing a response to his brother-in-law's letter of complaint. The truth is, he has a solution now, one that simply popped into his head down there at the kitchen table, probably out of the potent arak in that bottle. It's so simple an idea, that he can only write it down and see if it still makes sense in the morning. And so he drops hints of it in his letter to Sami, and with his excitement mounting, he delivers even greater promises in a letter to Niko.

But soon after he begins writing, Antoine loses his concentration, and his letter begins to drift from reason because he has had a fair bit to drink and, after all, his body is still exhausted from the very long journey he's just completed. He pushes his chair back from the desk and decides all of a sudden that he would like to see the stars over Béjaïa from the rooftop. He goes outside, bumping his head on the door frame, and there he lights a cigarette he has tucked behind his ear, he does not remember where or when, only that it's there. The pigeons in their cage are quieter than before. They must be sleeping. He smokes and looks up at the night sky, so vast and so clear and so full of stars, each one of them a possibility, and wonders which is Montreal. The birds ruffle their feathers as if to tell him it's too far off to bother trying.

The next morning he wakes up as the dawn is looming and the streets below idle with the passing chatter of merchants setting up their stalls for the day. The pigeons are in a frenzy, and the mosques are calling the faithful once again. At the table, he reads the letters, each making wild promises that he may not be able to keep. But they provide him with a goal, and a goal gives him focus, so he doesn't change a word. In any case, he can't stay here. These people have been too charitable with him already, and this morning his pride is beginning to rattle like a beggar's empty cup. He leaves ten thousand dinars on the table, pockets the rest of the money and the letters, and goes down to the street to start the next episode of his life.

He walks back down to the port, where the Frenchman sits in his caravan. "Back so soon?"

"I want to go to America."

"Impossible. Our ships can't go anywhere near U.S. waters, much less into one of their ports."

95

"Then I want to get as close as possible. Do you have any ships crossing the ocean?"

The Frenchman looks up at Antoine, as if to say, why are you putting yourself through all this trouble? Then he checks the log-book with the schedules and says, "The closest you can get from here is São Paulo. We have a ship leaving this afternoon."

"Can I get to Montreal from São Paulo?"

The Frenchman turns his chair around and draws Antoine's attention to a map of the world hanging on the fake wood paneling. "See, we are here," he points to Béjaïa.

Antoine walks around the desk to get a closer look. This is the first time he has had a chance to see his travels laid out for him so majestically. "So Beirut is here." In two years, he has traveled no further than the length of a thumb. "And São Paulo is here." Antoine reaches all the way across the ocean to just beneath the bosom of South America, more than an entire arm's length away from Béjaïa. "How long is the trip?"

"From Béjaïa to São Paulo, maybe one month, depending on weather. These are the open oceans we're talking about. It's not like the seas. Less predictable."

"And where is Montreal?"

Somewhat amused by this geography lesson, the Frenchman raises his arm to point at a little red dot inside a long channel. For a time, both men stand side by side, quietly studying the map. The world is immense.

"Looks like you're going to see the whole world."

"If that's what it takes."

He spends his remaining hours in Béjaïa walking the shady streets, as the sun grows stronger and more vigilant. He finds a post office and mails his letters, to let Niko and the Maleks know that he is on his way. In the envelope, he inserts thirty thousand dinars, to help them pay for Niko's food. The world is full of possibilities, he thinks, when you can see yourself on a map like the one in that caravan. He knows exactly where he is and where he has to go. After buying an envelope and a stamp, and mailing the letter, he asks the shopkeeper, "Do you have a map?"

"A map of where? I have a map of the city, and beyond that, the country."

"I need a map of the world. It's for a boy."

"In that case, all I have is this." From under the counter he pulls out a round globe the size of a melon.

Antoine picks up the globe in his hands and inspects it from all sides. The oceans and seas are a light blue, and the countries alternate between shades of orange, green, yellow, and pink. Each country features many dots, proclaiming cities. But he only has need for a few dots. Beirut is there, Béjaïa is there, and when he turns the globe around in his hands, on the other side he finds São Paulo and even Montreal. "It's accurate!"

"It should be," laughs the shopkeeper. "Otherwise, I'd be a fraud, selling you a world that doesn't exist."

With the globe tucked under his arm, Antoine Karam walks back down to the port, where he sits in the shade of the caravan and waits for his name to be called.

On a cool Thursday in late September, sixteen months after Sami Malek wrote his letter to Antoine, a gruff Québécois mailman enters the lobby of a Montreal North apartment building, and he waves his usual hello to the building superintendent.

"*Bonjour, Claude. Ça va?*"

From his wood-paneled office, Claude barely looks up from his *La Presse* newspaper and cigarettes. "*Pas pire, pas pire.*"

The mailman passes the faded floor-to-ceiling mural of a bright, autumnal forest shedding its leaves for winter, and enters a long, narrow mailroom. There, one by one, he opens every row of mailboxes and files in the appropriate envelopes, packets and flyers.

Halfway through this daily ritual, a mild-mannered Arab with a gray, receding hairline and a paunch walks in, sets his briefcase and tan trench coat down on the mailroom counter, and checks his box too soon.

97

"I'm not there yet," the mailman says. He has a job that he's been doing for twenty-three years and he likes to do it methodically. "You'll have to wait."

"I'm here and they're not," Sami bargains. "Did anyone else come down to say hello?"

The mailman relents. "What number?"

"324, Malek."

The mailman rifles through his bag and comes up with a small bundle, including one red-and-white envelope that requires a signature.

"Ah see, it's a good thing I'm here. Otherwise, you would've had to come upstairs.

"*C'est bien chanceux ça.*"

The mailman hands him a clipboard, points to a line, and after Sami has put down his signature, gives him what turns out to be a letter from the government.

In the elevator, Sami opens the government letter first. The envelope contains numerous forms to fill out and a cover letter that states that he and Yvonne have finally been accepted for Canadian citizenship. A ceremony, in which they will officially be sworn in, will be held in three weeks' time.

It is the news he'd been hoping for. Sami is relieved. The long and nerve-wracking road to citizenship is finally coming to an end. After years of paperwork and meetings and setbacks, they've finally succeeded in cementing a solid foundation upon which to build their lives. This cheap apartment in Montreal North, the hording of his savings from Lebanon, his doggedness to build a reputation as an honest businessman and a reputable architect – they've all paid off.

As the elevator doors open, Sami sees that the potential that was once the cornerstone of his years as a young and enterprising man, back in the sixties and before the endless wars, is there waiting for him once again, right in front of the modest door to their home. This apartment has served them well. Unlocking the door and stepping inside, he decides that soon they'll move to a bigger place.

Maybe they can even buy a house. He has the money saved, and now he has the stability and means to push his stake into the soil of this foreign country.

Sami Malek sets his briefcase and the remaining mail down, and looks out the window at the bright blue autumn sky. He takes off his shoes and he sits down at the table and thinks about how far they've come in the past year. The journey has been a long one, six of the hardest years of his life. This has been a good year, a year in which they've finally gained a strong foothold in this country's slippery way of life. A new school session is underway, and both Yvonne and Niko have returned to classes. His wife has almost completed her degree and she's started a new job, a better job, as a receptionist at a law firm.

To everyone's surprise, even Niko managed to graduate from his language class last June, and so earlier this month he began school in the regular stream, albeit two grades behind because of everything he missed. But the progress appears to have changed the boy's outlook dramatically. It was he who got Niko there. He was the one who put pressure on the boy. He taught him the French language night after night and made sure he got it. He went to meet Niko's teacher, had the lesson plans explained to him, and he tightened the leash on the boy. He hadn't expected that Niko would actually come around to the idea of being told what to do, but that happened too.

Awash in the pride of his own accomplishments, Sami gets up and sorts through the remainder of the mail on the kitchen table, which is mostly bills and advertisements. But among them he discovers a thin cream-coloured envelope with no return address. The receiver's name and address – his own – appear in Arabic in black ink, and then again in English to the side, in red ink. He carefully tears open the envelope and discovers a letter from Antoine Karam inside.

He looks at the sheafs of paper with mixed feelings, because in the past sixteen months it has taken a great deal of effort to get used to the idea that Antoine Karam had disappeared for good. Even Niko, the hardest to convince, has quietly accepted that conclusion. As a result, they'd been able to move ahead. The contents of this letter, Sami fears, will only set them back. He begins to read:

Sami and Yvonne,

My debt to you is irretrievable, what you have done for me and my son can never be repaid, a thousand pardons for not calling or writing, I have been working at sea on ships and there are few opportunities for me to make connections or settle down, we are always moving. Now I am in Algeria and I will not be here for long but I am getting closer to you all the time. Soon I will come for Niko. In the meantime, all I can ask is that you don't give up on him or me. Please take care of Niko, and do what you must to see that he doesn't go down the wrong path. He should not pay for my troubles. I am aware that I am asking, always asking, for charity. You have already been more than gracious. I don't live in a world of much certainty, and so it is difficult for me to make promises, even though all I want is to list them here for you. All in all, I am aware of what I have done to you and what you have done for me. I am your weakness and you are my strength. The strong must always remember to be gentle with the weak. True, this weakling, you might say, has built his own cage. I pray to you, Sami and Yvonne, don't forget me and take care of my son as if he is your own, for without you I am nothing but an empty cage.

Your humble servant,
Antoine Karam

p.s. I have enclosed some money for Niko's food.

What is he expected to take from this letter, Sami wonders. It contains little in the way of practical, useful information. The letter in his hands serves mainly as a confirmation of existence. But that confirmation offers no guidance, no stated desire by which they are to proceed. If Sami reads it correctly, they are to remember that Antoine is still out there, but that they should otherwise forget him in the everyday passage of their lives.

The envelope contains more paper. Sami pulls out several large bills, which he supposes must be Algerian money. They amount to thirty thousand of whatever the currency there might be, but in Canada, at most, to a token amount. The envelope also contains a second letter. He unfolds the page and finds a letter to Niko. At first, he's reluctant to read it, but should he really give it to the boy without first confirming that its contents won't hurt him?

My dearest Niko,

I am alive, by god am I ever alive! I have been traveling the seas as a sailor, battling storms and chasing whales and hunting sharks with harpoons, eating fresh fish and singing songs of the sea to keep up the spirits of the other men. This is how I make a living now, and this is how I will come for you one day. I will come by boat. I am in Algeria now. This is my first time on land in over four months. I have grown fins! I am staying at the home of a wonderful stranger who has showered me with charity. He keeps a cage filled with hundreds of pigeons on his rooftop, and he has trained them to deliver messages, which he ties to their legs. They are wonderful birds! But I will not stay here for long. It may take months on the dangerous high seas, but it is possible to take a boat across the ocean. But I will do it, and I will come find you. It saddens me to hear that you get into trouble. You must try harder to live a good life. You must try your hardest to stay out of jail, because once you begin to think like a prisoner, there is no way out. Perhaps you're old enough now to know that I have been living a life in which I have no control over my destiny, and that I sent you to live with your aunt and uncle because, as we traveled, I began to see the poisonous thoughts growing in your head. It took all my will to send you away, even if it was to give you a chance at a better life. You may ask, what is a better life? I will tell you. A better life is one where you can do whatever you imagine, without anyone standing in the way. You must make sure to dream of a better life for yourself, and to pursue it without hesitation.

Till we meet again,
Baba

Sami's first thought is that Antoine no longer knows the boy he's writing to. Too much time has passed and, in any case, boys grow up quickly. Second of all, Sami draws the conclusion that Antoine must be spending too much time at sea or in the world of adults to know children at all. This letter is more a philosophical tract than a communication to an impressionable boy on the cusp of thirteen. If he gives this letter to Niko, it will set him back with futile hope for a heroic father sailing the seas in his direction. And while Sami would like nothing more than to believe that, something tells him that even though Antoine Karam's sincerity can be taken at face value, it will take much longer for him to get his house in order. A boy Niko's age can't be expected to make that distinction.

Above all, Sami doesn't want to disrupt the delicate progress he's made with Niko these past months. There is only room for one role model in a young boy's life, and to bring up these vague promises of a distant father right now would only confuse him. It's taken two years, but Niko is actually doing better in school. He even has some friends. His nephew should be allowed to live like a normal child.

He has become quite good at taking the subway and then the bus back home from school every day. Some days he even stays after school to play soccer in the schoolyard. But on that particular day,

Niko is ambushed by an urge to rush straight home, and by the time he arrives back at their door, the school day has only ended thirty-five minutes earlier, and he's set a new record for fastest time ever getting home from school. He slides the key in the lock, turns the latch, pushes the handle, and there he sees, at the end of the short hall, his uncle seated on the sofa, looking down at a piece of paper.

At the sound of his hello, Sami raises his head, smiles knowingly, and discreetly puts the paper away in the side-table's drawer. Niko bounds into the apartment, dropping his schoolbag and coat along the way and kicking off his shoes. He runs into the kitchenette for his usual after-school snack: a spoonful of Nutella.

"Guess what?" he grins at his uncle.

"What?" Sami says, made curious by Niko's evident excitement.

Niko runs back to his bag, pulls out one of his subject folders, and retrieves a sheaf of paper. It is the math test for which they'd studied all last week. "I got an 89%!"

"That's excellent. Let me see."

Niko sits down on the sofa next to his uncle. "I only got three wrong."

"Where did you make the mistakes?" Sami says, looking over the test questions.

"Here." Niko turns over the first page. "I didn't invert this fraction correctly."

"Do you know how to do it correctly?"

"I think so, now that I see the mistake."

"Show me."

So on the back of the test, Niko explains how he would have handled the numbers if he'd had to do the equation again. "Is that right?"

"That would have given you the right answer." His uncle rests a hand on his shoulder, and that's how Niko knows he's proud of him.

"I knew it."

His uncle then puts the test down on the coffee table and looks at him expectantly. Has he done something wrong?

"I've got good news, too."

Niko's face brightens. "Oh yeah, what?"

"We've been accepted for citizenship."

"That's great!" Niko high fives his uncle. "Are we gonna celebrate?"

"Maybe we'll all go to dinner this weekend."

"Can we go to Pizza Hut?"

"Why not. But this doesn't mean you shouldn't do your homework. Tell me, what do you have today?"

"Some French, some math, and a bit of science."

Sami gets up and goes to the fridge. "Do you want a grilled cheese before we get started?"

"Yeah!"

"Alright, go wash your hands and I'll get cooking."

And so Niko hustles into his room to change out of his school clothes and into his home clothes, because Sami has taught him that one must have specific clothes for specific tasks in the day, and that if he is dressed in a more relaxed fashion, he will bring a more relaxed – and therefore open – mindset to his homework.

As Niko undresses on his side of the room, methodically putting away his school clothes in the old chest at the foot of his bed where he keeps all his belongings, he can't help but think that Sami is always right, even when Niko thinks he's wrong at first. It's as if his uncle has an uncanny ability to see into the future and decide its outcome out of sheer will. He never thought that a person could do that before. If his uncle can do that, if even he can learn to do that, then why can't Baba? But Niko is having a good day, and he would rather not think about Baba, so he quickly throws on his home clothes – an old T-shirt and jogging pants that are patched at the knee from too much crawling around in the hall with toy cars. He knows he's too old to be doing that so much, playing with toys cars at thirteen, but he can't help it: toy cars rolling across a solid floor and into the leg of a table or the buttocks of a sofa, rolling off freely until they crash. He got an 89%! This one thought keeps popping up in his head like a special news bulletin on the TV, over and over again. An 89. Just three years ago, that number meant nothing, and now it means everything. His new teacher is much more understanding with him than Madame Robitaille ever was. This, he believes, is why he's doing better. Plus, he likes playing soccer after school. In soccer, Niko estimates, I'd give myself a 95%. He wonders if this is how his uncle Sami thinks.

"Is it ready yet?" he shouts into the other room. Then he comes to the table, where his uncle is still looking over the test while preparing the grilled cheese, as if he's just as spirited and proud of the result as Niko is.

"I have hard science homework," Niko says. "Do you know about evolution?"

"Of course." Sami knows too much about evolution, traits and complications that aren't even in school textbooks. He puts a pan on the stove and turns on the element.

"Evolution is everywhere. Heat like this here," he angles the pan to spread the bubbling butter, "forces evolution. So does the desire to grow and become better, like your test. Evolution is everything."

"I'm evolving?"

"Sure. We all are."

They share the snack, one half apiece, and then get started on the homework, and this is how Yvonne finds them, still at the table and buried in books, when she gets home from the legal office.

Days before the citizenship hearing, they receive news from Lebanon that is already months old. It comes to them through a string of acquaintances. Yvonne's father has died. For some reason, she'd always thought that when the news came, for such bad news would inevitably come from the war-ravaged remains of their homeland, that it would be the result of a bomb or a bullet. Instead, her father simply had the bad fortune of being trapped in an elevator because of a power failure, and he had a heart attack in there. When Yvonne finds out, she locks herself in the bathroom, the only room in the apartment that affords the privacy of a lock on the door, and she bawls until she runs out of energy and then she starts all over again.

Niko has never known his aunt to be a sad person, but here she is letting out more sadness than anyone else he's ever known. It's horrifying to listen to, and as he and Sami sit awkwardly in the next room listening to Yvonne wail, he can't help but start thinking of Yvonne's father, for he remembers his jiddo well, and then he can't help but begin to think about Mama too because he's her dad, and how they're all gone, and with the miserable sounds of his aunt shrieking in the bathroom, he can't help but think of every single person in the world whom he loves and how they're all gone, and in the end Niko begins to cry a little too – even though he'd promised Baba he would never do that again – because no matter how many 89s he gets in school, he's still all alone in the world.

His uncle puts an arm around his shoulder and says, "Go ahead and let it out. It's okay to feel sad."

With weepy eyes, Niko turns to his uncle, the only person he knows who never loses control, and he says, "It sounds so scary. When do you think she'll stop?"

Sami looks at the swollen child and wonders what to tell him, and there's no reason to hide secrets at such times, and so what he ends up telling Niko turns out to be a sliver of adult truth, the kind usually kept from him.

"I suppose once she stops being angry at herself for hating him."

"But why does she hate Jiddo?"

"Because they had a big disagreement over something important, and they haven't spoken in seven years. And now he's dead."

"Do you hate Jiddo too?" He simply can't understand why anyone would hate his grandfather, who never did anything wrong to anyone.

"Your jiddo was my friend. Your jiddo, my child, once worked for my family."

"You were his boss?"

"Something like that. Your jiddo was a hard worker and he took care of his family, and we took care of him."

"Did Mama hate Jiddo too?" He doesn't think so, but who can tell what's right or wrong anymore.

"Oh, I don't think so. I think your mama and jiddo got along just fine."

"What did Tante Yvonne and Jiddo fight about that was so bad?"

Sami Malek thinks about this for a while and finally says, "You know what, it's not important anymore. He's gone now and it's too far in the past to matter. Don't tell your aunt I said anything." That evening, they go to the Greek-Orthodox church on Jean-Talon Street to pray for Jiddo. Saints abound in the stained-glass windows. Crosses adorn the walls and the smoke of incense and candles mingles in the air. It is a cold weeknight in a foreign country and no one else in the church knows about Jiddo and the fact that he died, or that his funeral took place well over a month ago, and so as they sit there in the uncomfortable pews, they feel their desolation more keenly, isolated from the world. A priest with a full white beard takes the podium. With frail hands he ruffles through the pages of a large book. Delivers a hymn. Reads a collection of psalms. And the sparse congregation bows heads in quietude.

Now that her father, her mother, and her sister are all dead, Yvonne decides that she will pray one last time for them all, and that will be that. Tomorrow she resolves to become a different person. How unfairly her father had treated her. She was the youngest daughter, the least valuable of them all, and so he had arranged a marriage for her and hadn't even bothered to ask her what she thought. All her life, no one has ever asked her what she wants.

She was born in one of those Shatila shacks in the Palestinian refugee camps of Lebanon. Her family came from simple peasants.

They worked with their hands, knew little of anything that didn't have direct contact with their lives. Her father was a stone-mason, building with stone and cement. No one in her family knew how to read. When she was born, it has been said, her mother had nothing to wrap her in, other than the dirty sheet they used for a ceiling. Her camp was on an ugly strip of land in a valley behind a sports stadium. It flooded with sewage whenever it rained. Every time they left, to buy food, to swim, whatever, they'd show identification cards. Her grandfather had been a trader, traveled by donkey. Her father had two daughters, and he went to work in Malek factories, which allowed them to leave the camps.

Four years ago, she had seen the massacre in Shatila on the news. Though her family hadn't lived there for years, it sent shockwaves through her mind: all those people, shot or stabbed or daggered with acid. All the dead buried quickly, so no one would know who or how many had died. She knew them. In her heart, she was still one of them.

Now, as she sits in the pew and listens to the psalms and quietly mourns, Yvonne thinks of all those people. She might as well pray for all their souls. An entire generation of friends and family, all gone. Tomorrow, she thinks, I will start a new life in this country where nobody knows the history of your name, what it means, and nobody cares where you come from. She is young still, not even thirty, and this land is ripe for a woman like her who's not afraid to try. It's not what her father would have wanted her to do, but now that he's dead she supposes she can do whatever she wants, even correct her father's mistakes. Yvonne peers up at the painted ceilings of St. George. In some ways, she decides, she has been looking forward to a moment like this all her life, an opportunity to make a clean break with the past.

Beside Yvonne, Sami sits just as still, numbed into silence by a wave of immense and sudden sadness. They are at a crossroads, and maybe there is some deeper meaning to be taken from this depressing news that has come to them now, just days before their citizenship confirmation. He has worked hard to get to this point, and yet sometimes he feels like he's gotten nowhere at all. In Canada he is little more than a blind man trying to thread a string through a needle's eye. The death of his father-in-law, along with the heavy-hearted psalms and ritual of the service, has turned his narrative of achievement into a lowly history of running away. He has left so many people behind, and he has gone through even greater pains to never look back.

My poor mother, he finds himself reminiscing. Bless her soul, she had many children, so many, seventeen, and she was the pillar of their family to the end. Not a single one of those children is in his life now, but at one point there were so many of them, together.

Seventeen children, seventeen different dreams, and then she had died. This is the myth he has made of his childhood, as useful to him as worry beads. It reminds him just how old he is now.

His own father had a stroke when Sami was thirty-one, and he was left an invalid. He took over his father's business, and its growth brought him to Beirut and made them rich, all as his father sat in the far bedroom of their apartment, staring out the window at the sun passing, his left arm useless, his face half gone. Sometimes he would drink on the front steps of their building, and wine would spill out of his mouth and stain his shirt.

He had a wife before this, too. Marie. He no longer believed in love, or made a place for it in his life, but back when he was young, not even twenty, he had loved Marie ferociously. They had married at a huge wedding that went on for days and had expected to share a long life together. And then she had gotten pregnant and then she had died just as Ziad was being born.

Ziad, he thinks, the war took him away, too. Or maybe Sami pushed him into it. Even a decade on, he still does not like to think of his son, and he finds it hard to pinpoint what happened between them. Ziad had disappeared into the violence of the streets. If he had waited for Ziad, he contemplates now, instead of taking another wife and leaving that godforsaken place, it would have all turned out differently. They might all be dead.

Sitting here now in this church, those memories belong to a

stranger; he is no longer the same man who lived them, and so he is just their keeper. His mother, his father, his siblings, his first wife, his son, and now his father-in-law – together they amount to his ghosts. Sitting here and thinking of them like this has made him the fixation of every stoic gaze of every saint in the room, and they all look at him with regret. The Byzantines have perfected this concept of oblique and omnipresent knowingness. Every time he comes here, he can't help but feel that, somehow, this room can see right through him and expose the weaknesses he has suffered so long to hide. Such is his fate for leaving the war behind. He has become a stranger to his family.

Beside Sami sits Niko, who conjures a time in the distant past where he can barely see over the pew. He holds onto a giant candle with both hands, flanked to one side by his mama, and to the other side by Baba. They're together again. Baba pats his head, since he knows that Niko is hungry.

He's wearing new overalls, new shoes as well. They are all wearing their best clothes. He has black whiskers painted on each side of his nose. He has an obsession for lions: lion picture books, lion-paw prints on his bathrobe, lion roars at the kitchen table whenever Mama prepared what big lions have for dinner. He is an *assad*. He's tapping his feet, counting the number of taps it will take to end the service so they can go outside, where he will run around with his giant candle like a torch in the arid afternoon air. He can only count up to ten.

Mama steps on his toes.

And then the last hymn draws to an end and the man in the tall black hat closes his big book. Bells shudder and the sweet waft of incense billows through the aisles. Back to front, rows file out of the church. He squints as they wait to pass through the large wooden doors, a scheme he's prepared for the onslaught of sunshine. To his satisfaction, everyone else is caught off guard and fumbling for their sunglasses. The militiaman guarding the entrance with his machine-gun, he notices, already has his big Ray-Bans on. He pulls on Mama's dress to tell her that he wants glasses like those. She knows. He's been asking for them ever since the first day he saw fighters in the streets. Again she tells him that the army makes those glasses for criminals and no one else. He says that he'll have to become a criminal then, and she says *never unless you want to kill your mama!*

Outside on the steps, Mama spots her cousin, who's with his wife and children. As the adults exchange stories, his mother's cousin's children and he stand awkwardly, eyeing each other's candles and shoes. He has nothing to say to interest two girls aged ten and twelve. He is incredibly shy in front of anyone who is not his parents.

Soon, his grandfather appears, dressed in a dark grey suit and a red tie. When Jiddo catches him standing forlorn behind Mama's dress, drooling with hunger, he picks up the little boy and mounts him on his shoulders. From up there, Niko can see the tops of everyone's heads. Jiddo pulls a lighter from his pocket, lights the boy's candle and his pipe.

Then Niko bends over and whispers in Jiddo's large, wrinkled ear, "What should I do now that everyone's gone?"

Jiddo looks up and whispers back, "You must do what's right for you."

When he holds the candle across his shoulder like a rifle, Mama scolds him to hold it straight.

He bends down and whispers in Mama's delicate, untouchable ear, "Will you be mad at me if I grow up?"

She looks up and says, "Not if it makes you happy."

A car explodes at the far end of the square, and immediately he's back on the ground, beneath his jiddo's arm. The car bomb is too far away to hurt anyone from the church. It doesn't appear to have been wired properly and merely smolders under a canopy of black smoke. The car horn has stuck after the explosion, a nagging reminder that a peaceful afternoon is ending. Still, for a moment, everyone in the square ducks down to his height, waiting for more, and he can see over their heads again. And then, the militiamen in the jeep run to see what's left of the car. People in the square brush off their good clothes and walk home, resigned to the fact that their brief time outdoors has come to an abrupt end.

Later, during the car ride home, Sami and Yvonne ask Niko if he'd like to become their son, if he would be happy if they adopted him.

"That way you can become a citizen like us," Sami says, by way of explanation.

"And we can be a real family, together," Yvonne adds. "In any case, we just wanted to tell you that it's a possibility, for whenever you want. It's for you to decide. All we'd like for you to know is that you're welcome to stay with us for as long as you like. You have a home here."

"Would I have to change my name?"

"You don't have to do anything you don't want to. All we're saying is that it might be something that makes you happy. But it's for you to think about. To decide if it will make you happy."

"Would it make you happy?" Niko asks.

"Of course it would make us happy," Sami says.

Niko says nothing more and, staring out the window at the passing factories alongside the road, mulls over what his aunt and uncle have just said. The idea scares him. Would his parents be mad at him if he changes families? What would Baba think if he ever came back?

"But what if I'm not an orphan," he finally says, evidently confused. "What about Baba?"

No one has an answer to that. In silence, they crisscross the thoroughfares of Montreal, all the way back to their apartment in the city's north end.

The day of the citizenship hearing, they all wake up early. After nearly two years together, they have slipped into a routine that makes the best of their limited space. Yvonne gets up first, uses the washroom, and makes coffee. Then Sami gets up and uses the washroom, and by then the coffee is usually ready. Niko lies there a bit longer, trying to ignore the day for a few more precious minutes of sleep. Then it is his turn for the washroom; his uncle typically knocks on his door twice as he leaves the washroom. On his way to the morning coffee, Sami picks up the newspaper waiting outside their door. After Niko washes the slowness from his eyes, he joins his uncle at the table, where his aunt has his breakfast ready for him: Froot Loops. Her men minimally fed, Yvonne then goes to put on her face, the longest task of her morning. And so Sami is left to read the newspaper quietly, sipping his coffee to the loud crunch of colourful cereal that is his nephew's breakfast.

Sometimes Sami uses this time to quiz Niko on his homework, especially if he has a test that day, but that day Niko is not going to school, and Sami has informed his clients that he will not be available, and Yvonne has taken the morning off from the law firm. What will happen to his aunt and uncle once they are in that room, wonders Niko. Maybe the officials will ask him about becoming their son.

He asks his uncle, "Will they take away your citizenship if you don't adopt me?"

Sami shakes his head. The boy has been asking questions like this, randomly and tragically off course, about the adoption ever since they brought it up. "Like your aunt said, you're free to do whatever you want. One thing has nothing to do with the other."

"But will you be different after you're a citizen? Can we still do homework?"

"Of course." Sami puts his newspaper down. "Things won't be too different. We might move to a bigger apartment or maybe a house. You can have your own room."

"But it'll still be the same?"

"You can go whenever your father comes," his uncle replies. "We won't stop you."

"Can you go back to your own country if you're a citizen?"

"Sure you can. Only here will be home, too, and we'll only go there for visits."

"Does that mean if I become a citizen, too, I can only go back for visits?"

Down the short corridor, he sees his aunt come back out of the washroom in a billow of steam, fully dressed, and of course she's overheard every word of their conversation because the TV's not on, and so she jumps in. "It means you can do anything you want, and no one will ever tell you no because of your passport."

Is that good or bad? Niko sits sullenly at the table, more confused than ever. It's a lot of pressure to figure out if he wants to become a Malek and a citizen on the same day, and he wishes just this once that Baba was there to help him instead of his Uncle Sami. Baba never became a citizen. How come? He has never thought about it that way before. There must be something bad about becoming a citizen, if Baba never wanted it.

"Do you think Baba's still alive?"

"I don't know, *ya habibi*," Yvonne says, sitting at the foot of their foldout bed and clipping on her earrings. "For your sake, I hope so."

She doesn't want to lie to her nephew, because in all honesty Yvonne doesn't know and she doesn't want to lead Niko on. Even if Antoine were alive, he couldn't get stable enough to stand squarely on his own two feet for long. Some people just don't have the discipline. But she couldn't say anything like that to Niko, that Antoine Karam isn't, in his own sister-in-law's opinion, the type to get it together.

"That's why it's most important for you to decide," Sami adds, looking from over the edge of the newspaper. "Your father will always be your father. But, if you want us to, we can be your parents too, while you wait."

Niko finishes his bowl of cereal and, feeling uncomfortable, goes back to his room to change into the clothes his aunt has laid out on his bed, something she only does now on special occasions, when he needs to be dressed well.

As soon as he leaves, Yvonne turns on the TV and, as Sami begins to change into a dress shirt by the hall closet, she walks over to him and whispers, "Do you think we've asked too much of him? Maybe he's not ready to deal with such big questions."

"It's important that he begins to think about these things."

"It breaks my heart every time he asks about his father. I never know what to say." It saddens her to think that Antoine would just disappear like that, without a word. And then she thinks he must be dead. "I can't help but feel like crying whenever he asks me those questions."

"He asks less and less, though," Sami says, sorting through his shelf for a properly pleated pair of pants. "We've got to keep him focused on school and growing up. When he's older, he'll be free to do what he likes. But right now he needs parents."

"Do you think he wants us to be his parents? Three days and he's been asking the same questions."

"In the end he'll come around because he knows better than to throw away a chance."

"I hope you're right."

They put on their coats and take the elevator down to the garage, where their rusting Chrysler LeBaron awaits them, and then they drive to the Citizenship & Immigration building, where they park the car and walk past the security guards in the lobby to the elevator that takes them up to the third floor, where the notice they received says the transformation will take place. Upstairs they wait in a long line with their documents ready, and soon they are called to a counter, where Sami and Yvonne present their papers and have their pictures taken.

"What about him?" the government clerk asks.

"Just us," Sami replies.

When Sami says that, Niko can't help but feel ostracized, even though he knows that's the only answer that his uncle can give. Now that he's here, he wouldn't mind having his picture taken or signing his name.

After the pictures are taken, the clerk says, "Okay, just go in that room and take a seat. Your citizenship card will come by registered mail in the next two weeks."

They enter an austere white room with high ceilings and blue plastic chairs in rows all facing a large desk. About half the seats are taken. Sami leads Yvonne and Niko to the three open seats closest to the front. They sit and wait in the same order as they always fall into when together: Yvonne, Sami, and then Niko, left to right.

Niko leans over and asks his uncle. "Will there be a party afterwards?"

Sami smiles. "Not here, but maybe later at home."

"Do I have to leave if I don't become a citizen?" Niko asks, still not sure how someone who is a citizen can live with someone who's not.

"You'll be alright. Today you're here to have a look, tomorrow you can do this yourself."

The only thing, Niko thinks, is that he would have to give up on Baba.

"Listen," his uncle confides, "I know this is not easy for you to sit here and watch this, or to think about your future now. When we get back home, we have a little gift for you, so you can have something special today, too. You deserve it, with all the work you've done at school."

"A gift?" Niko's eyes widen. It's rare that anyone gives him anything. "What is it?"

"We talked about it, and we think you're old enough to have your own savings account."

"A savings account?" Niko has never thought of having one, but he is just as glad to have one now that it's been orchestrated for him.

"That way when you get a job one day, you'll have a place to keep your money where it can grow."

"Grow into what?"

"Into more money."

"And every year on your birthday," Yvonne adds, "we'll add some extra on top of what you have."

Sami puts his arm around his nephew, who no longer pulls away when he attempts such maneuvers, and says, "You're a lucky man. I've already put $500 in there for you, so you have a good start."

It's what 30,000 Algerian dinars converts to in Canadian Dollars.

"But…" Niko hesitates, "can I still keep it if…"

"If what?"

"Even if I don't get adopted?" He lowers his head, ashamed to look at his aunt and uncle.

"You don't want to become our son?" Yvonne says, her voice unable to hide her disappointment.

"No," Niko whimpers, as politely as he can muster, "but thank you."

"Are you sure?" she asks.

He nods.

"It's for you to decide," his uncle says. He removes his arm from around his nephew's shoulders, and crosses his legs. Quietly, he then says, "Think about it a bit more."

They think he's making a mistake, but they don't see how he'd be letting down Baba if he became their son instead. He must think of Baba, because if he doesn't, no one else will. But he feels horrible, because they have given him a home and food and now a savings account, and he hasn't given them what they want in return.

A judge in a black robe walks into the room through a side door, and a bailiff stands up and instructs the citizens-to-be, "All rise."

They all stand up and pay attention to the judge, all except for Niko who sits on the bench, moored to the dock, dejected and staring at his feet because he is the only person here who cannot participate in the building of new futures. And so the boat leaves without him. In due course, the judge instructs everyone else but him to raise right hands and swear allegiance to a new country.

*

All around the ship, an unforgiving blue sea fills the empty expanse in every direction. Antoine looks up at the sky above, once brimming with stars. It has steadily marbled with little gray clouds, and the deeper they venture into the ocean, the more light they lose. Walking across the gently swaying deck to the other end of the ship, he looks ahead and sees only ominous blackness, an abyss. They've been at sea for over three weeks, and tomorrow they expect to see the Brazilian coast. But there is no sense of it out there now. They are charging into a storm tonight, he can hear it in the subtle whisper of a wet wind gusting across the water.

After smoking a cigarette with the wind's howls growing wilder against his ears, Antoine gets out of the cold and trudges down four levels, deep into the belly of the vessel, where he lies on his bunk, which is merely one of many that lines the corridors of the sailors' quarters. He pulls his curtain shut and turns on his flashlight, his only belonging, and even though he can still hear other sailors in conversation nearby or walking past his bunk, he has grown accustomed to turning his cubicle of rust and dampness – no more than three feet from bunk to ceiling and seven feet from head to foot – into a bastion of inward speculation.

As they cut across the equatorial Atlantic to São Paulo, the tropical waters grow fierce and unpredictable, and he can hear the waves outside rising higher. The ship sways, and Antoine tries to put the motion out of his mind. He pulls out his wallet and removes the dog-eared photo of his family from its pouch: there he is, a much younger man, standing proudly behind his wife Elise with his hands on her shoulders. On Elise's lap sits his chubby boy, the last Nakhle, no older than three when this was taken. With the sound of sea rain lashing the steel frame of the ship, he finally falls asleep.

When he wakes up again, it is to the sound of an emergency drill. He pulls back his curtain and jumps out of his bunk, and bumps into other sailors hurrying through the narrow corridor. Sailors run in every direction, yelling 'fire', 'flames'!

118

"We're taking on water!" one of them shouts, cursing frantically down the stairwell.

Antoine can smell smoke in the air. He straps on his life jacket. Soon the lights go out, and the emergency generator kicks in. He stuffs all his belongings into his bag, and then pushes his way up the stairs through a mass of shoving bodies. There they brace for balance on the open deck of the violently swaying ship, which rolls up and down, left and right, at the mercy of gargantuan waves and a shower of rain pouring relentlessly into their faces. Bright orange plumes of smoke silently begin to creep out of the portholes. They hold on to anything that's stable. Soon, the ship tilts dangerously to one side.

"Abandon ship!" the captain calls out.

One by one, men begin leaping overboard.

There is nowhere else to go. Taking a genuine leap of faith, Antoine falls into the sea, behind a curtain of total darkness. Saltwater floods his mouth. At first all he feels is a rush of warmth, something like being born again, he can't help but think, for there is surprisingly much room to think in his head at such a moment, more room than there has ever been. But then the cold begins to infect his skin. His lifejacket buoys him back to the roiling surface. Thereafter, his teeth chattering, he rolls up and down the massive sea, barely holding his head out of water as he waits for dawn. Hours pass at a pace that feels like days. As first light finally creeps up and a wan grey bathes the sky, Antoine can see where he is for the first time, and he sees only water rising and falling, fettered with flotillas of debris. There is an oil canister floating nearby. The ship is gone. The towering black waves are divided only by the distant voices of men calling out for help and the rumble of occasional thunder. By mid-day the thunder and calls of men are gone, and the sea is silent again, and all that remains along its roiling surface are floating islands of trash.

After that he doesn't see or hear anyone else. Striving for anything to hang onto that can confirm his existence, he latches onto a wooden ladder floating nearby, and so he pulls himself up and rests his tired arms by lying against its rungs. The sea calms, the clouds break, and soon the sun burns what is left of his salt-caked face. There is no land in sight, and not a single ship comes to the rescue. Towards the beginning of his second night, the winds pick up and it begins to rain again, and though the rain allows him to taste unsalted water for the first time since his ship sank, he finds it impossible to deny that time has finally run out on him, and there may not be a way out of this predicament. Out here, no one else is left but him. He hears a faint siren calling him, and he finds its reverberation across the open water serenely angelic in tenor and persistence. Thereafter, Antoine Karam begins to make preparations for his death.

Decadence

As SHE PLUCKS HER EYEBROWS, Yvonne gazes into a handheld mirror and concedes that even at thirty years old she could still be mistaken for Sophia Loren's cousin, as her friends once teased her when she was younger, back when she had friends. She still has the regal bones of a Spaniard, and thick auburn hair, her colour for this season. Next season it might change. Certainly they can afford it now, so why not. She isn't very tall, she concedes to the handheld mirror. No one in her family was ever tall: she comes from resolutely short people. Thank God she is still thin! Yvonne pulls her hair back to inspect 18-karat earrings dangling in the light. They are a birthday present to herself purchased ten days ago, when she received her pay-cheque.

Today is her thirtieth birthday, and Yvonne has a lunch with two sisters, Madeleine Khoury and Hanniah al-Sfeir, her cousins by some distant degree. The sisters are the grandchildren of her mother's great aunt. In any case, their families came from the same camp, and that's enough to make her feel guilty if she ever said no to them. They are meeting at a seafood restaurant.

All morning she has passed back and forth between the brightly-lit master bedroom and the *en suite* bathroom of their new house, trying on different blouses. She labours over the last details of her face, an increasingly complex conspiracy given the subtle wrinkles she's discovered around her eyes. Once Yvonne has attended to every last detail from chin to scalp, she smokes a Winston Light over the toilet, and as ashes fall into the water, she anticipates the coming afternoon down to its last detail, for she already knows how it will unfold: talk of families here and abroad, talk of houses, talk of husbands, and talk of civil war.

So this is what it's like to be a citizen, Yvonne thinks, cocking one arm on her hip as she studies herself in the bathroom mirror. In the past two years, their lives have grown comfortable in this new three-bedroom house, and as a result, somewhat predictable. She has her university degree now; she has a part-time job, a car, money to spend and to spare, and the appearance of a family. That bruised shade of brown hair is a nice colour on her. She's young still – when she wants to be. She drops the cigarette into the toilet. The bathroom fan siphons off what's left of the smoke. Taking her purse, she goes downstairs to the two-car garage and begins the long drive to the Town of Mount Royal, on the island, in her used Volkswagen Golf, their second car after Sami's Nissan Intrepid.

A half-hour later, when she enters the restaurant, she spots the sisters at a table by the far window, overlooking their husbands' cars. She greets each sister with a trio of kisses to the cheek. Madeleine moved to Montreal with her husband and three children in 1976, and Hanniah followed in 1985 with her husband and two children. Madeleine's oldest is only four years younger than Yvonne, and so these obligatory visits with the sisters often feel like afternoons spent with two old, doddering aunts. She tells them what they expect to hear, and then they filter it back to all their distant relations.

A waiter comes with water and menus. After much back and forth between the sisters over prices, they go peruse the restaurant's seafood shop next door, where the racks overflow with red snapper fillets, mauve octopuses, bass, swordfish, mussels, and a squid the size of large tubes of toothpaste. Yvonne orders the lobster, just to shock them a little. They're waiting for her to order first anyhow, so that they can order something less expensive.

Back at their table, Yvonne lights a cigarette, points at it with her free hand as she looks to the bar. She's been smoking more than she would have liked lately, but it's a matter of boredom, sure to pass. A smiling waiter catches her eye, and comes by with an ashtray. They all look out the window at their cars. It is a drab winter day, slushy and dark and windy.

Nonchalantly they exchange their news. Today, Hanniah says, they can afford to be a bit lavish: after three years, her husband has finally found a full-time job. "At his age, I was getting worried."

"Fantastic!" Yvonne says. "Now that your husband has a good job, you don't have to worry so much."

Madeleine cocks her brow. "Of course they can't all be as fortunate as your husband."

"No," Yvonne agrees. "Sami does have a talent for money."

Feeling obligated after that comment, Yvonne orders a bottle of white wine in celebration. Even if the sisters think she's rubbing her good fortune in their faces, it would be rude for them not to accept. They must still be talking about the new house behind her back.

"A new job *is* worth celebrating," Yvonne insists. She should know – at least she works.

The sisters smile, resigned to having a glass of wine.

The bottle of white wine arrives, and after a few initial sips they begin to talk more candidly than they usually do. The sisters hardly ever drink, and so a few sips is all its takes to make them tipsy, and it is not long before Madeleine and Hanniah are going back and forth in great detail about their brother, Mohab, who'd returned to Beirut for a visit.

"His old apartment was still in good shape, good enough to move back into," Madeleine says. "He says his neighbourhood has been more or less stable. He can still hear occasional gunfire off in the distance, but people know where not to go. He says life is returning back to normal."

"Even though there's still a war?" Yvonne asks.

"Even though," Madeleine confirms.

"There's still no electricity!" Hanniah says. "But everyone tells him it's better than it's been in a long time. If he doesn't find good work in Canada soon, he'll take the citizenship and go back."

Madeleine raises the possibility of her own visit. "Maybe next summer."

Hanniah isn't as certain. After three years of trying, her husband has finally found good work. "It would confuse the children."

Madeleine's son is engaged, and so she talks about how much she likes his fiancée, a good Lebanese girl who sits in Madeleine's kitchen all day gossiping and cooking with her future mother-in-law, and how she looks forward to her small family flourishing here, in this new country.

"And how is everything in your new home?" they enquire.

Maybe it's because she's had half a glass of wine by that point, or maybe it's because she doesn't feel like playing charades with the old ladies this afternoon, but Yvonne blurts out what that has been on her mind all month. "Well, to be honest," she begins, "everything is boring."

"Boring?" Madeleine scoffs. "You should be so fortunate to lead a 'boring' life here, after where you've come from."

"I know that," Yvonne says, taking another sip of wine.

"There's nothing boring about a husband who makes a lot of money," Hanniah laughs. "Is it boring to buy jewelry and expensive bottles of wine?"

"I work," Yvonne insists.

"You work, but at what expense?" Madeleine argues.

"You know nothing about my family."

"You never talk about them," Hanniah chips in.

Though Yvonne has only started on her second glass, she already feels dizzy. "Do you really want to know what goes on inside my house?"

The two sisters don't know what to say, for they have known Sami and Yvonne Malek only superficially for all these years.

"Our family ended the day we got our citizenship. My husband keeps to himself, doesn't really talk to me anymore unless he has to. He thinks as long as the house is paid for and we're spending money, no one has the right to question him. He used to at least take an interest in Niko, but he's stopped doing that. It's as if he feels he's done enough for us, so now he can forget we're there. We're . . . far apart."

And with that, she stands up, purse in hand, and walks to the washrooms. Ten minutes pass. Their food arrives.

When Yvonne finally returns to the table, her cheeks are a bit puffier, her eyes a bit sadder. In silence, they begin to eat, the crack of her lobster claws accentuating the awkward confession she's just placed on the table before them. She doesn't even know how to eat lobster. Why did she order the damn thing? The afternoon hasn't followed the script, and now she feels vulnerable for losing her veneer in front of the two sisters.

"So sad," Hanniah says finally, shaking her head. "Me, I wish my husband would shut up every once in a while."

"And how is Niko?" Madeleine asks. "How old is he now?"

"Fifteen."

Hanniah knows the story of Yvonne's nephew mainly through her sister, but has never asked Yvonne in any detail about him. Now she asks, "What about his father? Have you heard from him?"

Immediately Madeleine delivers a disapproving glance to her sister, but Hanniah ignores it.

"It's been almost five years since we heard anything," Yvonne tells them, taking yet another sip to finish off her second glass. "Before the citizenship, we at least had this hope of Antoine coming back. It kept Niko in line. But now, in this house, he shuts himself in his room all day and only comes out to have arguments with his uncle. He refuses to eat with us. He has no good friends, he tells us, and he hates the world."

"The poor boy," Hanniah says.

"He will grow up one day, you'll see," Madeleine advises. "My son was difficult at that age too. It's in their blood. Fifteen! One day, he'll come to his senses and realize his father is not coming back and that he has taken for granted everything you've given him. And then he'll come crawling to you on his knees, begging for forgiveness."

"*Inshallah!*" Yvonne says, ignoring her plate. She's no longer even hungry for this animal she can't take apart. Just restless.

"Maybe your house would not feel so empty if you had your own child," Madeleine suggests. "Never underestimate the power of a new child to bring people together."

"Well," Yvonne says. "I have my job." It doesn't help matters that it's been eight months since they've begun trying and she can't conceive, no matter how hard she tries.

Madelaine presses, "If you don't do it now, one day you'll regret it."

Yvonne says nothing, only plays with her lunch, which is proving much too difficult to eat. How she loathes the routine of sex for pregnancy. Changing the subject, Yvonne says, "I always thought that once we got the citizenship, that would be the end of my troubles. Outside the war, what else could be so bad? And yet, sometimes I think I miss struggling a little. It was a distraction."

"Now, now, my dear," says Madeleine. "Be strong. You're still very young. You'll learn yet that it's not all about dreams. You have to stand by your husband and the family you have, no matter what you think."

"Strong?" Yvonne scoffs, lifting the glass to her lips. "Do you know how I got married?"

The sisters shake their heads, hypnotized by this unprecedented openness.

"Sami was my father's boss. They arranged it between them and then, one evening, Sami takes my family for dinner to a chi-chi restaurant, a restaurant that we do not have clothes for, so we are forced to look like dogs. After the dinner, my father and Sami go for a walk through the hills. After the walk, my father tells me I'm to get married. My father, suddenly he's a businessman! Monsieur Malek, he says, is leaving the country very soon. I will look after the factory in his absence. You, my sweet, will marry Sami and leave the country. Me, I ask. Why me? So that he can raise his profile with immigration. This is how I got married. My father traded me for a factory. Romantic, no?"

The two sisters nod knowingly, as if to say, no, it's not romantic at all. Madeleine, of a generation to understand these matters more intimately, cautions, "You know, my husband, between you and me, only made sense to my family. Those days were different. You married for the welfare of your family, not for your own interests. It saved everyone involved a lot of stupidity and divorce."

"Still, he's a good man," Hanniah says, shifting subtly to her sister's side. "He has a good heart."

"Yes, he does," Madeleine agrees. "Listen, Yvonne. Be reasonable. Have children. I promise, with children in the house, all this nonsense about romance will go away."

"Maybe I don't want children," she lies, even though she wants a child more than anything. "You know, in the end, maybe it's not a romantic movie that I'm after. Sometimes I'm just curious. I can't help it. I've never lived by myself, without my father or my husband. Don't you ever feel curious about that?"

The sisters shrug, not really taking her seriously anymore because she's no longer talking like a woman who came from the same camps as them. Perhaps afterwards they'll say to each other, "That Yvonne can be very condescending sometimes."

Yvonne lights another cigarette. "Everywhere I turn, I see the modern woman making her own life. Why not me?"

"Go ahead and be modern," Hanniah says. "You have a car, a job, nice clothes. You even have a fifteen-year-old nephew who won't speak to you. This is just like having a modern teenage son."

Given the obvious tipsiness of their young third-cousin Madeleine feels a duty to offer more advice. "Everything must be allowed to age properly. You'll grow out of it. Just wait and see. Having family is better than being alone. Have another child, I say. You don't have to wait for romance with your husband for this to happen."

They're both judging her, Yvonne thinks, even as they try to feed her advice. She can hear it in Madeleine's voice especially. It was a mistake to assume that these women could think like the modern women she wants so badly to have as her friends. And they bring Niko into it, who's too old to treat her any differently than a cook, a chauffeur, and an open wallet. And her husband, she's convinced, looks at her differently now that they've tried to conceive and can't. As if her infertility isn't part of the arrangement he made with her father.

"I'm sorry," Yvonne says all of a sudden, checking her watch. "I have to go. Niko is waiting for me at the school, and I said I'd pick him up."

"But we haven't even had dessert or coffee yet," Hanniah implores.

"Family can't wait," Yvonne replies, with a hint of bitterness.

"Yvonne, sit down a bit longer," Madeleine offers, returning to that friendly, maternal tone that says I once knew your mother. "You've had a lot to drink. You shouldn't drive just yet. Wait till after the coffee."

"No, really, I have to go now." Tipsily Yvonne rises from the table, cigarette dangling awkwardly from her lips as she collects her purse. She tracks down their waiter and collects the bill for all three, which she pays with the credit card Sami has provided her. Then she's off to the parking lot, where she's certain that the sisters are spying on her from their perch, gossiping about what a bad wife she must be. Well, they can all go to hell for all she cares.

Where have these feelings been stored all these years, Yvonne asks herself as she fiddles with the car keys. She can't, for the life of her, manage to slide the key into the lock. "What's wrong with this car?" she hisses under her breath. Then it's in, and she's letting the engine warm while she gathers herself.

Now that the sisters have made her upset, it's as though she can't help but obsess over the obvious hole in the life that her third cousins imagine to be so perfect. She had always worked from

Sami's plan. It had been a given. Come to Canada, work hard to start a second life, get citizenship, get pregnant, buy a house for their children, raise them. Sami has managed his part just fine – they have the house. Only she's unable to honour her part of the arrangement.

Why did we even try to have children, she asks herself in the rearview mirror, why couldn't we have left well enough alone? Sometimes it's just better to look forward to things, rather than find out they can't happen. Citizenship was like this: a hollow reward.

She pulls the car out of the parking lot and catches a glance of her bloated eyes in the mirror. She's been teary since the lunch began, but she can't say for how long exactly. The wine may have been a mistake. She can't recall the last time she had a drink. The streets are wet and the other cars keep spraying her windshield. Maybe she isn't in a mood to drive just yet. She doesn't even know which road to take from here to get to Niko's school. She decides to soldier on, out of spite. Those sisters have left her seething! How dare they attack her like that after she opened up to them. All this time, Yvonne thinks, they've had these lunches, invitations to each other's homes for holidays, and look how little they actually know of one another in the end. If she'd known just a little bit more about them, maybe she could have dropped the posturing a long time ago and left all these old blood ties behind.

Now it begins to rain again. With so much on her mind and her windshield wipers not working all that well, Yvonne soon decides that she's far enough from the restaurant to pull into a parking lot and take a break from driving, without having to look like an idiot in front of the sisters. She finds a rundown business plaza and pulls off the road. With nowhere to park in front, she drives around back and pulls into one of the few remaining empty spaces.

Too agitated and too dizzy to think straight, let alone find her way to Niko's school, she turns off the engine and lets the rain beat down on the windshield. She breathes deeply, then exhales. There goes all her strength. She tilts her seat and rests for a while, with enough energy to simply stare at the ceiling's upholstery and, beyond that, raindrops tempering the glass. The cabin fills with the acrid smell of sour grapes. Did she pay for the wine? She hopes so, because it was she who forced the bottle onto those two condescending prudes. She can't remember. In any case, she regrets it all. She doesn't like feeling this way: dehydrated, adrift, weak.

Soon the windows fog over, and then she dozes off. She's not sure how long she's out for, but when she finally straightens her seat, through the steamy windows Yvonne notices that someone is in the next car. Whoever it is appears to her only as a dull silhouette, like someone not really there at all. That's how I feel at home, she thinks, like a ghost. She smudges a peephole out for herself and peers through, a little window into a private world.

Yawning, Yvonne turns the key and pulls out of the parking spot. In all the confusion of rain and wine and misplaced feelings, she drives right into the side of another car. Only a horn is left blaring.

Waiting outside his high school for his aunt to come pick him up, it begins to rain again, as it has off and on for the whole day. Niko goes back inside the building and waits on a stoop where some students spend their afternoons, trading tangerines and making jokes at the expense of passersby. The school day ended nearly an hour ago, and the only people left in the building are janitors and a few teachers, with the occasional student running past, in the school's athletic uniform, to a team practice. Once upon a time, his aunt used to never be late. But now, whether it's car trouble, overlong lunches, or preoccupations at work, there's always an excuse. He decides to call home to see if maybe she just plain forgot. His uncle answers the phone.

"Is Tante Yvonne there?"

"No," Sami says, "she's not coming to get you. She called. She had an accident."

"I'm still at school. Can someone come pick me up?"

There's a long pause on the line. Then his uncle says, "Fine. I'll be there in half an hour. Wait for me."

By the time Sami arrives at the school, it is well past dark out.

"What took you so long?" Niko asks as he climbs into the car.

"I had to finish up some work," his uncle says. "You'll have to bear with me a bit longer. We need to stop by the mall before we go home."

"Why? I'm tired."

"It's your aunt's birthday. We need to get a present."

His uncle says he's in the market for a portable television for the kitchen. Driving along the potholed streets of Longueuil, past strip malls, crumbling factories and neon signs, they arrive at an electronics outlet store, not far from their home.

"You think she'll like that?" Niko asks.

"Why not?" Sami shrugs. "She always complains that the kitchen is boring, so maybe this will help."

By the time they pull into the parking lot, another windy late-autumn evening is upon them. The outlet centre is roughly the size of three football fields and filled to the brim with a cornucopia of technological innovations from the last decade. Once inside, Niko finds it impossible not to find some minor appeal in door-crasher bins filled with electric razors and portable cassette players with unfamiliar brand names. He accepts a shopping cart from a greasy man in a polyester suit. So begins their search for the television section, down an aisle stacked eight feet high with blenders on the one side, and on the other with basketfuls of remain-dered VHSs.

"I think I hear the TVs over there," his uncle shouts over the din of salacious Québécois pop.

He points vaguely past a hill of stereo speakers, toward a section of the warehouse where Niko thinks he can make out the pointed complaints of Geraldo Rivera and his avid audience. Soon they're confronted with a wall of frowning moustaches.

A rail-thin Lebanese boy in baggy pants and a ponytail saunters over and inquires about the kind of television Sami wants to purchase. It takes Sami a full three minutes to describe the proportions with his hands, and to then speak poetically about the kind of picture he desires. For what seems like hours, the two of them haggle over the price and quality of every portable set in the store, while Niko wanders aimlessly through the store. By the time they leave and walk back to the car, the night sky of Montreal's winters has already settled in and their new television is tucked under his uncle's arm.

"Well, that took forever," Niko complains.

Sami starts the car. "You must have patience with family."

"We were in there for most of the day."

"And now we have a good present for your aunt."

"*You* have a good present. *I've* just wasted an afternoon."

"Well, why didn't you get her something while you were in there?"

"With what money?"

"You know, I asked that young man if they had jobs. He said they hire all the time." Sami produces an application form from his breast pocket. "Making money makes a person feel stronger. You don't have to sit in that bedroom all the time. It can't be good for you."

Niko takes the job application and looks at it. "I don't like being told how to live my life. You're not my father."

"Suit yourself. See where that attitude gets you."

"I can hear through the walls when you fight."

"We don't fight. You don't know what you're talking about."

"And then you go out and buy her a TV because you feel bad. Because you can't have your own kids."

Sami smacks his nephew in the face, not hard, but forceful enough to throw him off-guard.

*

Back at the house, Sami Malek parks the car and Niko jumps out before he's even come to a full stop. Exasperated, Sami turns off the idling engine. It wasn't supposed to be this way – complicated – when he bought them a home. Their lives were supposed to become simpler. This new house in a South Shore suburb of Montreal was supposed to make them better people. The day he was finally given the keys to this house was the climax of a lucid dream. He couldn't quite believe it was happening. After they had moved in, he spent entire days pensively walking circles across its two floors and unfinished basement, not fully convinced that the rooms were his to keep. He had an unfinished basement with its own hot water tank and furnace, where he would one day house his business. He had a garage jutting out of the front of the house that fit a car and, besides that, a table for tools, where he would one day build contraptions to bolster the house as it got older. In place of the mounds of overturned earth and rock outside their door, he saw a manicured front garden; along the uneven gravel lane where his car was parked, a clean black driveway; atop the ramshackle storm sewer ditch, a splendid white sidewalk; and over the washed-out gravel roads, a fully developed neighbourhood to call their own. It had been as mesmerizing to him as an empty canvas, and he was full of ideas, for he had been laying this house out in his thoughts all his life.

Now, as Sami pulls down the garage door and goes inside to where the house smells of roasting lamb and the preparation of the birthday dinner is underway, he can't help but think that he's deluded himself somewhere along the way into thinking this ambitious construction of citizenship could somehow cover up the fault lines in the foundations of their history.

"Smells good," he says, sticking his head into the kitchen.

"Mmm-hmm." Yvonne has a large piece of gauze taped over the left side of her forehead, just above her eye.

"Does it hurt?

"Not really," she says in a low voice, avoiding his eyes.

"You okay?"

"Yeah, I guess. I have a headache. Dinner should be ready in twenty minutes."

"Fine." He goes upstairs to his office, and locks the door behind him. The boy's pithy attack, no different from any kid his age, has nevertheless made him sour and over-emotional. If only they had a baby here to ground Niko, he thinks, to make him responsible like an older brother and make Sami himself more like a father to them all. Another child, he focuses on what has become a silent obsession, all I want is to become a father again. Niko will live here until he is eighteen, and then what? He would leave them, like a guest at a hotel.

Sami takes off his glasses, pinches the bridge of his nose, and amidst all the drafting paper and rulers that fill what is supposed to be his future son's room, he looks out the window for the soul that has seeped out of his dream. All he sees is the Jacques-Cartier Bridge, the bridge that his wife takes to work.

He sets the portable television on his desk and begins to search the room for wrapping paper, which he knows is in there somewhere, if he could only remember where. This can't go on like this forever, he tells himself while scouring through the closet for anything that could adequately camouflage the big box on his desk. Things are going to have to change around here, or else we'll all go crazy.

"It's dinner time!" he hears Yvonne call up unenthusiastically.

He goes downstairs where the dining room lights have been dimmed and his nephew sits sullenly at the far end of the table, already waiting for the meal to end. Presently, Yvonne carries in a birthday cake. She sets the cake down in front of herself and they begin to sing, an incongruous pair of voices around the dinner table. Happy Birthday. When the song reaches its finale, she blows out the candles in one breath, as if to say, there, the evening is that much closer to being over. Thirty thin trails of smoke waft through the air, followed by a halfhearted show of applause.

"Can I go now?" Niko asks Yvonne.

"You'll do no such thing," Sami says.

"I hate you."

"Niko!" his aunt gasps. "Both of you."

"You're ruining my life." Niko says.

Sami stands up. "Enough is enough."

"Hit me again. Hit me as hard as you can." He runs off, up to his room.

For a time they sit in silence, letting their food cool to the gently swaying light of the candles.

"I have a surprise for you," Sami says finally. He goes to the next room and comes back with the big box, wrapped in old newspaper, and he sets it down the squarely on the table. Already the week-old paper has come loose on one side, and the first few letters of the brand name peak through.

Something has to be done, Sami Malek decides twelve days later while waiting for the doorbell – something has to be done about all these ghosts. Sitting in what he has fashioned as the formal living room, Sami nibbles distractedly from the edges of a tray of baklava. He has decorated this room, where he greets his guests and clients, to look like an illustrious living room in Beirut. Light shimmers through the French mock-crystal chandelier. On the marble coffee table, imported from Thessaloniki, newspapers and magazines: *La Presse, Macleans, Time,* and *The Montreal Gazette.* For the bored, a bright book of crossword puzzles. On the walls, handwoven Persian carpets. Beside each window, marble columns crowned with replicas of centuries-old Levantine pottery. It is both impersonal and impeccably tasteful. A guest can feel at ease sitting in here, not at all like he's invading anyone's privacy.

The loud door-chime finally singsongs, and expecting it all along, Sami jogs into the front hall to receive his guest. A tall, burly man in a winter coat stands on the icy front porch, with a briefcase in one hand and his car keys in the other.

"*Istez* Halim Mahfouz, thank you for coming," Sami says, inviting him in.

"Think nothing of it."

Sami leads his guest back to the living room, and as Halim wipes his perspiring face with a handkerchief, Sami explains how Thursday afternoon is the only time they can meet because his wife is at work and his nephew is at school. "Needless to say," Sami concludes, as he offers his guest a seat, "these are private matters and I don't want to involve them just yet."

"And private it shall remain," Halim assures him, breathing coarsely. Seizing the moment, he asks for a glass of water.

Upon filling a glass, Sami says, "You know, when I met you back there at the club," referring to their Lebanese Business Association, "and I heard the story of your work, I couldn't stop thinking about it. How does one find people exactly?"

"Oh, it's not too hard. We have our ways, just like any profession. But it takes a while. Sometimes years."

"You must be a deeply methodical person."

"You could say that."

"Halim, I like that about you. Scotch?"

"Just a little." Halim pinches his fingers just so.

They toast their common sensibilities.

"Perhaps you see this in your line of work," Sami continues, "but for me, my interest in finding this person is more a matter of clearing my conscience than anything else. For now, I don't necessarily want to know more than if the person I'm looking for is alive, and maybe where he lives. Maybe something of what he's done all these years, too. Without at least knowing, he's a burden on my life. Have you heard that before?"

"Many times," Halim nods vigorously. "Or at least something like that. You know, you're not alone in this question. Wherever there is war, people who flee leave behind family. Keeping in touch is sometimes a luxury, but losing touch brings its own guilt. People don't know where to begin to resolve the whole matter, and that brings with it more guilt as the years go by. This is why people appreciate my work. It's a delicate procedure, this finding someone you've left behind. It's best to have an agent like me in between. Sometimes I succeed, and other times there's nothing I can do about it. I make no guarantees. It's a risk. There are some people who just don't want to be found."

"Of course," Sami says with great enthusiasm to be meeting someone who understands his predicament. All in all, this man, he feels, is being honest with him. He leans in closer and puts his hand on Halim's knee. "You know, all I want is to be able to put these questions out of my head and into someone else's hands so I can sleep at night."

Halim places his hand on Sami's, as if he knows the feeling exactly. "You look tired, Sami. Tell me about your family."

Sami sits back and sighs. For a time he stares into space and thinks about what to say, for he has never before been asked so directly to describe the collage that is his current family.

"Well, to begin, I would say that there are three of us living in this house, and that we haven't lived here long, but that once my wife and I became citizens two years ago, our lives became a lot easier, if only because we finally had some stability. My wife, her name is Yvonne. She is younger than me, thirty years old. Now, you probably notice, I am no longer thirty. You're correct. I'm fifty-six, I'm almost twice her age. We've been married for almost nine years now. We got married before we left Lebanon. Let me see – it was in 1979, to be specific. It was an arrangement I made with her family. I knew her father, that's how we first met. Her father worked for my father, and then he worked for me. The marriage was to help with the immigration. And it did. We moved here in 1980. We lived in a tiny apartment in Montreal North. It's not easy, starting over again at my age. Good thing I had money. But I wasn't ready to spend it in a country without the guarantee of citizenship. You never know."

"You sound like a very prudent man, Sami," Halim says, looking on with admiration. "You have built yourself a castle here on foreign land. You have conquered."

"I've done well for myself, it's true" Sami agrees, stroking back his thinning hair.

"And you say that you have a boy who lives here as well?"

"Yes," confirms Sami, "a nephew. Niko, his name is Niko Karam. His mother is my wife's sister. She's dead now. His father is a man named Antoine Karam, whom I've never met. When was it exactly? 1983. That was the year we got a frantic phone call from him. It was the strangest thing. This man who neither me nor my wife knew very well at all, calling us to see if we'd take his child. He was calling from a Greek island, it was so small I had to look it up in an atlas. We said to him, why don't you come, too? I even offered to pay. But he said no. He paid for his own son to fly here and he probably stranded himself as a consequence. From then on, only a note here and there. It's been two years since the last time. He's been gone for five years. I'd like to think that he's dead, but I don't know."

"And the nephew has lived with you ever since."

"That's right," Sami says, as if just now realizing the length of time they've all lived together. "It's been a long time."

Halim breaks into a conspiratorial grin. "So let me guess the rest. This is the big secret: you want me to find Antoine Karam, to see where he lives or if he's still alive, and to help your nephew find his dad."

Sami can see that Halim is following his eyes carefully, to see if he's snared a hint of truth in what he's said. And then Halim begins to laugh a little, cautiously at first because he shouldn't be thinking what he's thinking, but just the same he leans over and puts it out there, because it just might be the sharper of the two truths.

"Or, who knows, maybe just to get him out of your house."

Both men laugh uneasily.

"I have to warn you, it won't be easy."

"I can pay." Sami Malek's eyes wander the room in discomfort after he says this. Then he adds, "But you mustn't tell anyone."

Just then, there is a knock at the door.

"Excuse me." Sami gets up to see who it is, and is greeted by a police officer holding his nephew by the forearm. The front of Niko's shirt is stained with blood. His eyes are swollen shut.

"Is he yours?" the policeman asks.

Sami's instinct is to answer no, but all he manages to say is "What have you done now?"

The light edges forward and a foaming blue figure gels into being before him. It hovers at his side and uncorks his mouth. Saliva slides down his chin and neck. Immediately after, Antoine breathes in sharply for the first time. A woman's wet voice sounds an alien bag of patterns over and again in a steady, determined tone.

Antoine coughs, in an effort to say something, but nothing comes up except rasps and gurgles. He's too weak to move his lips. How tired he feels to have made it this far, however far this may be. Is this death? Now a cloth-like dampness presses against his eyes. He dozes again, too tired to fight. Death, a perpetual paralysis. His soul must still be trapped inside his body, unable to break free. He will have to push, force it out like a newborn child.

Days pass. He is innately aware of the higher blue beings. They resuscitate and gag him at will. Every time he wakes up, he can see a bit more clearly, and the woman's warbling voice is there again, sounding like the wash of the sea, always at his side. He feels her skin on his uniform. Her hand feels warm. He can see now that her voice and blue body blend together, that one is in fact the essence of a person and the other only a uniform. She's smiling at him. She tries to look through his eyes, looking for a way in. He looks at her frightfully, eager to see if she can decipher the message in his volatile eyes. He thinks she catches some clue of what he's trying to convey. She gasps, rushes out of the room.

She returns with a towering figure draped in white sheet. The new presence leans over Antoine's wasted corpse, shining a bright light in his eyes, trying to find the trapdoor that will let him out.

He injects him with a needle he can't feel. His heart catches fire. From a well deep in his chest comes a horrendous moan, at first feeble and then fearsome. He is filled, after all, with the anger of being alive.

"There," sighs the doctor, "you're back."

A rebirth. Not the first the doctor has witnessed. In Spanish, he asks, "Tell us, who are you?"

Who am I?

"Where do you come from?"

Antoine falls asleep. When he wakes up again, the doctor is there and so is a second man who stands further back, as if afraid of what he sees. The second man says, "You speak Arabic, no? You have spoken this language in your long sleep from time to time. Do you understand?"

Slowly, Antoine nods.

The doctor says something and then the man who knows Arabic translates. "Ask him, does he know what year it is?"

Antoine shakes his head.

The doctor frowns, and then begins to speak freely, and along the way the translator converts what he can.

"You are in a hospital. You have been in a coma for almost seventeen months. You arrived here on August 27, 1986. It is now April 22, 1988. You are in the city of Valparaiso. You are in the country of Chile. Furthermore, we have no idea who you are. But let me congratulate you, at least you're alive, my friend. It's a miracle. You're one in a million. No one expected that you would even wake up after all this time. Tell me, do you know how you came to be here?"

Antoine shakes his head.

"You were pulled out of the sea in a fishing net, by a group of fishermen in the Atlantic ocean. They say you were floating on a ladder over twenty kilometers from the nearest shore. They said they had no idea how you made it out there, so far out in the sea. You had no identification, and you were very nearly frozen. You had a pulse, they said, but nothing else. The captain of the Chilean ship couldn't decide whether you were dead or alive,the sailors were about to throw you overboard again when you began to talk through your unconsciousness. They said they couldn't pry your hands from the ladder. When they brought you in here, you were one of the strangest cases we'd ever seen. The whole city knows about your story: the man from nowhere, found floating on a ladder in the middle of the Atlantic. The newspapers here had never seen anything like it. Some people have come up with a story about how you might be an angel. We even kept the ladder for you, because some of the nurses believed it kept you safe. It is, you understand, truly a miracle that we're able to have this conversation right now."

The doctor walks over the near wall and brings the ladder to Antoine's bedside. "Do you recognize this at all?"

He leans the ladder over Antoine, as if introducing two old friends. Antoine looks at the wooden frame. It sparks nothing in him. 1988, Antoine thinks. He has apparently lost two years of a life he can't recall.

"Amnesia is only a wall," the doctor says a few days later. "You can climb it. You'll remember something soon enough, I'm sure. Then our work will begin."

Over the next few weeks, reporters from all across Chile visit his bedside to take photographs and ask questions. He has no answers for them. In their newspapers, which the nurse dutifully brings him every morning, they print stories about a man from nowhere. His translator reads him speculations about his own life that seem as foreign to him as the stories of strangers.

When the nurse tries to bathe him, he has a strong urge to grab hold of the ladder again. She scrubs bedsores from his back, and the urge disappears. Her name is Beatriz Gabriela Cruz. She tries to teach him words of Spanish, so they can at least communicate the basic necessities of his hygiene.

One night in the hospital, he has a dream about a pigeon and a lamb, but he has no sense of what they might mean. The next night, in an apartment that looks like a cage, he and the lamb and the pigeon all pace circles. Then someone knocks on the door, but Antoine can't figure out how to open its many locks. The person on the other side keeps shouting, "Come to the door, Antoine. Antoine, open this door," and so on and so on, but there is nothing to be done. I am Antoine, he remembers thinking in the dream. When he wakes up, the thought stays with him.

Before sunrise, he tries to climb out of bed on his own, if only to walk over to the window and see the room from another angle. Bracing himself along the metal frame of the hospital bed, he wobbles upon his unused legs, managing one step, then two. Then he tumbles down and once again finds himself on his back, staring at the ceiling, thinking that one thought over and again, the only truth he knows: I am Antoine.

A night orderly soon finds him, and lifts him back into bed. As his head settles back on the pillows, the orderly straps him down. The next morning, he tells the translator, "My name is Antoine."

Later that morning, the doctor comes to his room with the translator in tow. "They tell me you think you remember your name!"

"Yes," Antoine says, "I do."

"Tell me."

"Antoine." He's relieved to hear himself say it again, with even greater conviction. "I heard it in a dream."

The doctor stands back, a glint of pride in his eyes. "That's a big step. I'm sure more will soon follow."

In the afternoons, a nurse fills his empty head with Spanish. Everything that enters, sticks, and he learns quickly. She says, "My name is Beatriz." She touches her chest. "You are Antoine." She touches his chest.

One day, months later, a man in a brown suit comes to his bedside and introduces himself as Serge Maroun, from the Club Union Arabe.

"I saw in the newspapers that you finally remembered your name," he says, "and when I read it, I looked closely again at the picture, and I said to myself, yes, that's it! This man is Lebanese. "

"Do you really think I'm Lebanese?"

Serge Maroun bends over his bed to take a closer look. "No doubt about it. I've been following your story in the newspapers. Fascinating, a man in a coma found clutching a ladder in the middle of the Atlantic. He ends up at our port, and when he wakes up, he has no memory of anything. When he remembers his name, it turns out he's one of us."

"One of you?"

"Yes," Serge says confidently. "One of us. I can tell just by the way you speak your Arabic."

"Perhaps you're right. I don't know."

"You don't have to rebuild your life on your own. We can help. It'll take time, but we have ways to find out who you are."

After six months, the newspapers are no longer interested in his story, and people no longer stop him on the street. He's merely the man from nowhere, who can't remember a face or a name very well. Other than his name, there is not yet a single thing he remembers about his past life, but, now that he is out of the hospital, whenever Antoine dreams, he is waist-deep in the sea again. In his hands he holds a giant silver fish, what must be a sea bass, and as it squirms and snaps in his hands, the sunlight flashes off its scales in strident ambushes. The fish wants to break free from his grip, but he can't let it go yet. Then it gets away and even though he can no longer see it, he knows that it will die, and then it will float flatly on the sea surface alongside every other fish that escapes his grasp and rushes blindly into the wild.

He wakes to the shrill of a persistent car horn outside the window. Ever since he came out of his coma in the hospital, each new morning has opened up before him as an utterly new world. When he first opens his eyes, he often has no idea where he is. But if he stays calm and quiet and waits, some telltale sign will help him figure it out. There is only a low grey ceiling. There is a door, and beyond it a small kitchen, and then a balcony door that's been left open. He can see all this from his mattress on the floor, where he sleeps beside the nurse from the hospital.

Her name, he reminds himself every morning at around this time, just as the sun rises, is Beatriz Gabriela Cruz. She has written it discreetly inside his wrist. He must never forget this. She's the one who taught him a little Spanish, enough for Antoine to get through the day. When he was well enough to leave, she insisted that he come live with her. Beatriz. Beatriz Gabriela Cruz. She tells him that she's been born again, too. He arrived at her hospital, after her husband ran off. It was a sign.

Outside is Valparaiso. He can practically hear the whole of it yawning to life. The car horn is still bleating outside the window. He rises from the damp mattress and, in his underwear, walks out onto the front steps to see what all the noise is about. Antoine can hear it, down the hill. He reaches the railing across the street from their door that gives over the side of the hill, and from there he looks around. There it is, another accident, this time it's a produce truck and a motorcycle. Dozens of people have come out to collect oranges off the pavement as the two drivers, who appear to be arguing, duck in and out of the truck's cabin, most likely trying to figure out how to put a stop to the runaway horn.

He goes back inside. On his way to the small kitchen, Antoine walks through a cobweb, and so when he reaches the dirty sink, he washes his face and picks the web out of his oily hair. How is it made? These little details fascinate him, how cobwebs can suddenly tangle up his fingers like memory does his mind. Sitting down at the kitchen table still covered with yesterday's leftovers, the full impact of what he knows finally sputters back to motion, like the engine of an old car on a humid winter's day. He must get ready to do something, it occurs to him, what he cannot say but this must be why he's awake at this hour, and this must be why Beatriz is still asleep. There is a cross over the bed. There are crosses everywhere in this house. He goes outside into the small courtyard where Beatriz and her mother grow tomatoes in oil drums, and there, dutifully, he waits. Eventually he goes back inside and brews a strong pot of coffee.

From where he sits, he can look through the hall and in the other room, and he can watch Beatriz waking up. She rolls over on one side of the mattress and finally opens her eyes, her breasts swinging into her armpits. She strokes the barely-there bulge of her belly. He can ignore it when she's dressed, but not when she's naked. Every time he sees her belly, it looks a little bigger. It's his, Antoine thinks, his own child. It kicks at the rhythm of a ticking clock sometimes, as if wired to a bomb.

She gets up with a groan. "Why don't you put some clothes on?" she says.

"I can't remember yet what I have to do," Antoine replies.

"I'll get some clothes for you." She walks past him to the closet. "Here, wear this." She hands him the baggy mechanic's jumpsuit that her husband used to wear for work.

He slips into the mechanic's uniform. Beatriz wraps herself in a housecoat and they drink the bitterly strong coffee Antoine has prepared. As they do, the dishes in the cupboard begin to rattle. The earth shakes a little, as it does every few days in Valparaiso. No one other than Antoine pays it any attention.

"Remind me, where am I going?" he says.

"To the bottom of the hill, to the bus stop."

The information gives him a focus. He watches Beatriz rub her belly at the table, as if the baby can taste his strong coffee too. The baby, he thinks, it knows just as much as I do. He gulps down what's left of his coffee, dons the large coat and worker's cap that once belonged to Beatriz's estranged husband, and steps outside.

The sun comes over the harbour, and a warm morning light bathes the green valley. Down the winding streets of their hill, garbage bags scuffle to life with rats that scurry in and out of the burrows they've dug overnight. As he walks past two-story walls of homes just like his, homes that are pink and blue and green and red, Antoine ponders the coming baby. He can't help but long impatiently for whoever's inside. That child, he thinks, will help me figure out who I am.

Serge Maroun tells Antoine he must be Lebanese, but he has no memory of a Lebanon anywhere in his head.

"You're very lucky, Antoine," Serge Maroun often tells him. "Because of a loophole, you can probably stay here as long as you like. Just the same, I'll keep looking for your past."

"As you wish," Antoine replies blankly. In any case, here he leads a simple life. He's merely the man from nowhere. He doesn't have much need for a past, and though he doesn't know what's back there, there's an overwhelming feeling he gets from time to time that seems to say that he's better off not knowing. The ordinariness of having a roof over his head, a woman to talk to, and a responsibility to fulfill, all this gives him a sense of purpose he doesn't necessarily want to disturb. Still, he wonders, what will happen to him when that belly blows open? His life will change, won't it? But in which direction, he can't say.

As Antoine rounds a corner and arrives at the bottom of the hill onto a plaza lined with swaying palm trees, he puts up the collar of his coat, shrugs his shoulders, and looks primarily at his feet as he hurries past the traffic. The mornings are cold. It's windy today. He walks cautiously for several city blocks, to the open market by the bay. There, Beatriz has pointed out a special bus stop where the unemployed gather to meet farmers or contractors who come to the city in search of cheap labour. This is another thing he never forgets. Responsibility has a way of branding details upon his new brain. He has a desire for responsibility.

The winter morning has brightened a bit now, and the fog has begun to lift. The meeting point is relatively quiet, and when Antoine gets in line, there are only six men before him. "Has anyone come by yet?" he asks the next man in line, not sure what to expect.

The stranger next to him shakes his head. "No, nothing yet."

"There's no work anywhere," Antoine says in his cobbled Spanish, eager to open up to this man who might understand his plight.

"It's rough," the stranger agrees.

"Tell me, friend, where is it good to find work?" When the stranger ignores him, he presses with a measure of desperation. "I have a baby coming."

The stranger looks him up and down, and then says, "Why not try the docks? There, no one cares where you're from."

And then the stranger looks away and pretends Antoine is no longer there, and it is clear that he doesn't want to be seen talking to a foreigner – if that's indeed what Antoine is; he has no sensation of foreignness. Soon a produce truck arrives and takes the first two men away, and then only four of them remain, waiting. Then a van pulls up and takes all four of them to a vineyard an hour and a half away. The city of Valparaiso disappears behind them, as does most of his memory of it.

By the time Sami hears from Halim again, he's begun to think the case is going nowhere. But Halim says, "I have news for you. Come meet me and I'll show you what I've found."

"I'll be there in an hour," Sami says.

February has given way to March; it is one of those rare late-winter days when the sun, warm enough to thaw blankets of snow, leaves long stretches of pocked and polluted ice along the river's slow melt. In a haze of reality and recollections, Sami drives home across the Victoria Bridge, where the steel grid rattles beneath the wheels and the lanes have always been much too narrow, thinking just one thought, that he's about to change the boy's life. He's eager to find out what Halim has to tell him. If it's bad news, he speculates, then he wouldn't have called me downtown.

When Sami buzzes the apartment on the twenty-fifth floor, a woman's voice, thick with Syrian inflection, inquires who is there, and once he gives the proper code, the code he's been instructed to hand over at this juncture, the door springs open. Inside, the lobby stinks of ammonia. He stands in the claustrophobic elevator, fending off palpitations in his chest as he watches the yellow light shoot across the numbers as it approaches the twenty-fifth floor. Elevators make him nervous; on the way up, he thinks of a time long ago, before the move, another occasion he was riding an elevator, in a building that was bombed. It was the closest he'd ever come to death: waiting in a dark, airless box, between the seventh and eighth floors of a building that had lost its power. The doors finally part, and he slips out into a narrow hallway that shimmers with a sickly neon-green light.

He knocks on the door labeled 2520 and then waits. Soon the door cracks open the length of the door-chain, and a woman with a burka obscuring all but her eyes peers through. Without a word, she closes the door again and slides the chain, and when the door opens again the veiled woman stands to the side, in obedient repose, silent, draped in black cloth from head to toe, as if the very ghost he is after. After letting him in, she shuffles down the hall and disappears into a far room.

The stout, bearded investigator, this time in a white gown and sandals, bounds in to replace her.

"Welcome."

They kiss each other's cheeks three times, and then Sami says, "Halim, thank you for calling me."

"Of course, of course. Come. Sit." Halim leads Sami into a room that contains only an old Persian carpet, large cushions, and a large-screen TV. "Please, sit." Halim says again, motioning to one of the largest cushions.

"May I ask you a question?" Halim switches to Arabic. "Do you know that this man Antoine Karam looks a bit like you? Yes, it's true. I finally received some pictures of him, and there was your face in the envelope, or so I thought. You look very much alike."

"So he's alive! You have pictures here?"

"Well, it turns out that it's a bit more complicated than that."

"Hmm."

"Let me get the file, and I'll show you what I know." Halim Mahfouz walks into the back room and closes the door behind him. The veiled ghost of a woman enters the room silently, carrying a silver tray with coffee, and then leaves just as quietly, as if serving no one. When Halim returns, he carries with him a briefcase. Sitting back down beside Sami, he unlocks its clasps and withdraws a large brown manila envelope, which he places between them. Sami dons a set of thick reading glasses, and they begin to sort through the information that Halim has gathered.

First, Halim Mahfouz removes an enlarged photocopy of a photograph from the folder, a blown-up, pixelated black-and-white scan of an identification card. The copy has a hand-scribbled note on its top end, in Arabic, marked with Antoine's name, a birth date, and 'age 40'. The photo shows a gaunt man with deep-set eyes and a broad brow, staring out into nowhere and full of defeat. His open mouth betrays a chipped front tooth. He has a moustache and the beginnings of a beard coming in around his chin.

"He doesn't look like me at all," Sami says.

"You don't think so," say Halim, looking again at the picture. "Sometimes we don't know what we look like until someone else tells us."

But Sami can't see the likeness through the over-carbonated copy. "Do I really look like that?" he asks.

Halim says, "Around the eyes, yes, a little."

"So where did you find this?"

"This is from his file with the shipping company in Marseilles you told me about. There is more, too."

He withdraws another piece of paper from the envelope. "Turns out the Marseille company sent him to work in Algeria. He had some problems getting a resident's status in France. I got in touch with these people, and it turns out they're not exactly as legal as their European counterparts. They mainly deal in illegal goods, some weapons transport, some drugs, mostly oil and gas stolen from Africans and sold to the rest of the world on the black market."

"As you will see here," Halim continues, pulling out a third sheaf of paper, "this is the schedule for an Antoine Karam. He worked along the coast of Africa mostly. But then at the end, something changes and he signs up to take a ship to Brazil."

"Brazil? What's in Brazil?"

"I don't know. I thought maybe that would ring a bell with you."

"Brazil," Sami whispers again, mesmerized by the seeming irrefutability of the documents before him.

Halim allows a wry smile, happy to have pleased his client. "So I began to ask questions with several of the port authorities in Brazil, and I found this out." He withdrew a fourth piece or paper from the folder.

"What is this?"

"This is a record stating that the ship in question never arrived at any Brazilian ports."

"Where did it go?"

"Well, this is where the matter gets complicated. As far as I can tell, the ship in question didn't dock anywhere."

"You don't mean it's still floating around out there, lost at sea?"

"No, Sami, quite the opposite."

"There's no way of tracking it down?"

"When you're dealing with these less than legal elements, you don't always have as much oversight as you'd like. Now, I did look a bit further, and I managed to track down the log of every man signed to that boat."

"And?"

"And none of them has ever worked another ship."

"You mean it disappeared?"

"Something like that. I mean that it's most likely that the ship sank somewhere along the way. The ports tell me it's not unusual for boats to go this way, especially the independent shippers. Few of the men on these boats are people with connections to the rest of the world. No one asks questions, and so no one cares."

"When did this happen?"

"It's difficult to pin down an exact date. The ship left Algeria in September of 1986.

All this information results in a firm lump of anxiety in Sami's chest, and for a while he sits there sifting quietly through the documents with a shaky hand, waiting for a pain in his chest to pass before he can speak again. When he's finally able to speak again, Sami taps the picture and says, "So then Antoine must be dead."

"This is the way it is, sometimes," Halim says, as a means of consolation for being the messenger of bad news. "You go looking, and you don't know what you'll find."

All in all, Sami Malek has learned a lot in one afternoon. He sits back along the plush cushions and freshly vacuumed carpets of Halim Mahfouz's apartment, mulling an empty demitasse of Turkish coffee as he tries to read the future in the remaining grains. He sees nothing but black muck looking back at him. The boy is here to stay.

"I'd better go," Sami says.

"You'll be alright?"

"Yes, don't worry about me."

"Trust in Allah, he has a plan."

"Right," says Sami, slowly shaking Halim's hand goodbye.

Sami steps out of the building, where the wind howls by in waves. Already the sun is setting, and the constant mill of downtown traffic is fast approaching the feverish pitch of an impending rush hour. Heavy flakes of snow begin to waft toward the sidewalk. Sami buttons up the collar of his coat and digs his hands into his pockets, and then he crosses the street.

As he drives home, the road veers into the setting sun and a bright flash erupts against the windshield. Startled, he swerves. The car to his left honks at him, and an angry driver curses him. In the back seat, a buck-toothed teenager gives him the finger. If only he could have had such a bond with Niko. Reminders of his lot in life are everywhere. Winding through the insolent side streets of his neighbourhood, he soon pulls into the driveway where he houses another man's son, and where gusting winds have scattered sheets of newspaper into the snowy hedges again. He collects the musty newsprint and then unlocks the door to the dark house.

There is a mound of mail on the floor. No one has been home since he left. Sami collects the envelopes and takes them into the kitchen. He sets the pile down on the counter. Invoices, bills, credit card notices, letters from banks, junk mail, no one sends personal correspondence to them anymore. They are alone in this country, as they are in this world.

Then Sami walks through the empty house, turning on all the lights. Outside, dusk shutters down into mere darkness, and the whole house glows brightly from every window, exposing its hollow core. Back downstairs, Sami Malek sits amidst his decorative efforts in the dark, in an armchair he keeps by the bay window which overlooks the St. Lawrence River. Through the hall, he hears the front door open and someone coming inside. It's Niko, he can tell simply from the sound of his footsteps. It's strange, he thinks, I still behave like a father, I still worry like a father, but I'm not a father to anyone at all.

He gets up and finds Niko in the kitchen, searching through the fridge.

"Are you hungry?" Sami asks.

"Is there anything to eat?"

"Come, sit down. I'm hungry too. I'll make us something quick."

Sami goes to the fridge and pulls out a loaf of bread and a brick of cheese. "Do you remember this? You would come home from school, and we'd have a grilled cheese before your homework. You remember that?"

Niko sits at the kitchen table, preoccupied with the newspaper. "Huh? Yeah, I guess so."

"What do you have for homework these days?" Sami ventures as he slices the cheese and warms the pan. "Can I see?"

"It's no big deal. I can do it by myself."

"Is everything okay at school? Why are you getting into all this trouble?"

"The kids at school are idiots. That's all. Anyways, I don't think I'll be at that school for much longer."

Sami sets the butter in the pan and lets it sizzle. "Remember how we learned about evolution while watching this butter melt? Do you still know about evolution?"

"Yeah, you said heat forces people to change."

"That's right," Sami says, surprised to have lured Niko into a normal conversation for a change. "Sometimes we get too hot, and our balance and place in the world begins to shift from under us. Maybe you're too hot now."

Sami can tell that even Niko senses there's something behind his words. "What are you getting at?"

He sets the cheese sandwich down on the pan and presses it down firmly and listens to the butter seer its soft skin.

"Young man, I'm sad to say that your dad is dead," Sami announces. "He died off the coast of Brazil when his ship sank. It happened last year, I know this for a fact unfortunately. You're old enough to know this now, too."

Niko stares hard at the comics section of the newspaper, trying to figure out exactly what he ought to be thinking right then. Slowly, the pain he's been waiting to feel begins burning a hole in head, and then the newspaper grows too restless for his quivering hands, and he has to let it fall away. "But how do you know?" he croaks.

He can't help but look hard at Sami with dark, wet, disappointed eyes. Sami brings the grilled cheese sandwiches over to the table and sits down beside him. "I hired a detective to find him. I couldn't stand the sight of you not knowing anymore. It's ruining your life. So now you know."

Niko can feel his face contorting against his will. "What if it's not true?"

"My boy, it's unfortunately very true. I've seen the log of the ship that left from Algeria. Algeria was the last place your father was on land. The ship never made it to port. No one from that logbook has ever worked again. The ship went down at sea."

Then Niko can't fight it off anymore because the way his uncle is looking at him is just like the way his grandfather looked at him the day his mother died – and now everyone's dead but him – and so he puts his head down on the table and in his arms, and tries his best to disappear.

"There, there," says Sami, setting his hand on Niko's shoulder. "I know, it hurts more than anything."

"I loved them so much," Niko whispers through his arms. "What did I do that was so wrong?"

"You did nothing. We come from a bad world, and now you'll stay right here. You'll be a part of this family." By then, Sami has pulled his chair closer and is whispering right into Niko's ear, as if they're in their own secret world and no kitchen exists beyond their little hideaway.

Niko cries and cries, because it's been years since he's let himself go like this, because he made a vow of never letting himself cry again after his mama died. But now he just can't help it. "It's just not fair," he manages to let out meekly, choking on the flood of tears covering his face. "I tried so hard to be good for everyone. I waited for him, and he didn't come back."

"I know," Sami says, stroking his hair and kissing the top of his head.

"I don't want to be an orphan."

"I'll tell you a secret. I once had a son, a long time ago. And he died when he was just a little bit older than you. I miss him every day, just like you miss your dad. It's not fair, I know."

"What do we do now?"

"Now? We just sit here and let it all out, and then we begin again with new lives."

"How many new lives can we have?"

"I don't know."

They sit at the kitchen table and soon the room begins to grow dark and their sandwiches grow cold, but neither of them budges, and for a brief moment, Sami senses the boy falling asleep under his arm.

Sami holds his troubled nephew in his arms, and there in the kitchen on a darkening afternoon he remembers the day he lost his own son. It was November of 1975. Ziad was sixteen then, and he was forty-two. Eight months of car bombs and street-to-street gun battles had destroyed their neighbourhood, and they lived among rubble and ruins, their rooftops lined with snipers, their walls punctuated by bullet holes. The year before they had been able to walk freely to the sea wall in the summer night and watch the waves crash along the rocks while eating ice cream, and all you'd hear was the music pouring out of cafés. A year later, they ventured outside only sporadically, out of necessity.

He'd spent the day at the telephone centre and returned to the apartment in the late afternoon. Ziad was not there, but this hadn't surprised Sami. He'd sat and waited for the boy, all the while random bullet fire pecking at the streets below. He knew what Ziad secretly did out there, but he held his tongue. Evening came, and then the sun set, and the jackhammer of gunfire grew more insistent. Sami even remembers what he did while waiting: he lit candles and played solitaire on the floor of his hallway, away from the windows.

Finally at ten o'clock a knock at the door. Ziad was hurt, a man yelled from the other side. Sami had been afraid to open the six locks for a stranger, so he hadn't let him in right away. He had a peephole, and he'd carried on the conversation that way for fear of a revenge killing. He knew that Ziad had grown political.

And so Sami shouted back, "What happened? Who are you?"

He was the brother of one of Ziad's friends. On their way back home from a swimming pool, the man baldly lied, Ziad had lost part of his left hand to a car bomb that had exploded just as they were riding past on their bicycles. Two of my brothers are dead. He was the brother of one of the boys, but in a sense all of them were his brothers, he explained.

Sami hadn't known what to make of this. "How do I know you're not lying?" he shouted.

The voice held a bleeding supermarket bag to the peephole. For some reason, Sami remembered distinctly that it was a Safeway bag. The voice said he had two of Ziad's fingers with him. Sami let him in, and together they turned over the Safeway bag on the kitchen table. A bloody cloth fell out, something like the sleeve of a shirt, and out of that rag rolled two fingers still attached, in the shape of a 'V'. He knew immediately it was Ziad's hand. He recognized the silver ring it bore. It was his dead wife's ring. Sami thought he'd lost it. But Ziad had evidently stolen it.

"Where is the rest of him?" Sami asked.

"At the hospital," the young man said.

"Which hospital?"

"Ma'wa al-Ajaza."

"What were you doing over there?"

It was night, and Ziad was caught in a hospital on the other side of the city division in West Beirut.

"Because they want to kill us all," the young man said adamantly. He looked down at his pants and suddenly had to leave. The blood, he said, reminded him that he had to tell his family what had happened to his brother.

Sami let the young man out and thought about what to do next. He had no choice but to go. He wrapped the severed fingers in a clean dishcloth, and he drove to the hospital along the empty streets. In the hospital, the halls were crawling with women crying for their dead sons, and brothers swearing revenge. Amputees. Bruised faces, mouths swollen shut. The few doctors and nurses he saw that night were either in a panic or looked defeated. There were too many people to help, and no supplies to help anyone.

Flies hovered everywhere in the humidity. In this hell, Sami had found Ziad. He was lying on a stretcher in a hallway, and from one side he looked completely normal, like the son Sami was at the hospital looking for, but from the other side, beginning from the cheekbone at the nape of his nose and running all the way down to his left knee, Ziad was charred black. Like a newspaper held to flames, he was already flaking. His right arm was gone, torn decisively just above his seared elbow, and a doctor was frantically sawing away at the shoulder to stave off greater infection. At that point, Sami had realized that the two fingers in his plastic bag were actually from Ziad's good hand, that the boy he knew was lost forever. There was no anesthetic to give Ziad, and so he was screaming the most bilious and rancid sound a father had ever heard from his offspring. Sami had no antidote for this vision. To this day it still haunted the crawl space of his subconscious. Ziad began to convulse. The doctor bound his jaw with a leather belt. Ziad died a few hours later from blood loss.

For this reason, Sami never thinks about his former life voluntarily. The war for him is a painful reminder of a time and a place when he had no control over what was happening in his world. Ziad died much the same way he had killed his mother sixteen years earlier, during his complicated and overlong birth. Sami remembered now, during Ziad's birth, the midwife helping with the delivery had come out and said to him, 'What do you want? Who should live? Your wife, or the child?' How could he be expected to make such a decision? He'd thought about it, he'd had no choice but to think about it in all seriousness, this most difficult decision, and he paced the room as if walking would make the decision any easier. He remembers asking, 'Which one stands the better chance of living?' And the woman said, 'The child.' He said, 'The child then, save the child.'

The midwife ran back into the delivery room to carry out the instruction, and immediately after, Sami slid down into a chair, pulled down by the immensity of the mistake he'd just made. He could have no feeling for the child without Marie. He had thought to himself, this would have been the decision Marie would have wanted me to make. But right after, Sami knew that every time he looked at the boy he would see only his incredible misfortune.

Right then, in the dark kitchen, Sami kisses the top of Niko's head because he understands something of Niko's predicament, even though Niko must have no means of articulating it yet. The boy beneath him stirs and nuzzles even closer, unawares of where he sits and with whom – only that, for the moment, human warmth is better than solitude.

Then Sami hears the front door opening and Yvonne walking in, shouting, "Is anyone home?"

Yvonne walks into the kitchen and finds them sitting at the kitchen table, and straightaway she says, "My god, what happened to you?"

At the sound of his aunt's voice, the spell that had hung over Niko's sadness breaks and he looks at Sami as if looking at an intruder and shoots up from his chair. He runs past his aunt and up the stairs to his room, where he slams the door shut.

His aunt knocks at his door, asking over and over again if he needs anything. After she goes away, Niko lets go and his thoughts drift back into darkness. Mama dims the lights and from the fridge she pulls out a birthday cake and they begin to sing for him, both Mama and Baba, because in his memories of his boyhood, every day is his birthday and Niko is the centre of everyone's dreams. His grinning face glows in the candlelight, and once the song comes to an end, he musters all his breath and blows them all out in one fell swoop. What does he wish for, wonders the fifteen-year-old Niko. He wishes for all of them to stay together forever.

Once they've eaten the cake and Mama is busy doing the dishes, Baba says he has an activity for them.

"Is it a birthday present?" Niko asks excitedly.

"You bet," says Baba. He says it's a new game to tire them out for bed. "A man will go crazy if he doesn't get a bit of exercise." Baba laughs gaily.

"Yay!" says Niko.

He leads Niko into the front hall. Beside the door sits a huge dresser for their jackets and shoes.

"From now on," Baba says, "we will push that dresser against the door after we've set all the locks and bolts."

"Why should we do that?"

Baba leans down to have a private conversation with Niko, so Mama won't hear them in the kitchen. "So the ghosts won't get Mama."

Baba's plan works. After moving the dresser Niko is dead tired every time, and Mama is safe inside. Often he falls asleep in Baba's arms as Baba carries him to their room.

Whenever they hear strange footsteps in the hall outside or a mysterious rapping at the door, Baba tells Niko the local militia is just making sure they've moved their dresser into place. Nevertheless, every time they receive a visitor in the night, the first thing Baba does is cup his palm over Niko's mouth.

"Shhh," he says, "the ghosts are here."

Niko closes his eyes and pretends to be dead so the ghosts won't get him.

Then Baba slides out of bed and creeps slowly toward the door. In the next room Baba keeps a secret, which was his word for gun. Baba was adamant: they would not sleep in the cellar and allow thieves to take their apartment

"A person without a home has trouble being a person at all," he always said. This much is true, Niko thinks now as he lies awake half a world away. Niko feels that way all the time without Baba. A person with no home becomes whatever is around him.

The sea ebbs and flows between horizon and shore. In this magic hour, before the cooks call down for supper, Serge Maroun likes to stand on his balcony and observe the waves rolling forth and receding. There is much to see along the coast, up there from the marble balcony of the Club Union Arabe. Every afternoon at this hour, after all but his last calls of the day have come and gone, he brings his feet down from his desk, pushes away whichever case-file he's investigating on behalf of General Pinochet's Minister of the Interior for this province, and then he saunters over to the hobbyist's telescope he keeps on his private balcony.

His office is on the third storey of the Club Union Arabe, a charity organization for local Arab exiles that also monitors and sometimes deports illegals. The Club is located in a century-old mansion, a half-timbered Germanic construction that grows like the gnarled roots of a scrambling tree along the side of the mountain. It is situated between the twin cities of Valparaiso and Viña del Mar, and depending on which way Serge looks, he can see either the busy port of Valparaiso or the glamorous beaches of its younger, more attractive twin sister, Viña del Mar. His balcony hovers over the busy highway connecting the two.

Brown exhaust drifts up from the highway with the salt air. From high on his perch, Serge Maroun can smell and see the whole of Valparaiso's port: the yelling drivers, the train station, the tankers coming and going, the military exercises, the fishing boats, the stinking sea lions.

He peers into the telescope and watches a dinghy come in to the rocky shores of Valparaiso, and then veers it the other way toward the white sands and excitement of Viña Del Mar. The long shore there is crowded with families and the military. It is January, the time when everybody takes vacations. At this time of year, people swim far out past the waves, and sometimes they drown, and if he happens to be standing at his telescope then, he phones it in.

There is always something to see down there. He is, according to his wife, a workaholic. Along the main road, the police have pulled over a truck. Traffic is backing up and horns are honking. Someone is being arrested.

Inside, the phone rings. It is the building's operator.

"Mr. Maroun, we have a long-distance call for you," she says, her voice cracking within the building's old and unreliable wiring. The Minister of the Interior has given them this old building, but provided no money to fix it, and aside from its residue of ghostly elegance, a tasteful hint of more affluent times, the electricity flickers on and off every evening, and the phone lines bristle for days after an earthquake, which here tremor every few days anyways, which means the phones are always bad.

"From where?"

"The Lebanese Businessmen's Association in Montreal, Canada."

"Patch it through." He waits for the line to connect. "Hello?" he shouts, "This is Serge Maroun. Who is this?"

A wall of shifting static reproaches him. "Mr. Maroun?"

"Yes. I'm here," Serge shouts. "You must speak louder. We have a bad connection."

"My name is Daniel Efrem," the man shouts back, now sounding very far away. "I'm calling in regards to your departmental bulletin on a man named Antoine, no known surname."

"Yes, go on," Serge exclaims, returning quickly to his swivel chair and searching the surface of his messy desk for a pen. "What do you have? I'm listening."

The line dies, and he throws down the receiver in disgust, because you can never trust the phones in this damn building when you need them. But then he sets it back on the table and prays for the caller to call back. Presently the phone rings again. This time they have a better connection.

"I have something," the caller says quickly, not wanting to lose the line again. "I'm not sure what it is, but it's a name that came up in one of our searches."

Serge cocks his pen. "Give it to me."

"First name S-A-M-I. Family name M-A-L-E-K."

"Sami Malek," Serge reads back. "How close is he?"

"We're not sure. To be honest, it could very well be nothing, but it's all we could find. According to our sources, they were married to sisters."

"Great, a brother-in-law." They make for unpredictable connections. "How did you find him?"

"He hired an investigator to look for the man in question. The investigator says that this man has a son who lives in Sami Malek's house."

"A house where?"

"They live in Canada."

"Do you have anything else?"

"I'm afraid that's it. Say, is this in regards to that man of yours down there, the one who was found alive on a ladder at sea?"

"That's the one."

"Does he remember anything yet?"

"He says his name is Antoine, that he heard it in a dream, nothing else."

"Is that possible, for a man to remember nothing but his name?"

Serge sighs, because this is the question that's been troubling him all this while. "For all I know, he could just be keeping quiet."

"Well, I hope you're not in any rush," the caller chuckles on the other end.

"I've got all the time in the world." He puts up his feet and adds, "Listen, can you get me an address for this Sami Malek. I'd like to send him some newspaper articles with pictures of our man here. Who knows, maybe it'll ring a bell."

"Of course. Good luck, Mr. Maroun."

They hang up, and for a time Serge stares at the notes he's jotted down throughout the conversation. A son, he marvels. He walks back out to the balcony, where the sun has quietly begun its descent. He lights a cigarette and looks out to the horizon, and thinks that this could all end up, somehow, as nothing, meaningless unconnected information. Down below, the police have gone back to the barracks and the poor soul they arrested has probably been thrown into a dark cell in some airless basement for a few days. But, on the other hand, traffic is back to normal. The only reminder that anything has happened down there is the abandoned car on the side of the highway. By morning, that will be gone too.

If We Are United

IN THE DISCOUNT STORE, Niko strolls toward a section where basketfuls of remaindered VHSs are kept. He sets down his school bag and, under white halogen lights, begins to search compulsively through the bins. VHSs and cassettes: they form the spine of what he enjoys most when not strapped down to the sinking ship that has become his education. He comes across a slightly damaged copy of *Airplane*, peels the security sticker off the package and slips it through a tear in his raincoat. Then he picks up his bag and he's off to the wall of cassettes at the back of the store, into a den of remaindered popular culture.

INXS, *Moonlighting*, *Back to the Future*: the eighties have been a decade without meaning, a regret. He's seventeen years old, too old to steal, but not old enough to get into any real trouble for it, and so he passes his time perfecting his skills, even though he's pretty bored with the routine. But thieving has become second nature to him, like birds taking flight. Other students run track or play clarinet, shoplifting has cultivated his distinct set of talents. He doesn't get along with anyone at school or at home, most days the world exists merely to antagonize him. This month alone, he's argued about Bill Cosby's idealized portrait of fatherhood, the futility of an assigned bedtime, Weird Al Yankovic cassettes played too loudly, the pornography in *Police Academy* movies and Van Halen's "Hot for Teacher," one Jessica Hahn poster not so secretly pasted to the inside of his closet door, Iron Maiden illustrations left on the dining table, a Motley Crüe T-shirt that is three sizes too large. What problems he has to contend with! His worldview does not include lush meadows, adorable kittens or petting zoos. He never stops to coo at babies. He is impatient with puppies. He loathes those marathon media-fondled grieving orgasms that follow natural disasters: let those children boil their brown water in peace.

He moves on from one bin to another, his coat lopsided with the weight of his loot. In the cassette section, he sorts through stacks he's already pilfered from, searching only to confirm stock he's already seen. Once in a while, he comes across something new, and if it's attractive enough, he breaks the seal and pockets it.

This store is too big to properly secure, and in the three years since they've lived on the South Shore, Niko's discovered all the possible routes available to him to sneak stolen goods out from under the noses of the mostly bored weeknight staff. The trick is to slip out the employee exits, which lead into a series of tunnels and passages that make up the arteries of the shopping centre. Here security is non-existent. He can navigate one of a number of options, leading to loading docks, the public washrooms, or one of six halls leading back into the shopping centre's corridors of boutiques and stores, all without ever running into anyone. Anyone he does pass assumes he's an employee coming or going.

From where Niko is in the store, he figures he can be at one of these employee exits in fewer than forty paces. He looks over his shoulder: the coast is clear; the only employee he spots is buried in a magazine over in Large Appliances. Quietly, he makes his move. He heads for an infrequently used aisle along the far wall, which is mounted with typewriters and fax machines. The thrill he feels when he takes those first footsteps toward certain theft is unparalleled. At home, right under the supposedly watchful eyes of his increasingly intolerant aunt and uncle, the hiding spots of his room, the depths of his closet and the drawers of his desk, overflow with the trophies of his boredom. He's collected quite a few valuables along the way – sixteen cassettes, nearly a dozen VHSs, countless candy bars, dirty magazines, and a neglected gold necklace, stolen off a blue velvet neck at The Bay. His heart pounds faster just thinking about it all.

There he is, finally, at the employee exit, at the end of the aisle. He's passed through these doors enough times to know how to push them just so, to minimize the extra clatter of reckless swinging. This time, though, when he pushes through, an alarm fires off.

He turns and runs blindly into the tunnels. The corridors behind the mall's façade are narrow and winding, their walls caked with grime and dust, and his path obscured by broken boxes and garbage bags dumped out by store employees who only take their trash down the freight elevators to the giant compactor once a week. With every turn, his shoulder hits an unexpected shelf of canned goods, his hip a wobbling washbasin. Footsteps chase after him.

"Hey you!"

Niko runs deeper into the mall's insides. It's not as well-lit and shadows dance everywhere. He trips over an industrial-sized yellow mop bucket. His schoolbag goes flying. He gets back up and, limping, starts running again. Brazenly he turns back: he almost forgets his schoolbag behind. It is here that for the first time he spots the glaring eyes of the security guard, red in the face like a bloodhound and heaving for an honest breath, propelled around the corner by the momentum of his body fat and bounding down the dark corridor in his direction.

There are perhaps twenty paces between them, less now. His bag dragging behind him by the strap, Niko shoots through the nearest door and finds himself in an airless stairwell. At the next level down, he enters a white tiled corridor, a suicide dash that seemingly gets brighter as he races in full sprint. Just as he hears the security guard crash into the stairwell upstairs, Niko slams through a set of swinging doors at the far end of the hall and tumbles into a room, where a young woman jumps back. Hastily she grabs a T-shirt from the bench and clutches it to her chest. "Get out!" She yells at him as though he's a stray dog that's wandered into the mall by mistake. "Get, go!"

Desperate, he puts his hands up in the air, as if to say, I'm harmless. "I need to hide. Please."

She's not much older than he is. The T-shirt that she presses against her chest reveals the straps of her pink bra and her freckled shoulders. Footsteps are fast approaching, and now they can both hear the security guard shouting curses at him.

He glares at her pleadingly. "I'll do anything. Just buy me ten minutes."

Nevertheless she stands there and listens to the footsteps getting closer, batting him around with her eyes like a cat that can't decide whether to snap its prey's neck right away or let it struggle a bit longer.

Just when it seems that it's all a little too late, she shoots her chin over her shoulder in the direction of the showers. "Go in there. Hide in one the stalls. Don't say a word."

Niko dives toward the showers, where he kneels down and pulls a shower curtain closed behind him. This is it, he pants in a flash, either he gets me now, or I'll make it. If I make it, I'll never steal here again. That girl with the face he can't trust will either give him away or she'll save his skin.

From the shower stall, he hears the security guard burst into the locker room. Immediately after that comes the girl's sharp, exaggerated cry. She's screaming at the top of her lungs about perverts and rapists. Now Niko hears what must be the security guard fumbling for an apology, and then he's stumbling for a way out of the locker room so as not to lose his job.

Crouching down in the wet shower, Niko lets out a sigh of relief. In the belly of the mall, he's managed to scrounge together, out of sheer luck, a new lease on life. But that was close. He's never been chased before.

Then he hears footsteps again. The shower curtain pulls back. From where he's crouched down, her head blocks a halogen light that glows like a hallucinogenic white halo around her, obscuring her face.

"Coast's clear. He's gone."

Slowly he slides up. "Thanks for that."

"So what was that all about?" she says. "Why's he after you?"

"Oh, it's nothing really. He thinks I stole something."

"Did you? Why'd you run?" Her blue eyes hone in on his evasive glances. "You did. I can see it in your face." As he tries to walk past her, she steps in his way. "I can call him back here. I'm the only one who knows how to get you out of this mall without getting caught. Lemme see it."

"See what?"

"What you stole, you little thief."

He pulls out the cracked cassettes from his coat, and the VHSs. She looks at them and smiles sarcastically, he has no taste.

"Well, I guess I kinda wanted this one a year ago." She looks at the back of a Whitesnake cassette. "Consider it as your gift to me for saving your ass."

She tosses the tape onto her duffel bag and introduces herself. Her name is Barbara.

The blow-dryer whips Barbara's chestnut hair into a hot frenzy in front of a cracked mirror. Niko sits awkwardly on the bench running down the middle of the room. From time to time, he catches her eye in the mirror and she's not quite winking at him, but definitely doing something purposeful with her eyebrows and the flutter of her lashes, as if she can tell him what to do without saying a word.

"Where do you work?" he asks blankly.

"The Zellers. By the food court."

"Is this a Zellers change room? I didn't know they had change rooms."

"Yup, we're right under the Zellers actually. Fascinating, isn't it. Where did you steal those? Future Plus?"

"K-Mart."

"And the new alarms got you?"

"Yeah."

"You sucker," Barbara says, evidently pitying his lack of fore-sight. "They just put that in last week."

"So why didn't you turn me in? You could be in trouble too."

"Me? Please." Barbara rolls her big eyes. "Besides, I hate those lazy bastards. I'm most definitely not going to do their jobs for them."

"How long have you been working at the Zellers?"

"A year," she yawns. "How long have you been stealing?"

"Not too long."

"I wouldn't think so." She stuffs her blow-dryer and uniform into her bag. "I'll go check if we're safe."

And with that, Barbara brushes past him, pushing him with her shoulder, even though there's plenty of room for her to pass unobstructed. She's wearing some perfume that makes her smell like After Eight dinner mints. A moment later, she pops back in. "We're good. Let's go."

She leads him up another staircase, which involves cutting through the upper reaches of a boiler room. They finally emerge from the building by the back parking lots. It is well past nine o'clock now, and most of the shoppers and employees have already gone home.

"Come with me," she beckons. They walk across the tree-lined asphalt, skirting puddles that glisten in the bright lights of the lot's towering lamps. At the far end of the lot, under a tree, they reach a beaten-up Ford Grenada.

"I'll drive you home."

"Cool, you have a car."

"Sure do."

She gets in and unlocks his side from within. With a loud creek, he manages to unhinge the large passenger door.

"Biggest piece of shit on the planet," Barbara announces once he's in. She unwraps the Whitesnake cassette, tosses the case into the back seat, and then pops it in the tape deck. Hair metal whines out of the car speakers. As they listen to the first song, Barbara

leans across Niko's lap and opens the glove box. She pulls out a
Young & Modern magazine, and uses its back cover to roll a joint.
By the time David Coverdale is tearing into "Is This Love," the
cabin fills with smoke. She passes it to him. He takes it, assuming
it won't be much different than cigarettes. It isn't much different,
or at least not that he can tell. She finishes it and starts the car.

"So where do you live?" she says.

Where does he live, he wonders. "Not far," he manages to say.
He can't pull his eyes off the tape deck. All this time he's been
thinking, he realizes, about where to look. Finally he continues.
"Bridge Street. By the river. Should you be driving right now?"

"Not really." She giggles and he can't help but join her, even though
he feels a bit uncomfortable sitting in a moving car. "We'll go slow."

Glacially the old Ford reverses and then pulls out of the parking
lot. Once they're on the open road, Barbara concentrates intensely
on the task at hand, and given that he's quickly hypnotized by the
passing streetlights anyways, apart from a few jerky requests for
directions, the rest of the ride is devoid of conversation.

Once they get to the top of his street, he says, "You can just
drop me off here," even though they're nowhere near his house
yet. "I can walk."

She pulls over. "Hey, come by the store sometime and say hi.
I'm in cosmetics."

"Zellers has a cosmetics section?"

"Yeah, go figure. No one ever comes by, so it's pretty boring.
So come by."

"Okay."

With that he gets out of the car and slams shut the massive
door with a loud crunch. She drives off indecisively.

He walks through the suburban streets, in wet clothes and a
stoned stupor. The siren, the tunnels, the fat security guard, Barbara. It's been quite a day.

Perhaps theft is too risky. And just maybe it's time to get a real
job. Niko thinks seriously of the money he'd make. He'll need

money if he wants to move out and live on his own soon. If he gets a job, he can do as he pleases. Plus, Sami and Yvonne won't care if he moves out. They'll be happy to have their big house back to themselves. Stumbling along aimlessly, periodically pausing to stare at branches blowing in the wind against a turbulent purple sky, some twenty minutes later he finally arrives back at the bend of Bridge Street they live on. Unlocking the front door in a daze, he can hear the game-show chatter of the television coming from the den, where his uncle has probably fallen asleep. From the kitchen his Tante Yvonne comes in to greet him.

"Busy day at school?" she asks.

"Sure was."

"You look tired," she peers into his glazed eyes. "Are you hungry? There are leftovers."

He is very hungry indeed, he realizes. "Sure," he says, not convinced it's a good idea to be hanging around with his aunt right now. "Do we have anything to drink?"

"We've got pop!" Industriously she goes back into the kitchen, as if she's been waiting for a maternal mission like this all day.

At the kitchen table, Niko giggles for no reason and his mind races along, seemingly unable to ebb the flood of thoughts pouring into his head.

"Food's ready!" his aunt says cheerfully, somehow buoyed by his good mood.

His aunt sets a plate of microwaved lasagna before him, along with a glass of Pepsi. He demolishes the leftovers to his aunt's queer satisfaction with his healthy appetite for her cooking. Yvonne runs her fingers through his hair. She says, "Now that's the happy boy I want to see."

Barbara. Her lips are electric when they kiss for the first time. She may be only eight months older than him, but she's a portal to another world. Barbara already lives on her own. She has a car. She's never been outside the province, much less another country.

She is fully and completely a Montrealer, and as a result, when Niko's around her, he can finally see a life for himself in which he doesn't have to think about his parents or the stump of a life he's been dealt so far. In fact, he doesn't have to tell Barbara anything about his past, she doesn't ask too many questions between all the joints they smoke. Baked, they sit together in the dusty backroom of the arcade café, not too far from the mall, as evening settles into darkness and the street lamps come alive, as students from Champlain College filter out and begin their journeys home, only to be replaced at the front tables by old men who spend the night playing backgammon and chess.

She's telling him about her apartment nearby.

"I'd like to see it."

"Let's go there now," she teases. "I can show you."

They go over there. The halls of her building smell like a giant ashtray.

"Are you hungry?" she asks, looking through the freezer. "I've got a chicken pot pie."

"Yeah, sure."

The sensitive sounds of Kate Bush fill the room. She brings out a large bottle of lukewarm Labatt Blue and a homemade bong, and they begin to drink and smoke more weed. She has a number of interesting stories to tell about growing up in this neighbourhood, at least two rounds' worth, and so Niko just sinks into her ratty couch and thinks about the texture of the fabric against his skin and listens.

"What about you?" she asks.

Drunk and unable to think straight by then, Niko leans forward as if telling her great secrets. "I'd really like to visit the neighbourhood where I was born. It's pretty far away though. In another country."

"I'd love to travel," she confides. "It gets so boring here."

The timer chimes. Chicken pot pie, overcooked. After the warm Labatt, neither of them is much in the mood for dry pie. So, instead,

Barbara straddles Niko's waist and runs her ring finger into his lips and then she pulls it out even quicker.

"So you really like me, huh?" she says.

"Really really," Niko confesses, pulling up her shirt.

"Good."

Barbara climbs down off his lap to the carpet and unzips his pants. He winces for control, begins to see flashes of light. Moments later, as they laze on her futon bed, their bodies facing the ceiling, he wants to tell her that she overwhelms him, that he loves her madly and irrationally.

The next evening the city is engorged by a heat wave. During her break, Niko rides Barbara in the backseat of her car. His shirt is tangled up in his armpits, and beneath him Barbara's bra has twisted into a knot around her waist. She's alive with resin and goose bumps, which he can see shivering in the moonlight.

"I love you," he says, forcing the words to the back of her mouth with his tongue.

"You what?" she gasps.

They climax together, or at least Niko does and Barbara seems happy to leave well enough alone. By the time it's over, her dinner break has long ended, and her manager at the Zellers is most likely asking if anyone's seen her around.

"You're going to get me fired," she says, buttoning up her shirt in a hurry.

"Do you think you could get me a job?"

"I dunno," she says, hiking down her skirt. "Maybe. They're always hiring, so I don't see why not."

"Let's have a cigarette," he says.

"Let's have one as I walk back."

Outside they light a cigarette and blow out billows as they walk back to the superstore. At the entrance, they part ways because what they do on her breaks is, at least to her mind, still a secret to the rest of the store.

The next day, Barbara says, "They're looking for cashiers. If you want the job, my manager says it's yours."

"Just like that?"

"It's not rocket science," she shrugs.

On his first night at the brightly lit counter, Niko slumps in a daze of disbelief. It's only been a couple of weeks, but meeting Barbara has totally turned his life around. He used to be sad, trapped in a past no one else could see or understand, but now his past is just a period of time that's behind him, and he spends way more time thinking of the future. He's got this job, and he's horny all the time for Barbara. His only obstacle to being with her again: waiting out a slow shift while watching walls of TV screens quietly babble away in unison. As thirty-six Joan Rivers have confirmed to him before, he could do worse than work at the Zellers three nights a week – plus a weekend shift every other week. Besides rubbing himself raw against Barbara, his favourite thing to do ever, he pulls in $4.25 an hour, meaning that in the last two months, he's made just under $600. And that's not including what he's stolen from the Zellers. He's not doing so well in school, but at least no one's writing letters home to his aunt and uncle. Sami and Yvonne don't really bother him anymore unless it has to do with his school or the police calling. Most nights, they no longer wait up for him, and he comes and goes mostly as he pleases. All in all, he can't imagine how his life could get any better than this.

One evening two months later, Barbara rushes over to Niko's cash register while his manager is away, and she says, "We have to talk. When's your break?"

"Not for another twenty minutes." He can see her heart beating an aspiring, anxious rhythm in her neck. "What's wrong?"

"Meet me in the food court when you're off."

Twenty minutes later, Niko finds Barbara sitting at the far end of the smoking section, tapping her foot over a half-eaten cheeseburger.

"I'm pregnant," she says.

"How?" he says.

"How do you think?" she snaps.

"I'm sorry," he hears himself saying, but by then he doesn't know what's going on, he's just talking.

"I come from a very religious family," Barbara warns. "If my dad finds out, he'll kill you."

Niko gulps.

"I want to get rid of it," she says. "You got me into this mess, and you're going to get me out."

"How much does it cost?" He doesn't have much money right now. "Did you take a test?"

"A lot and of course."

"I want to see it."

"Do you think I'm lying?"

"After work, let's go back to your place and take another one."

At Barbara's apartment, they smoke weed and watch game shows. After the initial intensity wears away Barbara says, "I'm too nervous. Let's wait a while first."

Niko agrees. Barbara passes him another joint. He takes a few drags, passes it back, and sinks into the couch. Soon after, they begin to make out, not because of some urgent need for togetherness, but just because it feels good, and because they don't know what else to do with that question lingering between them other than to act like it was never there.

Afterwards, Niko says, "How long have you known?"

"A few weeks." Barbara says slowly.

"Why did you wait so long to tell me?"

"I was hoping I'd miscarry. You can if you get drunk enough."

"That's the stupidest thing I've ever heard," Niko says

She looks down at her stomach in fear. "It's not the first time," Barbara says.

"What do you mean it's not the first time?"

Ignoring him, she complains, "What will I tell my parents? They've already paid for one, but only because I was fifteen." Out loud, Barbara thinks it through. "But now I'm eighteen, and they wouldn't pay for a second one, no way. I'm Catholic for fuck's sake. How many children can I kill before I'm damned to hell for all eternity?"

"How many times have you gotten pregnant?" Niko asks.

"I'm not a slut," Barbara insists, with a glare of annoyance. "I'm just not an virgin like you." Then she takes his arm and returns to the problem at hand. "Niko, we'll have to take care of it quickly, without telling anyone."

"It'll be our secret," he says.

"We're in too far now. We say nothing and soon it will be gone."

"Like it was never there," Niko adds.

They relax again. They're both quite high by now, and even though the idea of being pregnant is still at the center of their every thought, they're more easily distracted by Alex Lifeson's intricate guitar work and, besides, the burden of not knowing doesn't weigh as heavily on their shoulders when this old sofa is so very comfortable to lie back on and sink in to. They stare at the ceiling while Geddy Lee's nasal wailing calls out to Tom Sawyer. But then, just as randomly, she slides back into frustration.

"I don't have the money," she frets. "Everything I make goes into the rent and the car and the food in the fridge and, well, this very nice pot. Niko, you'll have to pay for it. If you love fucking me that much, well then, you'll have to be a man about this and find the money somehow. After all, it's almost certainly yours."

"Have you slept with anyone else?"

"I don't know, Niko. It's summer. There's just too much going on. Stop bugging me with the stupid stuff. Can't you see I'm trying to figure out something huge?"

"Take the test," Niko says. "Take it now so I can go home already."

Hazily and with much interruption from the seemingly endless distractions of her apartment, Barbara finds her way to the bathroom and there, without fail, is the pregnancy test, just where she's imagined it to be: under the sink. She tears away the plastic wrapper, and then sits on the toilet and holds the fateful popsicle stick between her legs into her pee. And then she brings it out and they wait. Three minutes pass. There they are: twin pink lines staring back at her in eager conviction.

It's too hard to go through accidental pregnancy a second time, Barbara complains to Niko – and the longer she waits, the more difficult it becomes. She can already feel the child growing inside her, the little ripples of a sprouting womb. Niko's eyes well up with hopelessness whenever he imagines this happening. Last night Niko had a dream about the baby. It was grabbing him by the leg, a faceless baby boy dragging him down.

"Please tell me you have the money," she begs Niko at the mall, where they smoke cigarettes in the cold shelter of the loading docks.

"We don't get paid for another five days." He paces back and forth, thinking hard. "Even then I won't have enough."

"Can't you ask your parents?"

"Me?" He can imagine Sami and Yvonne sitting in their formal living room, listening to him confess the news of the mess he's gone and found for himself. They wouldn't even talk to him. They'd kick him out and he'd have nowhere to go. "Why not you?"

She can't. Barbara's parents would murder her if they knew she'd gone and done it again. He flinches in aggravation every time she says that, because it somehow feels unfair that she's gone through this before and yet here he stands with her, going through this for the first time. Between paying customers, Niko deliberates feverishly over what to do next.

The next evening, Barbara calls him at Zellers. She sobs into the receiver. "I thought going through with an abortion once before would make it easier the second time, but it's not like that at all. At least when I was fifteen, I somehow managed to not pay attention to what I thought afterwards. This time, I know how I'll feel if I kill it. It's enough sadness to die from."

"I'll get you the money," he hisses into the phone. "Just give me a little more time."

"How do you know I wouldn't make a good mom or you wouldn't make a good dad?"

"I wouldn't make a good dad," Niko argues. "I wouldn't love it. I would run away and leave it."

"You wouldn't," Barbara cries back. "Once you saw it, you would change your mind. The government would give us money. We wouldn't have to work."

He hangs up. Niko decides he must do something drastic. He will have to steal the money from his uncle. All this time he should have been saving, but $600 a month is not that much to live on. That night after work, he takes the bus home. Now that he's lived with the idea for several days, the thought of having a child horrifies him. He's no good at looking after himself. How can he be expected to look after someone else? At home, he watches television, and then helps himself to some food in the fridge. It's been forever since he's had some proper non-mall food, and so the sandwich Niko makes goes a long way toward clearing his head. But it also makes him tired, and he realizes right then that all he wants to do is sleep for a while and put his problems off to the side.

Niko goes upstairs, gets into bed, and passes out soon after his head hits the pillow. Somewhere along the way, he gets snagged by a dream in which he is standing in the middle of a wide and empty room, in a country that looks like nowhere but feels like Lebanon, and there in the afternoon light that pours in through the tall windows, before him on the marble floor, lies a collection of hands severed at the wrist. He counts them. There are seventeen in total. They lie side by side in two rows, the feckless five fingers of the swing voter between them. He walks around to the other side of the collection and bends down to inspect each one in greater detail. The hands, he senses instinctively, have all been his at different times in his life.

Then he can hear a boy scratching at the other side of the door, whining to come in, like a cat. Niko goes to the door, and the boy rushes at him and tackles his leg.

"There you are," Niko says, ruffling the little boy's hair. "Say, what's your name?"

"Nakhle!" the boy shouts.

Niko tells the little boy the story of the first Nakhle in their family, who worked the fields of Adam. "You've been chosen by grace," Niko tells the little boy in his dream.

With the boy latched firmly to his leg, Niko limps down a winding staircase, and then they go outside into a parking lot sheltered on all sides by tall buildings, and there they kick around a flat soccer ball, which the boy chases with delirious squeals of joy.

He wakes up with a start. It is almost morning, and still Niko can't get his mind to stop fretting. He climbs out of bed and stands by the window in a pale sash of moonlight, watching the St. Lawrence River spit chunks of white foam into eddies, bank them off standing waves. Even as a thirteen-year-old, Niko had this same double bed, as if the Maleks had planned this to be a guest room from the start. All he ever wanted was for someone to stick around and guide him. He remembers, for a moment, their old apartment in Montreal North. His uncle used to take an intense interest in his education then. He hadn't enjoyed school, would have left it if given half a chance. Niko's life had revolved around waiting for a phone to ring, to be invited back by his father. But now, all that waiting has resulted in one big mess.

Niko decides that somewhere in this house there must be some money he could borrow. He leaves his bedroom and furtively shuffles down the creaking staircase to the first floor of the house. Niko enters his uncle's office and feels his way to the armchair overlooking the river. The room stinks of stale tobacco. Pale moonlight washes a celestial glow over the large desk and chair. He switches on the desk lamp and sits down. A notebook rests open before him. He browses through the pages, not knowing what he expects to find. Pages upon pages, filled with addresses, names, dates, speculative musings, arrows connecting scribbles, references to government offices, to-do lists, even what appears to be shopping lists.

Niko decides that if there were any money here, the drawers would be the most obvious place, and so he starts rifling through them. There's nothing but pens, batteries, an eraser. In the left drawer he finds envelopes. He pulls them out and begins to search each one for money. In the second envelope he comes across a newspaper clipping. It falls out onto the desk. When Niko opens it, he's surprised to see a grainy newsprint picture of a man who looks conspicuously like Baba. In the same envelope he finds a letter addressed to his uncle from a man in Chile named Serge Maroun, who belongs to something called the Club Union Arabe. Reading in the glow of the desk lamp, Niko discovers that an Antoine has turned up in the city of Valparaiso. It's dated from the spring of last year. Why has his uncle been hiding this from him, he wonders. What's he been up to? Niko looks at the letter in closer detail. "Does this man resemble," it asks, "by any chance, the Antoine Karam you're looking for? If so, I think we may have found him."

According to the latest field report on Serge Maroun's desk, the man from nowhere leaves his house every morning at 5 a.m. At that hour, he descends into the pre-dawn fog that encircles the hills. He lives in a tin-plated bungalow near the top of one of Valparaiso's poorest hills, with a woman named Beatriz Gabriela Cruz, the nurse from the hospital where Antoine was first admitted upon his arrival to their country. They will soon have a baby together.

The shacks up there, Serge is well aware, have no numbers, and so the report details the characteristics to look for in order to tell Antoine's residence apart from the rest: one has to look for a black door with a white ladder on it, drawn crudely in spraypaint on the door's lower half by local children who tell long stories about the legend of the angel from the sea. Otherwise, there is nothing to really distinguish the home from the otherwise unbroken wall of black doors and windows along this cobblestone street.

Antoine works down at the port, where Serge Maroun has arranged for him to work, and where entry and exit records are meticulously maintained. He arrives at the port's gates, and there he joins a grizzly line of hardened faces, all waiting. The port authority, which consists of two clean-shaven marines in navy uniforms, arrive by jeep at six-thirty, no earlier, no later. The port authority rubber-stamps the men's paperwork. Most of them are like Antoine, transients working off temporary work permits that will conveniently expire once their secret pasts are revealed.

The sun rises then. The first truck arrives to peruse the available workers. The grizzled driver of the truck leans out his window with a megaphone and loudly explains the nature of the work. This first job of that given morning has to do with moving sandbags. Lots of heavy lifting. It's only a few hours' worth of work. Those who are interested are asked to stand up. Every man stands. The crew captain steps out of the truck to inspect them for stubbornness in their eyes, workhorse brutishness and muscularity, as if buying oxen. He taps the ones he wants on the shoulder. Then without saying a word he climbs back into the car, and a chosen few jump onto the bed of the truck.

Sometimes the jobs last for hours, and other times they appear to stretch on for days and weeks. Antoine never knows where he'll go that day when he leaves for work in the morning. Replacing sick or injured crew members, manning the boiler rooms of ships, helping out on offshore drilling rigs, cleaning bathrooms on freight ships, handling hazardous chemicals, moving cracked or leaking or illegal cargo, loading munitions for the Navy, unloading freight canisters, hauling fish: his record indicates he's done all that and more during his time down at the port.

In the evening, Antoine shuffles past the port gates, weary and broken from the day's chores. He walks back up the hill, at times pausing to sit on a curb, to have a cigarette or a random conversation with a shopkeeper. Antoine (otherwise known to the Ministry of the Interior as Case File #007658) appears to have something of an elaborately cultivated home life, the monthly report concludes, for someone who could be a spy. Maybe things are too good to spoil, the sympathetic reporter sighs in his slanted handwriting in a section entitled "Comments from the Field." Maybe the ladder man thinks that if he remembers too much, someone will come and take his wife and coming baby away.

Then again, there are instances when, through his powerful binoculars, the field reporter thinks he can see a disturbing signature of recognition flash across the ladder man's face. Antoine will drift away from his work, and he'll look over his shoulder with a forlorn gaze that indicates he can feel the eyes of others constantly on his back. They could very well be his own eyes. Perhaps his amnesia has begun to let little slivers of his past bubble up from its depths. If this is the case, he has been able to push them back down so far and say, no, not now.

Maybe the ladder man has found that he can do this at will, forget things. Perhaps that's why people say he's angelic, unlike them. Who does the baby bring to mind, the field reporter wonders on paper. This angel's mind, the field reporter speculates, must be like black pools of still water in mountain caves. There, the crown of a memory's head can float up into view from the depths, only to disappear once again, unnoticed by all except for a lurking premonition left to the angel himself, who momentarily feels the brush of past wisdom blow against his ear like a kiss from God.

He kicks, and her head gets caught under his arm. She straddles his waist as they turn, umbilical cords entwined. Then comes another push. Their walls close in, pushing them out until they are trapped in a corridor, caught one against the other, and slowly they inch, struggling backwards, clawing, biting, fighting, until finally a light pierces through in the distance, a blinding pinprick that drags them towards it, and they suck greedily at what remains of their mother's fluids, she slipping ahead, he falling behind. As she escapes her mother, she pushes away from her grandmother's hands, which deliver her into the world. Her grandmother pulls her free and raises her by the ankles, upside down, an index finger uncorks her cheeks. The world fills with new sounds, replacing the gurgling and swishing and squirming of the womb, excessive sounds that make her scream in alarm. It is then that she learns, to her surprise, that she too can make sound. A giant blade rises to cut her short umbilical. Her grandmother wraps her naked body in a towel, and she passes her along to a second pair of hands.

"There's more," says the grandmother with alarm, as Beatriz continues to scream and push. And then a second one dribbles out, but there is nothing to be done for him, and straightaway the grandmother deems him born dead, strangled by their umbilicals while waiting for new life to begin.

Who could that weakling of a boy have been, Antoine wonders the day his unexpected twins are born, but a shadow of myself. We are both too delicate for the cold air of this world. He has no money to give his son a proper burial, and so the next day Antoine walks down the hill, with the dead boy in a pillowcase, down to the water's edge where he borrows a dinghy from one of the fishermen there, and he paddles backward out to sea. The waters are hazy and calm, and the old boat bobs up and down languidly to the rhythm of his strokes, lurching toward the open seas, out past the edges of the bay to a deep chasm carved by a fault line long ago, before any of them were there, a chasm where freight ships never pass and the sea lions never come to feed. There, surrounded by the whiteness of the bay's fog, Antoine throws the pillowcase overboard as if it is the sum of all his demons. For several moments it floats awkwardly near the surface, peaking through at him from just under the glaze of topwater as if to give him one last chance to change his mind, and then the boy sinks into the blackness below.

Rowing back, Antoine is in a strange state of regret and mourning all at once. He shouldn't have done what he just did, he thinks, but he couldn't have let anyone else do it either. He can't put a boy, who never had the opportunity to live, in the ground. And yet, having expected only one child all along, in a roundabout way he had got exactly what he wanted.

He resolves to leave these mysterious feelings at sea, where they belong. The undertow of why things happen the way they do is very much out of his control, and who is he to argue with fate. Fate gives with one hand, he tells himself, and takes away with the other. His life must've always been this way. He senses that he's known these feelings for a long time.

Who is she, this strong little girl? Antoine wonders later that day, holding in his bruised arms the energetic twin that survived. He would think of them as twins always, like the bright and dark sides of a moon.

"What do I do, Doña Julia?" he asks his mother-in-law in the Spanish that has become his everyday language.

"Just rock her gently so she stays calm," Doña Julia says, looking into the bundle of flannel. "She's okay. Just be natural with her."

Everything about her – the little twitch of her fingers, the drooling, awkward breathing, the redness of her skin – mesmerizes him. She has won him over, just like that, in seconds. She is his, his greatest responsibility, the beginnings of a family that will stretch out past him long after he's gone.

Antoine carries her out into the front room and begins to introduce his new daughter to the neighbours who've gathered in their home on the rumour of a birth, because as this day has shown him, he belongs to this neighbourhood, where people will arrive at his door with plates of food and second-hand baby clothes and goodwill. All around, people he barely knows, most just from passing nods in the streets, coo and straighten at the sight of his new invention.

"She's so beautiful," they say.

"You're so blessed."

"*Si*," he can't help but agree. "She's an angel."

"She's the one who saved you at sea," they tell him. "She is your angel."

His angel, Antoine thinks. He would have never thought about it like that, but he supposes it's true. He's laughing as he says this, but after hearing the words come out of his mouth a second time and then a third, he realizes that they're genuinely true. He can't help but let his pride show: she is a ball of angelic potential, his potential. He has a baby girl and Beatriz and even Doña Julia; it all adds up to a family because of her. This baby brings it all together.

"Her name is Elise," he tells admiring neighbours. "She's beautiful and she's mine."

The celebration continues well into the evening, with the neighbours all taking turns having a toast with Antoine the brand-new father, who stumbles from one *salud!* to the next. By the end of the night, after the last guest has left, after mother and child are resting together in the next room, he goes outside on the stoop of his shack to smoke a cigarette, and in all the darkness of the hills, Antoine can see the steady gleam of street lights roll down the hill, down to where the tallest buildings hold offices who leave their lights on all night, and beyond that he can even make out the docks of the Navy base. Yes, everything's different now, Antoine decides out on the stoop in the cool night breeze, looking out at the amphitheatre of lights at his feet. From the moment Elise was first handed to him, he was renewed. The old Antoine, whoever he was, lies dead in a pillowcase at the bottom of the sea.

Every evening after that, when he arrives home, he plants a kiss on his woman's smiling head, and then nuzzles down deeper into the face of his new daughter. This baby illuminates his life in a disarmingly genuine way. There is an old willow tree near their house, and there he often takes Elise in the hour that Beatriz and her mother finish preparing the nightly meal. There, they often lie on a worn blanket in the evening light, with crickets chirping to keep them company, and in those passages it's as if the rest of the world beyond the blanket ceases to exist. It must be a case of love, the next report states in bold type, as the baby girl drools freely onto her father's stained shirt in the half-cast shadows of another warm night.

According to Barbara, Niko no longer has a choice in the matter. She simply can't go through another abortion, and the money the government will give her for having the child is more than Zellers will ever pay her. She has made a decision: she will have the child, and with the guidance of her parents' hand they will raise it and become responsible adults. "My father wants to meet you, so we can all sit down and discuss the future."

Two nights later, Niko and Barbara walk to her parents' home. There, her mother tries to be agreeable, offering him a beer and asking about his family, and though he delivers the basic outlines, he only appears to disappoint her, because she had at least hoped that her daughter had been knocked up by someone of better pedigree, and in the end she excuses herself to the kitchen and doesn't return for a long time. With her mother gone, Barbara scowls at her father, the continuation of some private argument they've been having over the past few nights, to which Barbara has already alluded on the walk over here.

"I can't believe you're making me do this," she says. Barbara then follows her mother into the kitchen, and Niko's left to sit awkwardly across from her father, who does indeed look like a fearsome minister. The man kneads his knuckles, ready to strangle Niko. Then he stubs out the last of his many cigarettes, and through the haze of smoke in the room, begins to talk sternly of the ultimatum he has arranged.

"Listen boy. I don't care where you come from or if you love my daughter or not," he says, "but from now on the two of you are going to do what I say, or God help me, I'll kill you with my own hands."

Niko nods bleakly.

"My daughter says you forced yourself on her, so you'll agree that you've made quite a mess for yourself. Now I know my daughter, and I don't know what happened between you two, but I know that this time I'm not going to make the same mistake again, whether you like what I have to say or not. Do you understand what I'm saying? I can always call the police and be finished with you, like that."

He snaps his fingers.

"First, before this child is born, you and my daughter are going to get married at our church, and you're going to do right by this child in the eyes of God. Next, the two of you are going to move into this house. We have room for you in the basement, and this is where you'll live. This way my wife can make sure nothing happens to the baby, and that our daughter and you don't get messed up with drugs and drinking all the time. From this moment on, all that is behind you. Third, you will come to work with me at the paper mill. I have already spoken to my boss about this mess, and he's agreed to take you on. The money isn't bad, and this way my wife and I can be sure there's enough of it for the baby to be raised properly. Our daughter will quit her job and raise the kid. The two of you will become proper parents, whether you like it or not."

The clarity of the arrangement unnerves him. Barbara's father takes him down to see the basement, ostensibly his future home. It is a damp room with cement floors and rough wood beams. The only windows slide open at the very top of the far wall to let in a little air, but nothing in the way of light.

Later, as Niko and Barbara walk back to her apartment, he notices that the pregnancy has already begun to show.

"Is this what you want?" he asks.

"Who knows, maybe they're right."

"Do you think we'll be happy down there?"

"I'm tired," she sighs.

In a way, he's relieved to hear her say that, because he doesn't feel anything like love for her anymore, only constriction. He leaves her at the entrance to her building, as there is no question as to whether he'll stay over or not, and begins the long walk back to the subway station.

That night Niko wakes up covered in sweat. There's no way he'll live in that basement with those people. He'd rather die. Or at least disappear, like Baba. If only he could leave for Chile right now, just get his passport and leave. But what about the baby, he hears the voice of responsibility ask. The baby, sighs the voice of his dreams, that baby will be better off without you.

*

It's taken forty days of planning, but he hasn't told a soul what he's about to do, for if his plan is to work, he must undertake it in untarnished secrecy. On the last day of that year, Niko goes downstairs and leaves the Malek house for the last time. It is a dark and hollow shell of what once could have been, had they been better people. Then, with a bagful of clothes on his back, he leaves. It's a Monday, New Year's Eve 1990, and that evening he's working the closing shift at the Zellers. He arrives at the mall and sits at his counter, waiting for 6 p.m. to roll around so that he can collect his paycheque, which he expects to come in around a measly $150 – not enough money to act upon, at least not on its own. But having worked at the store for more than a year now, he has in the past six months taken on the responsibility of tallying his till. Furthermore, he has a lazy shift manager, who is really just a university senior with a part-time job, and more often than not, he skips out early to go study for exams or meet friends.

So, after his last customer pays for a headset, Niko casually counts the cash sitting in his till, which he's supposed to do periodically anyways, to make sure he's balanced, and he arrives at the figure of $643.27. Mondays are slow, and tonight it is snowing out, so with the mall not that busy, the store has eight people working cash registers. All of them have a plan to finish up as quickly as possible because it's New Year's Eve, to just deposit their tills in the safe, along with the Ziploc bags of profit. Only in the mornings does the store manager come in and sit in the back room to collect and count all the bags. But tomorrow is a holiday, and so the store will be closed. He has been the last cashier left in the store on several occasions, and he knows that the back room will be deserted if he wraps up last. The only person left in the store will be the security guard waiting for Niko to leave so that he can draw the steel lattice down on the doors and lock up the place for the year.

By his figures, provided all goes according to plan, he stands to collect quite a score by the time he's through. According to store protocol, each cashier is expected to leave three hundred dollars in bills and change in his till. eighteen dollars of that is pennies ($0.50), nickels ($2.50), dimes ($5.00), and quarters ($10.00), which he'll leave behind, meaning that by the end of tonight's shift, after he fakes some calculation errors that will keep him re-tallying until the last cashier has left, the open safe will hold eight tills, each containing $282 of usable money, amounting to a grand total of – and here Niko does the math on unused receipt paper – $2,256. When he adds into the total the bags of nightly profits, he should have approximately $5,000 to work with. Add onto that, he thinks again, the fact that the safe holds the weekend tills as well, ready to go. On the weekends, all fifteen cash registers are active, so there are seven more tills in there for the taking, bring his total take up to $9,700. That could very well be more money than anyone's ever made working at the Zellers.

At 5:45 p.m., fifteen minutes to close, his shift manager shows up at his cash counter, as he does most days now, hands over Niko's paycheque and announces that he has to go to a party. "You'll be okay, right?"

"Don't worry about me," Niko says.

But the shift manager is off in a world of his own, and is already walking away as Niko replies. Then the mall sounds the announcement to close and the remaining customers all begin to leave. To get to the back room, five of the cashiers – all those working at the front – have to walk past his counter. The remaining two are anyone's guess, but given the sleet outside, he's hoping that by quarter past six, they'll have all finished up and left the store. He waits until the digital clock of his register glows 6:15. Then he begins the fateful walk to the back room.

One remaining cashier is in the room, a skinny girl named Oliviette. "Slow night, huh?" she says.

"Yeah, super slow."

He sets down his till and pretends he has something stuck in his shoe.

"You going to any parties tonight?" she says. "Wanna come to a party or something?"

"Um, I've gotta get back home." Niko says quickly. "We're doing a family thing."

"Well, see ya later," she chirps. "And have a happy New Year!" And then Oliviette turns on her heels and finally leaves.

He waits for her to disappear down the aisle and then closes the door. Feeling panicky, he empties the tills into a Ziploc bag, and then the large coins into another one. It takes longer than expected, and it seems to him like he's making a lot of noise. But no one comes. Finally, he stuffs several bills in his pocket and pushes the Ziplocs into his knapsack and leaves. The security guard at the store entrance is busy reading a comic book, and pays Niko little attention, other than to bring down the steel lattice once he's out. He goes outside into the rain, where he finds a lone cab at the taxi stand.

"Where to?" says the driver.

"The airport," says Niko.

The driver turns on the meter and they drive off.

Tonight, I'm safe, he thinks. In two days, they'll know everything. At the airport, Niko stands in front of the departures board. It seems so simple when he thinks about it, but he hasn't even checked to find out where he ought to land. Valparaiso is nowhere to be found on the board. He asks one of the ladies at the airline counters. "How do I get to Chile?"

"Going on a little adventure?" She looks at him strangely, and then she says, "Go to the Delta counter. Ask for Santiago."

"Thanks."

He finds the Delta counter, fearful that he'll have some explaining to do, but the man working there doesn't want to discuss the reasons behind his trip at all. He merely processes Niko's passport, asks if he has any other luggage, and sells him a ticket that costs more than a quarter of his money. Then he's off through the metal detectors, and then he's exchanging all his money into American dollars, because that's what the exchange officer suggests he do for Chile. That cuts his money by another third. He has two hours before his flight boards.

Oliviette, his missing Ziploc bag in the roll-in safe, the security guard, the taxi driver, the Delta counter: these are all the places he left clues behind as to his crime and his method of escape. Provided the police don't show up to arrest him in the next little while, he'll be getting out of Canada by the skin of his teeth. Niko hunches up in a ball and pretends to be invisible.

After they've searched the entire house and called the school, Yvonne asks, "Where do you think he could be? Niko's never gone missing for this long."

"I have no idea," says Sami. Outside, a gale wind has stirred a grey, stormy sky and the plastic garbage can they keep just outside the screen door has fallen over and rolled noisily away. "I hope he's at least not outside somewhere."

"What about his work?" she frets. "We can check there. I can't just sit here and do nothing."

Sami breathes deeply, mindful of the dull ache that's been building in his chest ever since they began to wonder why Niko hadn't come home. The first night was New Year's Eve, and they assumed he'd stayed with friends. But now, after a third night, something feels terribly wrong.

"Alright," Sami sighs. "I'll drive down to the mall and see what they know."

Alone in the dark, Sami backs the car out of the garage, wondering all the time if Niko's sudden disappearance has anything to do with the papers in his desk. He hasn't told Yvonne about any of that; she doesn't know about Halim's discovery, the newspaper article, or the letter from Chile. But early on the second morning Niko hadn't come home, he woke up before her and went into his office, locked the door behind him, and checked the drawer with the correspondence in it. The contents of the drawer were arranged differently than he remembered, or so he thought. In any case, the hunch was there and it was the only piece of the puzzle that made sense.

As he drives to the mall and traffic lights sway in the evening wind, he can feel the secret eating away at him. If his hunch turns out to be true, then he's responsible for putting the boy's life in danger.

At the mall, Sami walks around the brightly lit store, not quite sure where he ought to go or whom he ought to speak to. At a cash register, he asks of the employees, "Is the manager in? Can I speak to the manager?"

"Sure." He gets on the intercom and puts out a call for the manager to come to the cash.

A few minutes later, a slightly older teenage boy comes sauntering along. "What can I do for you, sir?"

Sami pulls the manager along by the arm and they begin to walk slowly down one of the aisles. "I'm Niko Karam's uncle. He works here, doesn't he?"

"Yeah, well, he did. I don't know if he works here any more."

"He hasn't been home in three days. Have you seen him?"

"Nope. But if he does show up, I'm supposed to call the cops."

"What did he do?"

"Come back here," the manager says, leading Sami to the back of the store. "Lemme show you something." In the back room, there's an older gentleman sitting in front of several small televisions. "Alain, can you pull up the footage from the robbery a few days back?"

"Robbery?" The pain in Sami's head grows sharper.

"Just watch this," the manager says, leaning in toward the screen. "Here he is," he points. "That's him."

Niko is on the television. The footage shows him unloading bills from cash registers and stuffing them into Ziploc bags, and then stuffing the Ziploc bags into his knapsack.

"How much did he take?"

"Almost $10,000."

Sami takes a deep breath. "Can I sit down for a second?"

The manager gestures toward an empty chair. "Go ahead."

Sitting down, Sami puts his head in his hands. "Tell your boss that I'll pay back whatever he stole."

"Okay. I don't know that it will get him out of trouble though."

Soon after, as Sami sits in the car, he finds that he can't even summon up the energy to start the engine and drive home to his wife. How can he tell her all this? It's enough bad news to take down a person. He winces at the recurring pain in his chest. He'd never, not in his wildest imaginings, thought that Niko could go off and make a mistake on such a grand scale. Looking back over their years together, Sami can't help but wonder if those bad judgments could have been passed down from his example. He doesn't think so. Then again, it doesn't look like he knows much of anything about his nephew.

At that, Sami turns the key in the ignition and begins the drive home, driving slower than he's ever driven before. I am destined to be the father without children, he thinks. This self-inflicted sadness will be the death of me.

Feeling deflated and defeated, and unable to fathom how he can break the news to Yvonne, let alone make it through the next day or week, he steps into the house and musters all his energy to make it to the kitchen table, where he slumps down in a chair and sets his head in his hands. When Sami was younger, even in war, he'd never imagined that he would turn out like this on the way to sixty: inflexible, yet overflowing with mistakes. He had expected these to be years of growing family and the reaping of his hard work's rewards. He takes a deep breath, for every one of these little discoveries adds a little more pressure, and then he tries to calm himself down.

"You're back," Yvonne says, rushing down the stairs. "I fell asleep. I couldn't help it. Did you find out anything?"

"Yvonne, listen," he begins, "it looks like Niko's gone off and stolen nearly $10,000 from the store."

Yvonne sits down and doesn't say anything for a short while. "That doesn't sound like Niko."

"Well, that's who Niko is."

"So where do you think he ran away to? I mean, I don't understand why he couldn't have come to us with his problems. We would have helped."

"I think we over-estimated our place in his life."

"What should we do?"

"I don't know, Yvonne, I don't know." He suddenly feels very tired. "I have a feeling he went to find his father. If you ask me, he's not in the country right now, otherwise we would have heard from him."

"But his father's dead. What's to find?"

"It's a long story," Sami mumbles, but it comes out unclearly. He tries again, and then he breathes too deeply. He puts all his weight on the table and stands up, but he can't stand long. Weakly, he whispers for help. He topples to the carpet, his fingers caught in a spiral of tablecloth.

As an immigrant to the afterlife, you half-expect the home you left behind to stand still in time, preserved solely for you and the luxury of your return. But as the car winds through the narrow roads over the mountains that separate the Bekaa Valley from the sea, and the sight of Beirut below begins to emerge through a haze of pollution, Sami Malek can already see the pockmarked buildings and the dead cars along the sides of roads, and he realizes that this expectation is nothing more than a dead man's wish, a way to feel that a relationship exists between a person and a place. But here in the afterlife, no such relationship exists, and places move on just as people do, for they belong to no one.

So this is where I was meant to go when I die, Sami thinks. Back here of all places, I wonder why. A man whose face he can't see drives the taxi, speeding dangerously down the sloping hills that overlook Beirut's suburbs. There are imported European cars parked in front of crumbling apartment buildings, and brightly coloured signs have already sprouted out of patchy cement walls, advertising everything from nail polish to supermarkets to stereo systems. The sun is out, and once they enter the city, they hit a wall of traffic and car horns jostle in constant conversation for space, and there are no traffic lights or signs. He looks out the window ponderously to find remnants of what he remembers. It is all strangely familiar, yet drastically different. Now they are driving past Sin El-Fil, one of Beirut's neighbourhoods in the east. And now, as they drive along, Sami sees ahead of them the downtown core of the city he once knew. It has been completely demolished and doesn't exist anymore, and in its place is an endless stretch of broken concrete, old tires, and overgrown weeds.

The service taxi pulls over.

"Where do I go?" he asks the driver whose face he can't see.

"Start walking, *istez*, you'll know when you get there," says the driver without turning around.

Sami climbs out of the cab. The city streets bustle with activity, and when one car bleats its horn, they all do. Syrian officers are trying, unsuccessfully, to set up a roadblock as a thicket of cars try to force their way through before the gap finally closes for good. Sami threads his way carefully through the cars to the other side of the street, where more pragmatic drivers are beginning to turn around. He walks along, looking up at all the buildings and, between them, the slumping forms of those that can no longer stand. There is always some little detail here, no matter where he looks, to remind him of the person he once was.

Soon he enters a part of the city that's a bit quieter, where some tables are set outside and old men sit around reading newspapers or just watching people walk past. There, he comes upon the jewelry store at the base of a fifteen-story apartment complex. The alleyway at its side is narrow, winding back into a maze of balconies and flowerpots and laundry hanging to dry. Walking along the dirty back streets of the city of his youth, he hears the twitter of a little bird, a titular, circular song that punctuates the clutter and clanging of someone fixing a car nearby. It is among the saddest soundtracks he's ever heard, as if the bird singing longs for the days it was wild. He follows the song to a window with yellow shutters and when he looks up, Sami sees the bottom of a birdcage.

This must be it, something deep inside tells Sami, the apartment where I was born. Inside the building, Sami looks up the spiraling staircase and sees only hazy clouds of dust swirling lazily in the air. Gripping the railing, he makes his way up to the second floor, and after catching his breath he finally knocks on the door.

On the other side, he hears someone eyeing him through the peephole, and then the door opens and a suspicious-looking man with closely cropped hair and a missing left hand says, "What do you want?"

"My name is Sami Malek. I was born here, and now I have just died."

"Welcome home, Sami Malek. We've been expecting you." He steps aside and extends his hand in invitation toward an empty room.

Sami steps inside. The apartment is small and completely unfurnished. "Where is everyone?"

"No one has lived here for years."

"What do we do now?" Sami asks.

"Now I take you to be reunited with the ones you love most."

His chaperone leads him inside. The large apartment that is his afterlife is silent all around, and all he can hear in the distance are the squawks of pigeons nesting on the rooftop. They cross a long hall to an open room in the back, and Sami begins to jog a little, because it has been so long since he's anticipated this moment of passing, of leaving his worries behind, and the moment has taken hold of him. He can't wait any longer than he already has, which has been much too long.

In the room at the end of the hall, though, he discovers only a lone woman clad entirely in black, lying across the velvet arm of a chaise longue, grieving. She has a funereal black veil upon her face, and so when she speaks to him, Sami can only faintly make out the movement of her lips through the black curtain. But he recognizes her nevertheless as his first wife Marie.

"You needn't have run," she says. "You're right on time."

Sami falls to the ground and grabs onto her knees and kisses them. "Marie, I've waited so long for this. I'm sorry, so sorry."

"There is no past here," Marie smiles through her black veil. "And there are no wrongs. Go there."

With an arch of the chaperone's arm, he gestures to the other end of the room. "Join them."

At the other end of the long room, two coffins rest side by side. The chaperone leads Sami to the coffins.

"This one," he sets his hand on the larger of the two, "is yours." It is open and empty, awaiting him. "You can climb in whenever you're ready to rest."

Sami moves his hand to the smaller of the two.

"And who is this one for?"

"This one is for all the sons you let slip away." It is closed.

For a long time, Sami stands there, simply looking at the two coffins as if he can't see them for what they are, and then, as he tilts his head askew to look at them from a slightly different angle, the sadness of what sits before him begins to set in.

Turning around, Sami wipes his face dry with a handkerchief and falls into another daze. There is a fire growing yet again in his chest, and he must sit down. He can't say what has just happened, but somewhere along the way he must have made another mistake because being here doesn't feel right anymore. I have to leave, he thinks. It's not time yet.

When Sami wakes up again, he finds himself confined to a hospital bed, and a thin blue curtain separates him from the next patient, whose complaining, in irritation, has brought him back to life. There are tubes coming out of different parts of his body and a deep pain in his chest that prevents him from moving in any direction. A heart monitor beeps stoically off to one side, and on the other side, sleeping awkwardly in a chair with her purse clutched tightly to her chest, is Yvonne.

"Hey, wake up," he croaks.

She stirs slightly, and then her eyes flutter open.

"What are we doing here? What happened?"

She sits up straight, yawns, and then decides to pull the chair to the side of his bed. "You had a heart attack," she says sleepily. "They had to open you up. You had to have surgery."

"Will I be okay?"

"The doctor says it's up to you. You have to take it easy and relax and eat well and get lots of sleep."

"Have you heard from Niko?"

Yvonne shakes her head.

In the Afterlife of Our Origins

A STEWARDESS OFFERING a breakfast tray prods Niko awake. Out his window a wafer of blue light radiates along the horizon. At first he's disoriented. A quick shot of panic rings through his ears. But then he remembers Barbara, the baby, the store, and the money, and the burdensome sense of purpose returns in all its waves. He's running away. He looks at the blue box of sky, at a view that has yet to take shape. He's been up in the air now for much of the last fifteen hours. Out his window, dawn slowly materializes, the jagged Andean mountains, their peaks strewn with snow, the clouds snagged upon them spanning out as far as his black eyes can see. Within the hour, the Boeing 747 descends into a sea of cloud.

The fog is dense that morning, and he can't see the airport's runway even as tires touch ground. Outside, the humidity cuts right to his tired bones. In the terminal, a wall of taxi drivers negotiate in a slanted, eager Spanish Niko has no hope of understanding. He chooses one, and his new escort carries his bag to a van. They drive past ghettos and smoke-billowing factories toward the heart of Santiago, passing workers walking along the highway's shoulder as Volkswagens and Nissans speed past. In the city, the taxi crosses the Mapocho, a mighty, mangy turquoise river. Broken furniture litters its banks and garbage bags flow down its ceaseless charge.

They arrive at a hotel recommended by the driver. Inside, the over-friendly hotel concierge hands Niko a tourist map and begins extolling the virtues of the *pisco sours*, a local specialty made by the hotel's rooftop restaurant. Right then, however, Niko just wants to sleep. The concierge takes Niko up to a room on the third floor, where he warns him to lock the door at all times. Exhausted from the long flight, Niko lies down on the damp mattress. In Santiago it already feels impossible to avoid the dampness of mornings, and he tosses and turns as the ubiquitous boom of car horns rises up from the streets. He is in that ironic state of being too tired to sleep. International travel has not been a pleasant experience. Lying here in a strange Santiago, Niko deliberates on how much trouble he'll have getting back into Canada. He thinks about this for a long time while lying there, if only because he feels so far away from home, wherever that may be. Then he falls asleep.

It's still early in the afternoon when he wakes up hungry. The room is stifling hot. Niko decides to forego the hotel's restaurant and ventures outside. There, he finds himself in a shadow of the modern cities he's now used to, amidst streets pockmarked by poverty and grime. Everywhere he is shouted at by blithe restaurant owners, brushing him into their small establishments. He has fried fish and rice among an enthusiastic crowd of soccer fans huddled around a black-and-white television. Later, along a backstreet, he sees a cow strung up from a truck, stripped clean of its skin and disemboweled, its entrails splattered into a wheelbarrow below. Hungry dogs lap at the pools of blood around it, chew upon saw-mangled bits of meat and bone, until the pavement is clean again.

Afterwards he sits down at a canal bench and tries to imagine Baba here. He looks around in exhaustion and amazement. So this is the rest of the world. How different his father's life must be here. He's never considered that they might be strangers if they meet again. But in fact they probably will be. With that, he begins to doubt coming here. The dream had been a quick one, more of an escape hatch at the bottom of the realization that his life had become a trap. But now that he's here, he's cast himself too far off. Somewhere along the way in the past year, everything had gone off track. Niko sits there in the warm sun and thinks about that for a while. His thoughts feel a lot like the river that flows before him, jumbled with garbage bags, dog shit, weeds, old tires, broken bicycles, soiled shoes, rusted cans, mounds of withering pigeon carcasses, and most of everything else that is left to waste here. He sees a dead dog in the water, its skin gone slack and leathery like an inner tube. A dead baby comes down, bobbing in and out through the current. Then he sees its bobbing plastic head and hands, and it turns out to be just a doll.

The next day he takes an orange bus toward the coast, to Valparaiso, passing vineyards and rolling green hills along the way, to where he can't say, his only clues a newspaper article and a name from a letterhead. As the bus fills with a soundtrack of Spanish pop divas he closes his eyes, thinks of Barbara, and hopes beyond hope that she's forgiven him for this. Back in Montreal he was convinced she'd tricked him, but now that there is some distance between them, he isn't so sure anymore. The highway winds in every direction, up, down, left, right, past tin shacks and evergreens and endless reams of wire cable. An hour later the bus approaches Valparaiso. Soon the bus pulls into a dusty terminal, and Niko steps out into the hot sun, and is immediately bombarded by a crowd of gypsies pushing everything from fortunes to massages into his face. Trying to appear relaxed, he pushes through the small crowd. He has a map of the city, but he's reluctant to pull it out, for fear of looking like a tourist and getting mugged.

Leaving the terminal, Niko tries to navigate the Valparaiso streets, which are choked with minibuses, a hair's breadth shy of crashing into one another. He hails a taxi, a rickety black-and-yellow car that could've been older than him, and asks for a cheap hotel. The driver pulls into traffic and immediately begins honking at the other cars while he yells over his shoulder. They careen through narrow cobblestone passageways and up hills, for everywhere in Valparaiso there are hills and soot-covered Victorian greystones and neglected monuments to bygone soldiers. Soon they arrive at a large, cobblestone square. The driver points at a pink, three-story building above a pharmacy and says, "Reina Victoria." Then he hands Niko a ticket stub with the fare on it.

He stands before a colonial-era building and looks around. Behind him, much of the square is used as a parking lot for the Palacio de Justicia, itself nestled into the side of a green hill. Several guards mill outside between two palm trees. Opposite the courthouses are the docks, an asphalt plain divided by a labyrinth of giant canisters and fenced with barbed wire, all leading to a benzene-dappled oceanfront of piers, at which military and commercial trading vessels dock. Two police officers in green fatigues ride past on dirt bikes.

Inside the hotel, the chandeliers emanate a decadent glow across marble counters and antique furniture. A dapper, silver-haired gentleman in a charcoal suit appears at the counter.

"Welcome to the Reina Victoria Hotel," he says in manicured English. "Do you have a reservation?"

A reservation Niko does not have. "Any chance of a spare room?"

"Of course. Let me see what we have available." He pulls out a ledger and begins turning through the pages. All but two rooms on the third floor are available. "A slow season," the concierge says, a sly reference to the twenty-seven years of dictatorship that have pushed his luxury hotel into a perennial winter. "Would you prefer to overlook the courtyard or the street?"

"Whatever is cheapest."

"Very well. The street, then."

The concierge waves for a bellboy, who takes Niko's bag and leads him up two flights of stairs.

Once he's alone, Niko pulls open the curtain and spies the Valparaiso docks from this new perch. He is close. What will he say if they meet? Now that he's here, he's not even so sure that he's ready to meet Baba. A father, he can't help but think, isn't someone who runs this far away. Now that Niko's done exactly that himself, this town feels more like the place where people who don't want to become fathers come to hide from the world. He peers closer at the figures walking along the docks: one of those dots could very well be Baba.

The sun begins to set over the harbour. One by one, the street lamps flicker on. Niko feels a sudden shudder of loneliness that beads with sweat and agitation. He hasn't had a meaningful conversation in days. He is hungry again, always caught in the end by the problem of hunger. He ventures out. A few blocks away, he finds a restaurant. As he eats, a young boy tries to sell him a page of an old newspaper for a few coins.

After the meal, Niko walks down to the waterfront, where buoys of lounging sea lions bark at the moon. From one end of the bay to the next, the hills shimmer with the warm vibrato of so many yellow street lamps. Somewhere up there among those lights, he presumes, is his father, looking down at him.

Somewhere in the back of Antoine's mind, someone foreign is lurking, and that someone must be his old self. He's been recalling more details about that man whenever a new fact or whim or word triggers a disturbing equivalent buried in his past. The other day, for example, a neighbour came over to their house with a camera, the only camera on their street, he proudly informed them, to take a picture of the family, a portrait, and once the flash went off and momentarily blinded them all, it registered an indelible image in Antoine's mind. I used to work with cameras, he thought to himself, as if he had known it all along. I used to own a shop that sold cameras and camera equipment, he recalled later that day. Now as he walks down the hill to the port where he works, Antoine obsesses over these rediscovered memories. The camera shop, he suspects, was close to where he once lived. He can see it, at the bottom of a building: it was his. It had a glass display counter, upon which he could show off every camera in the store. Looking down inside the display case, he sees the expensive lenses. Behind the counter, on several racks, are all the new cameras. He can see it all so clearly, as if he's standing in that room right then. Across from where he often stood behind the counter, there is a display of various camera equipment – bags, tripods, an entire shelf of film stocks. Where has it all gone, he wonders. How did I lose it?

A few days later, he pays a visit to the house of the neighbour who took their picture and says, "Can I look at your camera?"

"Of course! Come in."

The neighbour hands the camera to Antoine enthusiastically, obviously proud of his marvel of technology and eager to explain all its many functions.

"Tell me," Antoine says, holding the delicate machinery in his hands, "where do you develop these pictures?"

"I do it myself," his neighbour says proudly.

"Show me."

The neighbour leads him to the back of his house, past the kitchen door and through the small backyard where they keep only a few chairs and a barrel in which they burn tablescraps, and they enter a dark shed no bigger than a washroom stall.

"It's a darkroom," the neighbour says. He turns on the red light and all the chemicals and containers come to life, with drying pictures hanging on the short line above their heads.

"It's magnificent," Antoine says.

But for all their aura of authenticity, these flashbacks complicate Antoine's new life and the domestic simplicity he once enjoyed with his family has become more difficult to appreciate.

"You look distant," Beatriz says to him one evening. "Does your head hurt?"

"It's the long days," he says.

"They work you too hard, poor thing."

"The money is better than before. I'm saving." Without thinking it through, he confides in his wife, "I think I want to open up a camera shop one day."

"What do you know about cameras?" she laughs nervously. "You'll go and lose all the money you've made, and then who'll feed the children?"

Beatriz examines him with fearful expectation, wondering from which depths such an idea could bubble up.

"Maybe you're right," he says finally.

Beatriz breathes a sigh of relief, sets their baby on his lap, and goes into the kitchen. The baby drools and giggles as he bounces her up and down on his knee. He has never produced anything so beautiful in his life as her. Or has he?

Where does all this love come from, Antoine wonders. The baby twists and writhes in his arms, and he sets her down on the floor. Elise has already started to crawl. With the guidance of a table's edge or a chair leg, she can even stand up on her own two feet. She holds on to his fingers with her little hands and giggles fiercely at the prospect of balance. He loves to watch Elise amused like this, enthralled by first discoveries. He often feels the same way. She will learn to walk on her own soon. There's a man inside his head wobbling on his unused legs, too, and straining for the same equilibrium.

Beatriz Gabriela Cruz has been watching her husband lately, and what she sees has begun to worry her. Some nights she feels for him in the dark and finds that he's not there beside her. Her baby sleeps on the other side of her, but the man who completes their family is nowhere to be found. She gets up as quietly as she can to go look for him. She peers into the bathroom and finds that he's not sleeping in the old bathtub, which is where her previous husband used to be whenever he was not in bed, and so Beatriz continues on. She tiptoes through the creaky old house, into the kitchen, into the main room where they sit and eat and talk and play with the baby, but he is nowhere to be found. She pulls back the curtain and looks out the window, and there she finds him, standing curiously beneath the street lamp, staring not up at the sky, which is full of stars, but simply looking down at the bay, as if hypnotized by something in the dark that no one else can see.

She goes out and stands beside him, but it's as if he doesn't sense her presence at all, and the present is not in front of his eyes, but something else altogether. Beatriz scans the valley between this hill and the next, strewn with oil drums and mangled heaps of sheet metal. Tin roofs, some rusted through, others painted back to life with vibrant colours, grow out of the hillsides like weeds. A dog barks somewhere. From somewhere else, another dog barks back. At the foot of the hills stand a few larger buildings and the docks, the cranes, the stacks of containers that stretch across the length of Valparaiso. Beyond the docks is the harbour itself, a bay speckled with fishing boats and larger ships.

"What are you looking for?" she asks gently, trying to lure him back inside.

"I don't know," he replies.

"Are you confused?"

"I think so."

"Who is Elise?" Beatriz pushes, for she has often wondered from where so adamantly he came up with their daughter's name.

"She's the best thing to ever happen in my life."

"But who *was* she?"

"I'm trying to figure that out," Antoine confesses.

"It's cold tonight, and you have to work in the morning. Let's go back inside."

She takes his hand and leads this confused man in her life back into their home. She hopes he still thinks of it as their house as well. She takes his cheeks in her hands, and kisses him. "Stay with me," she pleads.

"Where would I go?" he chuckles.

"Stay with me," she says once more. "Don't leave us."

"I'll try," he says worriedly.

Then they go back to bed, where she holds him tightly as they fall back asleep. Who does he think is down there at the bottom of that hill, she wonders as she wraps her legs around his knees to form a cocoon.

A constant clanging comes from down the road. It gets closer still. Clang clang clang clang – what is that sound, Niko wonders. Around the bend comes an old man on a motor-cart, pushing a steel bed of propane canisters up the hill. As he drives, he strikes the canisters with a metal rod. Drawn out, a young woman in a floral dress comes into the street, waving a bill. The old man pulls over, carries a canister into her house, and then continues on his way. Clang clang clang, all the way around the bend, where the road branches off to shadowy staircases and archways and back streets leading only to more turns. And then the searching sound fades and all is quiet again.

He is on his way to the Club Union Arabe of the letterhead, which is in a neighbouring town called Viña Del Mar, up the coastline. Once he makes it down to the bottom of the hill, Niko waits at the side of the main road that runs between the two towns, roasting in the mid-morning sun as minibuses rush past. The streets are filled with such buses, and he has been instructed to look for a specific number and then flag it down, which he tries until he gets one of them to screech to a halt. Niko hops in and takes a seat and holds on for dear life. They are off. The driver sings along to a cassette player, a disco version of a George Michael song, something by Wham! At stops along the way, young boys climb on to sell ice creams or band-aids, whatever exchange endears them beyond begging.

The bus veers along the seaside road and its honeycombed rocks, rococo banisters, and crashing waves. There it is: a wall emblazoned with gold-plated lettering spelling CLUB U ION AR BE. He rings the bell and the bus screeches to a stop along the road. The property juts from the rock face of the hill, an old mansion. He walks up the driveway to the tall wrought-iron gate and rings the intercom. The gate shoots loose with a buzz. He walks further up the long driveway, and over the fence the boundless Pacific comes fully into view, gleaming along the horizon as waves come in and pull back.

A man in a brown blazer comes out of the mansion and stands at the top of the driveway, hands in pockets. "*Salam alaykoum.* How can I help you?"

"I'm looking for Serge Maroun."

"And who are you, my friend?" he says. "What's your name?"

"Niko Karam."

He looks at Niko again, closely this time, studies him from all sides as if studying a marble bust: a young man now, he has grown a head of messy pitch-black hair, serious eyes, a troubled disposition, flaring nostrils. "Come inside."

The man in the brown blazer leads Niko into a room with high ceilings and marble floors. At one end stands a bartender, polishing glasses.

"Wait here," he says, then disappears up a circular marble staircase, as the bartender brings over a cold glass of water and a bowl of sunflower seeds on a silver tray.

Presently, a tall, daunting man with a deep tan and thin goatee comes down the staircase. He has a thick head of brown curls and he wears immaculate rings on both hands.

"I'm Serge Maroun," he says, sitting down. "So you're Niko Karam. Tell me, how can I help?"

"I am here looking for someone. You sent my uncle a letter."

"And who might your someone be?"

"My father. His name is Antoine Karam, but you wrote that you know him only as Antoine."

"Well then, Niko Karam, we've been waiting for you for a long time now." Serge Maroun looks carefully into Niko's eyes. "You resemble him. It's uncanny."

"Is it true that he lives here?"

"He does. But his situation is delicate. We don't know enough about him. You see, he arrived to us as the survivor of an accident at sea. He has lost his memory. The only thing he knows about himself is his name. So I'm just telling you this because he might not know you. Tell me, does he have any other family?"

"Just me."

"You should also know this before you see him: he has a family here."

"A new family?"

"You look tired. Why don't you join us for dinner here? We'll eat, we'll drink, talk. And then we'll see what we can do to help you and your father."

At dinner, Niko manages to pull from Serge Maroun a sad portrait of a man, a man with no control over his own fate. It's all very strange and unexpected for Niko, who was looking forward to a father who was more upstanding, more pious and together — a famous photographer or at least a shop-owner. He doesn't know quite what to do. All this time he's resisted building a new life in Montreal, and now he comes here to find out that his father has no memory of him and that he's started a new family. It seems unfair.

"He sounds so different from the man I remember."

"Tomorrow, let's go see his family," Serge says. "They've been wondering about you."

"They can't know I exist. You said he doesn't have a memory at all."

"That doesn't mean they haven't suspected it. We all have. You see, we really have been waiting for you, all this time."

Beatriz Gabriela Cruz is in the kitchen preparing supper when there is a knock at the door. She wipes her hands on her apron, turns down the stove, and goes to see who's there. Standing before her is Serge Maroun, the man from the Arab association who comes to check on her husband every once in a while. And beside him stands a young man with a familiar, fearful look in his eyes.

"Hola, Señor Maroun."

"Señorita Cruz." Her guest tips his hat. "I come here with a special friend of Antoine's. From years ago, from Libano."

"Ah! Libano?" Her face darkens at the mention of her husband's supposed country, as the young man's face gradually reveals the telltale features that relate him to the man she knows. Reluctantly, she asks them to come in off the street.

Because she has been frying food all afternoon, the inside of the house reeks of vegetable oil. She waves toward the kitchen and wipes her hands against her apron, then disappears for a time, ostensibly to tend to the food, but mostly to compose herself. All along, from the time she first met her husband in the hospital, she has known this moment was inevitable. Now it has arrived. She swallows hard, and then goes back into the main room to face her guests.

Beatriz sits down with them. She can tell, just by the look on the young man's face, that he has been judging her house: a ragtag collection of old furnishings, water-damaged walls, musty curtains, a box of broken children's toys and overflowing ashtrays. The man he's looking for lives in a large shack, where apart from a collection of wooden icons the walls are bare, a symptom of her Christian modesty or mere neglect.

"*Lo siento, señors*, but Antoine is working on the ship. He will return in two days."

Serge Maroun quietly translates. Then he says, "This is Niko Karam. He knows Antoine from Libano. He has come all the way here to see your husband."

"How old is he?" she asks Serge Maroun.

"My dear, he is old enough," he replies with a knowing look.

"Oh good, *bueno*," she sighs without enthusiasm. In her hands, she twists her apron into knots. Quizzically she then looks at Niko, but says to Serge. "He comes here all the way from Libano?"

"No, no," Serge answers on his behalf. "He came here from Canada."

Beatriz sits up straight. "Vacation?"

Niko shakes his head. The young man looks relieved and disappointed all at the same time.

"How long have they been together?" Niko inquires through Serge.

On this subject, Beatriz is eager to open up, to give the young man the impression that her family is no joke, and that he ought to tread very carefully upon what is important to her. She and Antoine have been married two years, soon after he came out of the hospital. Together they have one child, a baby daughter.

The room fills with the stench of burning potatoes and tension.

"The food!" she says in urgent Spanish.

She scurries out of the room, barely able to contain herself. The interminable act has finally come to an end, and she has made it through without imploding. Resting her head on the cabinet door, Beatriz contemplates how to survive the next minutes or hours or however long it takes to get them out of her house. She takes a deep breath and wipes the corners of her eyes, because she is usually a strong woman, resilient they call her, but this is proving harder than she'd ever anticipated, and she does not want to lose her family now, just as it was growing into something she could be proud of. If only she could explain to him how rich their home is, how much love squeezes in between these rotten walls, then maybe this boy would let her keep what she and Antoine have built together. Maybe, just maybe, he will leave them be.

Just then a very old woman shuffles through the door, carrying in her arms a baby girl in a bright dress, who crawls off in search of her mother as soon as she sees strangers in her living room. Beatriz comes out from the kitchen, a wooden mallet in one hand, looking fraught and distracted. She and her mother stand before the two men in the living room. The older woman's hair is shockingly white. Now, Beatriz's mother absorbs the sight of the men with grave suspicion, while her daughter searches for the right words to explain. Beatriz finally whispers something in Doña Julia's ear. The old woman meets her daughter's eyes with an incredulous gaze, and then looks toward the young man seated before her. She guffaws in disapproval. Beatriz introduces her mother as the oldest woman on the hill: eighty-two. The old woman mutters something back to her daughter. She settles into a chair, holding her purse in her lap. Neither Serge nor Niko knows quite what to say, and so for a period they sit in awkward silence.

The baby girl who'd crawled into the kitchen now peeks out at them through the doorway, these two strange men sitting on their only couch. Beatriz brings a hastily assembled plate into the room, sets it down on the coffee table in contempt, and then sits down, resolved to protect her home with everything she has.

"Please, eat," she announces, as if daring them to accept her hospitality.

Cooing, the baby girl peeks out from behind her mother's calves and delivers a toothless smile.

"This little one is Elise," Beatriz says. "Tell me, do you know that name?"

After Serge translates, Niko says, "It was the name of my mother."

"And where is your mother now?"

"She's dead," Niko says.

Involuntarily, Beatriz breathes a sigh of relief.

He was never wanted here, Niko realizes, not by this woman and probably not by his own father. There is no plan for his return, and there never has been. His father has this other girl. She's got the name of his mother, and the only person left out of the picture is Niko. From where he sits, Niko can see through the open door of the only other room in this shack: their bedroom. It contains only a twin mattress, a nest of yellowing pillows, bed sheets, and tangled clothing. They all sleep together. Rashly, he tries to imagine himself sleeping among them, but it only saddens him.

He says to Serge, in an effort to hurry the rest of this visit so they can leave, "Please, just tell them already, I'm here to see my father."

Serge translates. The room goes silent, and then Beatriz nods and confirms she's known it all along. "You look like him. You have his eyes. Señor Maroun, tell him please, we have always known that he, or someone like him, would come one day. Tell him we have been waiting for him. Tell him we are proud of what we have, and that his father has no memory of the past, otherwise he would have gone looking for it. Tell him his father is a good man, a hard-working man, an honest man, and that we are proud to have him among us, but that this reunion he wants greatly complicates matters for us because we have a family here, and that family will not be broken, not as long as I live. We are married and we have a child," she says mostly to Serge now, "and I know that gives me the right to keep my husband here with me."

Quietly, Serge translates all she has said, and all the while Niko looks at the little girl and tries to see a resemblance to his mother, but sees only a thief. And then he understands what Beatriz has said and they sit in silence, because he has nothing to say in response, and he supposes she's right in a way, because he has nothing to offer his father other than confirmation that his past once existed and that it has not gone away. On the other side of the window, a cat complains, pawing at the glass and demanding to be let back inside.

Niko says, "You have a very nice family, but I had one too. It's gone now. My mother died a long time ago. I have no family now, while you have my father and this big family."

"I can tell you right now," Beatriz says through Serge, "you will destroy him. His life has been much different than yours. If you meet him now, you will be disappointed and that will crush him."

"All I want is to speak to him,"

"You will only bring him more suffering," Beatriz says, begging now. "If you care for his peace of mind, say what you must and then leave him to live the life he has."

"We should go," Serge interrupts. "Tell Antoine to call me as soon as he gets back."

Beatriz walks them to the door. On the stoop, she apologizes. The invitation into her home was a mistake. If Niko had any sympathy for the life his father has led, she says, then he wouldn't have come.

"If you knew the life he led before you," Niko replies, "then you wouldn't say that." He pulls a silver ring from his pocket, the silver ring that Baba once gave him long ago when it was still his mother's wedding band. "Please, give this to my father. Tell him it's from Niko."

"What is this?"

"He will know. Just give it to him and tell him not to worry."

Beneath a blanket of stars, they begin their journey back down the hill.

The world constantly disappoints him. He has no appreciation for any of it. Perhaps in the end Niko has held the world to an impossible standard.

"There's nowhere left to go," he says, holding his head in his hands.

"There's always someplace else to go," Serge Maroun corrects him. "You'll see. Your uncle keeps calling. You can always go back there."

"I've made big mistakes back there. I stole money."

"You're young, you'll find your own way yet. People forgive youth. You came here to find something, and now you know. At least you can move on with your life."

"I don't know where I'll go."

That night Niko dreams that he is on a ferry again, pushing past the plastic bags and swollen rolls of toilet paper that fill the sea off Beirut. His chin barely reaches over the railing, and his arms wrap around Baba's leg. As the ship moves further toward open sea and the booms and crackles of Beirut fade away, all that's left to see are flashing lights. Stripped of their sound and consequence, on this clear summer night the little boy and Baba watch a bright display of firepower rise up and blend with the sky to create a false constellation over the city.

Baba runs his fingers through Niko's hair and says, "Come, let's go sit."

They walk back to the deck chair and pull a blanket over their legs. Niko burrows deep into Baba's lap, digging around for the warmest position he can muster, for it is a cold evening out at sea.

"Baba, what do I do now?" he asks.

"Become someone else, Niko," Baba says simply. "There's always another life to be had after this one."

Once he's settled down, Baba tucks him in with both hands. They are a ball, a bond, inseparable inside the thin wool cover. The further out they venture, the more beautiful the lights over Beirut become, presenting a carnival in full swing. Now they glow like the insides of a factory forging steel. Now those lights betray a city industriously in the throes of being rebuilt.

Niko wakes up thinking that maybe Serge Maroun is right: anything is possible. It's all in how you look at it. But during the day, the feeling passes.

The next day, Serge Maroun invites Niko to a special dinner that the Club Union Arabe is hosting, a seasonal gathering of the membership and their families which is really just an excuse to dress up, have a lavish meal, and talk.

"You should come and see what the rest of us are like. I think you'll enjoy the conversation, and these people will be pleased to see a new face." The evening, Serge informs him, usually attracts a small but tightly-knit group of emigrants who span all sects, boundaries, and religions. For them, there is no distinction between Druze or Christian or Palestinian or Syrian; they insist that to see each man as a corpus for a country or a sect drains him of his vitality and asks him to defend the fabrications of a culture that will, in the end, leave him with nothing in return. And so they come here and eat and speak freely, as if they were born on no land, as if they are forever flapping their wings to keep their feet from touching the ground. They refer to themselves as the birds of Valparaiso, representing no one or no line of thought in particular.

That evening the old mansion leaning out toward the Pacific fills with the club's businessmen, and also with grandmothers and wives and cousins and children and grandchildren. Many of them were born of transplants and have never visited the land that attaches them to this club. As Serge Maroun explains it, many of them prefer it that way. To visit the lands to which they belong at this point would ultimately disappoint them, as they would have to take down the elaborate portraits of villages they've conjured from their parents' or grandparents' stories and replace them with a drab and conflicted reality.

And so, the fifty faces in the hall that evening depict a background of mixed bloodlines and mixed heritages. The youngest children, furthermore their children's children, will one day fade into an implacable exoticism. Here, outside the protracted Arabian struggles through an unforgiving century, as the so-called dream of an Arab renaissance caved in to greater antagonists – the full-fisted Arabism of the Baathists, the empty showmanship of Yasser Arafat, the odium of Lebanon's sectarian friction, the militancy of the Muslim Brotherhood, the ruthlessness of the Zionists, the opportunism of the Americans, the disappearance of Old Europe, the corruption and complacency of the Gulf – they have been able to flourish while waiting.

As the wait staff circulates trays of hors d'oeuvres and wine glasses, a great many of the older women, some of who resemble his own grandmothers, pull Niko aside to express their gratitude for this unexpected visit. To look at someone like him is for them a reminder of a bygone era that they never thought to encounter again. He brings with him a walking aura of their youth. Many of them haven't seen a young Arab face in decades, and so they're openly delighted to see the likes of him. At the stroke of eight a bell rings, and their attentions are directed toward the great mahogany doors of the main dining hall. The doors swing open, and the guests are invited in to sit around a large round table.

At the behest of his parents, a young boy stands on his chair and sings an old Arabic folk song in a language he's never known. Then, Serge Maroun rises to offer a toast. "Ladies and gentlemen, I salute you and your accomplishments. For you, for us, the future is bright. Our time to go back was not meant to be during this life. If you have felt slighted or powerless here in this afterlife of your

222

origins, if you have felt cast aside or condescended upon, then rest assured that there will always be a next life in the wings. Together we have made a virtue of waiting for the next life. Someday, some caste of our lineage, whatever shape they may take, might fly back to where we once came from."

With deep smiles and heavy hearts, they all raise their glasses to the afterlife of their origins.

When Beatriz hands him the old wedding band, at first Antoine doesn't recognize what's in his hands. But then, as he rolls the silver ring with his fingers and senses an afterglow of the skin that used to once press against its insides, its fate begins to pour back into his thoughts and he has to set it down. It has power.

"What happened to her?" asks Beatriz, looking on curiously.

"She died. She was coming out of our building and a car exploded, right out front. We had a son together."

"Yes, I know. His name is Niko. I met him. He came to our door while you were away, he sat on this couch, and he gave me this ring."

"He's here?" Antoine sighs and sits down. "So it's finally happening."

"He wants to see you."

"Yes."

"Is this the end of our family? Are you going to leave us and go back to your old life?"

She holds him for a long time, willing him with her embrace not to leave them, and when she finally lets go, Antoine sees that her eyes have impressed wet circles in his shirt.

Later, he walks down the hill, kicking a pebble along the way until he loses it in the crevices between cobblestones. He can do nothing else but think of the family he once had. They were all born in the wrong time. When Elise died, he had no chance without her.

Collecting all that he can remember of his son, he tries to build a picture of the young man who has come in search of him. The only composite he can construct is that of a little boy who used to watch Tom and Jerry cartoons and chase flies around their apartment. The longer he thinks about it, the less of a clear picture he conjures up. In the end, Antoine realizes that he is afraid to meet this young man who carries so many expectations of him. He must be here looking for a father, but Antoine is not sure what he can provide. It shames him to not remember more. It frustrates him that he can't just shake his head and loosen the cobwebs of his memory. It's all in there, he's noticed, but the darker a particular past, the more trouble he has bringing it back up to the surface. What happened between us? He can't recall how they came to be so far apart. The prospect of having to ask his own son how he ended up on the other side of the world only confirms his immense failures. Whatever it is I have done or failed to do, he fears, it must be among the biggest mistakes of my life. I have been unfortunate with boys, he decides, God must not want my lineage to grow.

That night as he stands at the stern of a cargo ship moored at the far reaches of the bay, Antoine looks up at the clear black night and all the white stars, and he pulls the silver ring from his pocket again and looks at it shine in the moonlight. It is a sign of a promise to another woman and another life, and in this manner, he can't blame the boy for coming here to defend the stake of his mother and their past. In the boy's place, Antoine hopes he would have done the same. His many lives since those beginnings have not been easy. But he has a dedicated wife and a daughter and a houseful of people here who love and depend on him, and this he must treat seriously and with respect, because without Beatriz and Elise and Doña Julia, he would have no one and life would not be worth living.

The moon up there is so bright tonight, a full moon. From where he stands, he can look out across the vast expanse of the sea in one direction and, in the other, up into the hills of his home. He kisses the ring, furtively, like a secret. He presses that ring against his lips with affection, as if it belongs to a lifelong mistress. There is room in his heart to love many people, some of whom have hearts that beat stridently in his memory, and others who greet him every night when he comes home and make sure his bathwater is warm enough.

Then comes the call for work and the spell of the quiet night is broken, and Antoine can hear the footsteps of many men congregating, getting ready to haul barrels from the depths of the vessel, up to the deck. He goes back to work and tries to push all these choices, the first he's had in years, out of his head.

In the morning, a letter comes to the Club Union Arabe, and it is delivered to Serge Maroun's desk. He opens it over a working breakfast.

"It says that he's willing to meet you tonight," he tells Niko later. "What do you want to do?"

"Tell him I'll be there."

Niko spends his morning of waiting inside the Club Union Arabe, watching television and hiding from the heat. Serge Maroun sits beside him, dozing on the sofa. Several other old men sit around the lounge chatting, periodically peering over to the television screen but not showing much interest otherwise. The only foreign newscast shows the first anniversary of the end of the fifteen-year civil war in Lebanon. The whole story fits snugly into less than a minute. A journalist tackles the question of what comes next for a country in its first year of peace.

"What will you do to him?" Niko asks, because he senses now that Serge has a lot of power over the fate of his father.

"He's lucky. The old government here is gone, and the new one wants to change everything. So many files are getting lost along the way. I think if he wants to stay, he'll be okay."

History forgets people all the time.

Later in the afternoon, after the sun's heat tapers off, Niko leaves the club and goes for a walk. At this hour of the day, the families of Viña del Mar come out in droves and walk together, relish the day together, young and old. Walking along, he notices that he's periodically greeted by the curious stares of the elderly, as if they too recognize something of a conflict in him that has yet to be resolved. He sees this quality in their faces as well. Perhaps they see it in each other because they intrinsically know what to look for. They are adrift in the same afterlife together. Momentarily he feels like a little boy again. This is a feeling, he decides, that he wants to snuff once and for all. Whenever he forgets which mask to wear, whenever he grows comfortable behind the cloak of his fabrications, he aligns himself to a forecast of false stars and wishes for successes from a sky of imminent failures.

Early that evening a thick fog drifts in from the bay, and suddenly Niko can't even see past the boardwalk to the ocean. As he walks back to the clubhouse, people and places fade in and out of the fog. He takes a taxi back to Valparaiso, past the waterfront hotels and the fish markets, past the university and the technical schools, past the lonesome boardwalk with its barking sea lions and the abandoned docks with their teams of stray dogs, past the old waterfront boulevard lined with palm trees, pink and blue and yellow buildings, past the port and to the cable cars leading up the hill.

Niko sits in a small funicular compartment, his breathing palpable and nervous. His palms sweat and he can't help but tremor a little. Beside him sits a woman carrying grocery bags, and beside her a man reading the evening newspaper. The funicular crawls up the hill at a workmanlike pace, jolting along as the view of the city emerges faintly through the mist and then a shadow of the harbour appears from behind the downtown buildings. They push upward still, through the evening's cloud of yellow smog, to the outpost at the side of the hill that is the lift's destination.

From there, Niko walks up the hill to his father's house as if walking through a strangely familiar maze, cast beneath a dim streetlight and netted with a century's worth of telephone wires and electricity cables never taken down. A small tremor shakes the earth as gently as a baby's rattle, the hills as nervous as he is, but no one seems to notice. How thick this fog can be. Along the way, dogs follow him for a time and then drop off, returning to the streets they know. He arrives to a part of the hill where he can no longer hear the sounds of the city. There are fewer street lamps and even fewer passersby. Clang clang clang clang. The last propane truck of the day makes its rounds. The clanging fades away.

Near the top of the hill, the fog suddenly ends. When Niko turns back, it looks like he has broken through a floorboard of clouds and into the heavens themselves.

Soon he turns onto Baba's narrow street. Then he is here, standing in front of Baba's door. The curtains are drawn and the house is dark. He knocks and he waits, and then hears what sounds like the scraping of a chair against the floor. But no footsteps come. Quietly, Niko presses his ear against the door and listens again, hunting for signs of life inside. He imagines Baba doing much the same from the inside, that they are listening for each other. If he listens closely, he thinks he can hear breathing in there.

Again Niko balls his hand into a fist and knocks, harder this time so there can be no mistake, and then disappointment beads in the corner of his eye. But then, there is a footstep inside. And then another. He holds his breath. The lock is unlatching, then the handle is turning. He steps back off the stoop. The door cracks open. A suspicious eye peers out. The door opens wider, but Niko can see nothing of the inside through the fallow gloom. The only light he has to guide him emanates from the sputtering street lamp a few houses down. And even then, he can only make out the whites of his estranged father's eyes. How Baba cowers under him, how much taller he's grown above his own father's height. How haunted and severe and skeptical his baba's gaze looks. How dark and mitigating those pupils feel against his skin, looking up, like the fingers of the blind. Eyes like those, Niko senses, have been watching him all his life.

They sit in the main room of Baba's home, each of them not knowing what to say to the other after all these years. Their Arabic, their mother tongue, has grown weak from disuse, and while Niko is most comfortable now in the French against which he once rebelled so fiercely, Baba's inclination is to lapse into the Spanish of his new family. They are forced to make up for the gap between them with hand gestures.

Baba says, "Tell me, did you know what happened to me?"

"Serge Maroun told me once I got here. They say you lost your memory. Do you remember me?"

"Now that I see you, I remember. But before you showed up, I had trouble."

"Were you really lost in the middle of the sea?"

"That's where people say they found me. I don't remember being there, or how I got there, but they say I was lost at sea."

"He said they found you clinging to a ladder."

"That's what they told me. I don't remember any of it, but they saved the ladder. Would you like to see it?"

"Let's see it," Niko says.

They go out back, through the kitchen, to where the evening stars are flaring up in the dimming dusk, and a ladder leans against the shed. It's no taller than eight feet, and much of its paint has peeled away, but if they look closely, they can still make out a bit of the yellow that was the color it was originally painted.

"Can you believe *this* saved my life?" Baba says, feeling the grains to the graying wood. "They say it was a miracle."

"Do you remember how you used to tell me stories all the time?"

"Did I? Did you enjoy them?"

"I thought they were real."

"What was real at that time wasn't so great. I don't want you to be devastated. There's a good chance, after everything that's happened, that I'm not the person you expect me to be."

They stand there for a while longer, looking at the ladder and not saying much. Then Niko walks back down the hill.

The next day, they go for a walk. They spend the afternoon sitting on a bench on the cross bridge, reminiscing over the tribulations of their long journey in the milk-warm air of the Chilean spring.

Once they relax a little, Baba tells Niko stories as they pop into his head, stories that Niko has never heard before and that Baba didn't even know he could remember. Niko had never known, for instance, that as a young boy Baba owned a pet gazelle; it was a birthday present from his father, brought home after a trip to Oman. Or that he hadn't learned to swim until the age of thirteen. It turned out he had a fear of the sea; once when he was six, he was dragged down by an undertow and almost drowned. As a young man, Niko learned, he'd once spent two weeks working at a farm in Cyprus. Baba claimed those were the happiest two weeks of his life, where he'd finally realized that he loved Elise and wanted a family with her. His life was so full of possibilities then, so many choices to choose from. Where had they all gone? He tells his son all this in a tentative, slow manner, as if recalling the stories only moments before they left his lips.

"I haven't thought about any of this for a very long time," Baba says. "But now with you here, it's all coming back to me. I thought I was nobody before, but now I see that's not true."

After all this time Baba still looks sad at the mention of Mama's name. He loves Beatriz too, but differently. Beatriz is meant to be his partner in this life, Elise his great love. In the end, he confesses, life is too short. It passes too quickly. And yet, if he were offered the chance to live forever, he wouldn't take it. Some things are meant to remain unfinished.

For Niko's part, he's compelled to remind his father of all the time he'd spent teaching him as a boy. "I'm mad at you for many things, but there are other things, like learning math and swimming and watching cartoons, which are my favourite times."

"Really?" Baba says. "Tell me."

He knows he hadn't been the easiest of children, and that together they hadn't had the easiest of households, but that his relationship with his parents, his ghosts, is much like his relationship with Lebanon: Niko wants to memorialize it and forget it all at once.

"Were you trying to get to me all this time?" Niko asks.

"I think so," Baba replies.

"Do you remember the summer we spent together at sea, Baba? We went to Cyprus, where you taught me to swim, and then we went to the Greek islands and fished."

"I do now. That was a difficult time for us. We lost everything."

"Maybe I was too young," Niko confesses. "I remember it was a great adventure. For me, that was the best time ever. I never wanted it to end. I thought we would build a house together on one of those islands and eat fish from the sea and fruit from the trees for the rest of our lives."

As they arrive to a balcony overlooking the valley below, Baba can't help but put his arm around his son. "That would have been nice," he says. "Too bad that didn't happen. They say you live in Canada. Tell me, how is your life now?"

"To be honest, it's not so good. "

"You know," Baba says, "when I sent you there, I thought you'd forget all about me and become a doctor. I thought you'd have everything waiting for you there, opportunities at your feet. You were supposed to go on and do great things."

"Life is different there," Niko shrugs. "There are too many rules, and no one is happy, but we all have a lot of money to live well and we all complain. I don't know how to explain it, but even though there was no danger to our lives, we still found ways to make mistakes."

"I'm disappointed to hear that."

They return to the house and Baba invites Niko in to spend some time with his new family. Niko takes a few steps inside, but once he's confronted with the jealous eyes of Beatriz and her clinging baby, he changes his mind and leaves the way he came, back down the hill. The distance is there still.

They are lifelong travelers, thinks Niko that night while lying in bed and looking out at foreign stars, they're travelers whose trajectories have been involuntarily turned adventurous. Thousands of years ago, the first Nakhle was a nomad; they belonged to a nomadic people. Here they are, nomadic again. Their responsibility is to breathe in, breathe out, to continue this delicate double entendre of the body's machinery as it courses from one generation to the next. They are troubled, others find them troubling. Their responsibility is to find the strength within themselves to reconcile the conflicts the world has thrown at them, and to lead better personal lives.

On the third day, Baba shows up at the gates of the Club Union Arabe. When Niko comes out to meet him, eyes bloodshot from crying in his sleep, he shouts, "I'm angry at you, Baba. All this time, you could have done more. I could have done better if I had known what you wanted. All this time, I was waiting for you."

"I suppose you're right," Baba agrees. "I could have done more."

"And you went off and started a new family. I waited for you, and you left me."

"For years now I've had no memory of you. It's strange to say, but my life became much easier once I forgot the past. I was hoping the same happened to you."

"I couldn't forget. I tried. It was impossible."

"Now that I know again, I suppose it will be impossible for me too."

"Why did you leave me?"

"I wanted to give you a better life."

"All I wanted was to be with you."

"I was not good for you. I wanted to give you something better."

"You tried too hard."

"I made a mistake."

"I made a big mistake too. If I go back, I'll go to jail. I'll be a father to a kid who will dream up fantasies of who I am. I'll be like you."

"What other choice do you have?"

"I thought I could stay here with you."

"You won't be happy. You're a grown man now, and I have responsibilities to all these other people who live here. They are my family now. It would only make you sad."

"I can't go back to being a kid with you, but I also can't move forward. What should I do?"

"It's painful to hear, I know, but think of where you are now and where you should be going in the future. I love you and your mother more than anyone, but our family wasn't meant to last. Don't make any more decisions based on the past."

"I don't know if I can do that."

"You're only eighteen. You still have your whole life ahead of you. So much more is waiting to happen. Don't let down your child like I let you down."

"I'm sorry I came here, Baba. "

"I'm happy you came here. I'm happy to see you again. I never thought it would happen. You've made me so very happy. Remember I taught you to float? Well, you're floating now. I can tell."

"I love you, Baba."

"I love you too, Niko."

"But it's not good for me."

"Sometimes that's the way love is." Once again, Baba invites Niko up the hill. "Come," he says, "eat with us. You're part of that family, too."

Later that evening, Niko returns to Baba's house and knocks on the door. When Beatriz answers, he doesn't run away and instead of staring him down, her eyes light up and she invites him in with her natural warmth.

"You've been through a lot," she says. "Come, let's sit down and start over again."

He sits down at the table that's been set, and soon candles are lit and a bottle of wine is uncorked. Then, all of a sudden, there's a baby on his lap, drooling onto his hands and staring up at him in wonder, as if he's the most important thing in the room.

"Look at how she admires you," Baba says.

"It's because she doesn't know me."

"That's the best part of having children. You get to be someone new."

Elise stretches in his arms and gurgles, and then she squeals in delight and wraps her tiny hand around Niko's finger. He lifts her up over his head and presses his ear up against her chest, where her young heart beats away. Thump, thump. Thump, thump.

After she hangs up the telephone, Yvonne rejoins Sami in the living room, where they have been waiting for the phone to ring a long-distance ring for days now. It is ten-thirty at night, and they are ready for bed.

"Was it him?" Sami asks straightaway, sitting up.

"It was him," she confirms, smiling a little.

"And is he okay?"

"He says he's fine. He says he's met his father, and they've had long talks. He says it was hard and complicated, the hardest and most complicated thing he's ever done."

"What are his plans? Will he come back?"

"He says he doesn't know what to do, but that he's thinking he will probably come back. He says he'll call back in a few days, after he sees Antoine a few more times. Do you know Antoine has a new family? It turns out he got married and had a child. Niko has a half-sister. Anyways, it's as you suspected, he's afraid to come back because he's gotten himself into a mess here with work and that girl. He says he got her pregnant."

"When he calls back, tell him we'll take care of everything. Tell him, whatever it is, we'll take care of it. It won't be easy, but we won't let him down again."

"I'm so happy he called," Yvonne says, sitting down next to Sami.

"Me, too," Sami says. "We'll take care of this problem with the store for him, and then find a way to help him with the child too."

Sami's not sure why he does what he does next, but he kisses Yvonne. It's a different kind of kiss, and he's embarrassed for behaving that way. But he learns something about her while their lips touch that he's never been able to see before: it's as though Yvonne has been longing for someone's lips to kiss her that passionately all her life. He'd never known that about her.

"Maybe we've made some mistakes along the way," says Sami.

She presents a ready excuse for him. "Maybe it's good to say it out loud. Otherwise, you'll always be like this, questioning and waiting and never knowing."

And against her will she begins to cry a little, because she's the kind who always cries at endings, and this kiss she didn't even know she'd been waiting for has the feeling of a bona fide ending to the long journey of getting to know each other. How clearly she remembers the night they first arrived here, to Montreal, how cold it was that January. When Niko came over, his flight was delayed. He looked petrified to be there, to be anywhere at all. He was like a cat, she remembers. She felt like that too when she first got here, and now Yvonne wishes she'd told Niko that when she first met him. It's new. It's normal to be scared. At least she had arrived with Sami. She was glad to not be alone in being scared, and they've been scared this whole time, Yvonne realizes, right up until that kiss.

"I have something to tell you that might not make you very happy," she confesses.

"What is it?" he replies with a look of genuine concern.

"I'm pregnant, too."

"Really?"

She nods again. Yvonne looks to Sami for approval, and he nods emphatically because, after so many years of marriage and of trying, he knows what will calm her and make her happy, and that's all he wants to do at that moment, make her happy.

"I'll be a father and a grandfather," he says. "We're going to have a bigger family than we ever thought."

"You know," she confesses to him, nuzzling closer than they've ever been, "I thought I lost something a long time ago. When I thought I couldn't have children, I didn't know what reason we had to start a life in this country. After we grew old, what proof would there be of our coming here?"

"Now, now," he says. "We came here to live freely. We came here to lead ordinary lives. Nothing would have been lost."

"You're right, but I wanted it to go on, after us. Is that wrong?"

"Well, now it will. We'll have a full house. I want to be a husband and a father and a grandfather."

"Do you really?"

He raises her head off the sofa and rests it back down across his lap. He holds her hand and he strokes her hair.

"Sometimes," she says, "I feel like we're living on the moon, like we can never go home again."

"My dear," he says, "it is not us who left, but our homes that are gone. We have nothing to return to."

"Still, I think it's perfectly normal for a grown woman to be curious about the place she was born. Without origins and children, what do we have?"

Sami bends down and plants another kiss on Yvonne's lips. She giggles tearfully like a schoolgirl. What is this warm laughter? He's never heard such a sound from her the whole time they've lived in this house. They'd been so busy trying to establish themselves that they'd forgotten the purpose of marriage. He does it again, kisses her, and this time he giggles himself. They are like children hiding from their parents. Listen to me, he thinks, I sound like an old fool! He is an old fool. He has to admit, in the end, that sure, he could have done better. A lifetime ago I lost everything, and now I have a wife and two children and a grandchild. I can always do better. His life and the choices he's made haven't been perfect. But a person must bend sometimes. Sometimes he can't foresee repercussions, and some decisions are made in moments of spiritual fog. This is why people are designed to carry mistakes, and this is why people should keep a room in their souls for what they might have done differently.

ESPLANADE
Books

THE FICTION SERIES AT VÉHICULE PRESS

A House by the Sea : A novel by Sikeena Karmali

A Short Journey by Car : Stories by Liam Durcan

Seventeen Tomatoes : Tales from Kashmir : Stories by Jaspreet Singh

Garbage Head : A novel by Christopher Willard

The Rent Collector : A novel by B. Glen Rotchin

Dead Man's Float : A novel by Nicholas Maes

Optique : Stories by Clayton Bailey

Out of Cleveland : Stories by Lolette Kuby

Pardon Our Monsters : Stories by Andrew Hood

Chef : A novel by Jaspreet Singh

Orfeo : A novel by Hans-Jürgen Greif; Fred A. Reed, trans.

Anna's Shadow : A novel by David Manicom

Sundre : A novel by Christopher Willard

Animals : A novel by Don LePan

Writing Personals : A novel by Lolette Kuby

Niko : A novel by Dimitri Nasrallah

Stopping for Strangers : Stories by Daniel Griffin

The Love Monster: A novel by Missy Marston

A Message for the Emperor : A novel by Mark Frutkin

New Tab : A novel by Guillaume Morissette

Breathing Lessons : A novel by Andy Sinclair

Swing in the House : Stories by Anita Anand

Véhicule Press